"We got hoodwinked, Jess."

Daniel Stone pulled away from the Quinn Real Estate office and glanced at the golden retriever sitting beside him on the front seat. "The old man never said anything about a woman and two children sharing the house with us."

The dog grunted in reply.

"Not concerned about an invasion of privacy, are you, girl?" Daniel scratched his loyal companion behind her ears as he turned onto Beach Road and pulled into the driveway of the big corner house. "Never mind, girl. We'll simply ignore our neighbors and go about our business. We may have come east to start over, but that doesn't mean we want a lot of new people in our lives."

The truth was that Daniel wanted nothing more than a calm, uncomplicated life. A summer at the beach should have provided him with such a life. Except Mr. Bart Quinn had ruined that possibility.

Why couldn't he have rented the downstairs apartment to a quiet, retired couple instead of a couple of kids and a woman whose hair—what exactly had Mr. Quinn said? Oh yes, a woman whose hair had dancing red lights in it.

"Why would we care about that, Jess? You and I know no one can ever replace Nikki."

Dear Reader,

Summer at the beach! What could be more fun than spending two glorious months in the sand, sun and surf? Fun is what Shelley Anderson is hoping to provide for her children when she rents the first floor of Sea View House a year after her divorce. The kids haven't been adjusting well, and the house is perfect—right on the beach in Pilgrim Cove, Massachusetts, a town that welcomes newcomers wholeheartedly, summerfolk included. At least, that's what the Realtor tells her when she signs the lease.

She's not so sure he's right after meeting Daniel Stone, the man who's renting the top floor of Sea View House. The man definitely wants to be left alone. He's obviously less than thrilled by the instant rapport between his beautiful golden retriever and her two active kids.

Welcome to Pilgrim Cove! Or welcome back! The ROMEOS still have all their fingers in every pie, and Matt and Laura (*The House on the Beach*, Harlequin Superromance #1192) are gettting married. Neptune's Amusement Park is up and running for the summer season, as is Little League Baseball. So come on down and be part of the action in a place where people know their neighbors and care about them.

No Ordinary Summer is the second in my four-book PILGRIM COVE miniseries. If you missed *The House on the Beach*, you can order it through eHarlequin or through your favorite bookseller. I hope you enjoy visiting Pilgrim Cove as much as I enjoy writing about life there.

See you on the beach,

Linda Barrett

I'd love to hear from you! Please write to linda@linda-barrett.com or P.O. Box 841934, Houston, TX 77284-1934. Check out my Web site at www.linda-barrett.com

No Ordinary Summer
Linda Barrett

HARLEQUIN®

TORONTO • NEW YORK • LONDON
AMSTERDAM • PARIS • SYDNEY • HAMBURG
STOCKHOLM • ATHENS • TOKYO • MILAN • MADRID
PRAGUE • WARSAW • BUDAPEST • AUCKLAND

To Pauline and Andrew—

who had the good sense to fall in love, get married and GIVE ME GRANDCHILDREN!

Thank you, thank you, thank you.

ISBN 0-373-71218-9

NO ORDINARY SUMMER

Copyright © 2004 by Linda Barrett.

This edition published by arrangement with Harlequin Books S.A.

® and TM are trademarks of the publisher. Trademarks indicated with ® are registered in the United States Patent and Trademark Office, the Canadian Trade Marks Office and in other countries.

www.eHarlequin.com

Printed in U.S.A.

CAST OF CHARACTERS

Shelley Anderson: Boston teacher, leases ground floor of Sea View House

Daniel Stone: Law professor (Harvard), leases top floor of Sea View House

Bart Quinn: Realtor for Sea View House
Father of Maggie Sullivan and Thea Cavelli
Grandfather of Lila Quinn Sullivan
Great-grandfather of Katie Sullivan

Laura and Matt Parker: Hero and heroine of first Pilgrim Cove book

Maggie Quinn Sullivan: Bart's daughter, Lila's mother
Partner in The Lobster Pot

Thea Quinn Cavelli: Bart's daughter
Partner in the Lobster Pot

Lila Sullivan: Bart's granddaughter and partner

Dee Barnes: Manager of Diner on the Dunes
Recently married to Rick "Chief" O'Brien

THE ROMEOS:

Bart Quinn: Unofficial leader of the ROMEOS

Sam Parker: Matt's dad, works part-time with Matt

Joe Cavelli: Thea's father-in-law

Rick "Chief" O'Brien: Retired police chief; married to Dee Barnes

Lou Goodman: Retired high school librarian

Max "Doc" Rosen: Retired physician

Ralph Bigelow: Retired electrician

Mike Lyons: Retired engineer

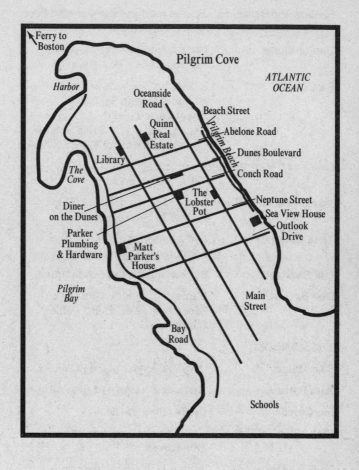

Ferry to Boston

Pilgrim Cove

ATLANTIC OCEAN

Harbor

Oceanside Road

Beach Street

Quinn Real Estate

Abelone Road

Dunes Boulevard

Library

Conch Road

The Cove

The Lobster Pot

Diner on the Dunes

Neptune Street

Sea View House

Outlook Drive

Parker Plumbing & Hardware

Pilgrim Bay

Matt Parker's House

Main Street

Bay Road

Schools

CHAPTER ONE

"ARE WE THERE YET?"

Shelley sighed and glanced into the rearview mirror of her five-year-old Toyota Camry. Both kids were squirming in their seat belts despite the books, tapes and games she had brought. They'd stopped for a fast-food snack along the way, a very infrequent choice when Shelley was in charge. But she wanted to provide Emily and Josh with a fun day. And if that included shakes and fries, so be it.

"Look out the window and tell me if *you* think we're almost at the beach."

Silence reigned for a moment, before Josh said, "Well, the trees are shorter than ours. And there's sand along the side of the road."

"I see sand," said Emily.

"There's a sign coming up on the right," said Shelley, slowing the car. "Can you read it, Josh?"

"I know how to read, Mom," Josh replied, exasperation in his voice. "It says Welcome To Pilgrim Cove. Population: Winter—5000. Summer—Lots Higher."

Shelley chuckled. A town with a sense of humor. "I have a good feeling about this," she said. But her son didn't answer. She glanced into the mirror again and sighed. Josh was as sullen as when they'd left the house. Of course, he'd been hoping his dad would surprise him with a call or a short visit even though it was Carl's "off" weekend. Finally, Shelley had suggested he call Carl. Josh's expression had reflected his hope against hope. But in the end, he'd taken the chance and dialed.

Shelley had seen the disappointment on his face and immediately blamed herself. Maybe she shouldn't have encouraged him to call his dad. It was so hard to know exactly what to do! In the year since the divorce had become final, she'd tried so hard to protect her children. A year of counseling, play-group therapy and keeping their lives and routines as normal as possible. And now Josh was sitting in the back seat of Shelley's car at the end of a two-hour drive from Boston, his unhappiness visible to everyone. Her son didn't want to acknowledge "on" and "off" weekends. Josh wanted the family the way it used to be.

She'd been so damn naive when she'd met Carl in the college bookstore. He'd been a confident, ambitious law student aiming for a big career and she, an undergrad working in the store, nose always in a book, mind on her grades. He'd pursued her after their first encounter. Won over her hardworking parents, bringing them hope for their son when her hormone-raging adolescent brother started looking up to Carl as a role model.

And her brother had straightened out, was now married with kids. Carl still took the credit when her folks spoke of those days. He knew how to play up to her family just as he knew how to play up to a jury.

"We're on Main Street now," said Shelley, picturing the map she'd studied the night before. "A very long street that continues down the entire peninsula. Lots of waterfront here. The Atlantic on one side and Pilgrim Bay on the other."

Josh grunted.

Shelley sighed again. She felt like the head cheerleader of a very reluctant team.

"Come on, Josh. Help me find the place. Quinn Real Estate, on Main, past Abalone Street." Shelley slowed down again to read signs as they crossed intersections. "Neptune, Conch, Dunes, Abalone!" she recited, tapping the brakes again. "Good. We're almost there."

"I see the place, Mom. On the right."

"Good eye, Josh. Thanks."

Her son gave a weak smile, and Shelley decided right then to learn every baseball term useful for building a boy's confidence. She was sure it was the "good eye" that had coaxed Josh's small grin.

She pulled into a spot in front of Quinn Real Estate and Property Management, as glad as her children to have arrived. Stepping into the sunshine, she closed her own door, walked around the car to help Josh and Emily out on the curb side.

"Okay, troops. Let's see if Mr. Quinn really does have something we can afford right on the beach." During their phone conversation earlier in the week, Bart Quinn had been encouraging without making any promises. Shelley was willing to accept any house in the vicinity of the beach, no matter how tiny. An uninsulated bungalow would do. She was convinced a change of scene and a change of activities were what they all needed. A summer at the seashore would certainly provide those.

BARTHOLOMEW QUINN LEANED back in his oversize leather desk chair and rolled it and himself to the large open window. A spring breeze tinged with sunshine and ocean had been teasing him all morning, and he'd resisted its lure until now. He closed his eyes and inhaled the best perfume in the world. If he were a younger man, he'd close shop for an hour and hit the beach in full stride. In fact, he had the urge to do it now. At seventy-five years, he still walked with a spring in his step! Plus a twinge in his knee.

He continued to dream, his mind's eye like a movie camera, capturing every foot of shoreline on the peninsula. He knew the shore in every season, the ocean in all her moods. The fair ones and the foul. Just as he knew every street in town. He chuckled at the thought. Since he'd lived in Pilgrim Cove all his life, he'd be hard-pressed not to know every street, road and thoroughfare. He'd be a lousy real estate agent to boot!

Finally opening his eyes, Bart stood up and peered out the window. Main Street was quieter today than it was in the middle of the week. Most of the businesses were closed on Sunday—Parker Plumbing and Hardware, the Pilgrim Cove Savings & Loan—but not Quinn Real Estate at the start of the busy season. He and Lila, his granddaughter, had been answering a constantly ringing phone since the beginning of March as people yearned for sunshine and summer vacations after a long New England winter.

Bart sighed with satisfaction. Life had been good to him. His parents had emigrated from County Cork long ago with not even a potato in their pockets, and now their son ran the business they'd established—the oldest and largest real-estate sales and property management company in the county—in partnership with their great-granddaughter! Now, how many families could boast that?

He turned from the window and started to push his chair back to the desk, but a slamming car door made him pause. Bart moved back and stared at the street directly outside. A woman was gathering two children from the back seat of a sedan. He glanced at his watch. Probably his noon appointment arriving at almost one o'clock.

He watched as she bent close to the children,

talking or listening, he couldn't tell. She had a cap of short dark hair, red highlights dancing whenever she moved her head. Then she straightened, took a child's hand in each of hers and looked up at the sign on the agency's front door. She didn't move for a second, in fact, stood very still as though plucking up courage before leading the children up the few steps to the doorway.

Bart shook his head. Poor girl. Could be she'd gotten lost. She certainly looked lost. Lost and scared. But also determined. A not-so-brave mother lioness.

"We'll see. We'll see," he murmured, checking his appointment book for her name before walking out of his office to greet her. He turned right and right again ten feet down the corridor toward the front of the building. The distance to the front door was the price he paid for the corner office with the cross ventilation, and he didn't mind a bit.

His granddaughter stood at the entrance, already chatting with their visitors and leading them down the hall toward him. "Oh, there he is," Lila said. "Granddad, this is…"

"Shelley Anderson," Bart completed, extending his hand to the young woman with the shiny hair. "Welcome to Pilgrim Cove."

"I'm sorry we're late," she began, a tiny frown creasing her brow, a shadow darkening her eyes.

"No matter," said Bart quickly. "We're a little slow today anyway. In fact, right now is better for me." Lila's astonished expression would have made him laugh if he'd allowed himself to look at her. So he didn't. Bart knew people, had learned to trust his instincts years ago, and still believed in a man's gallantry to women. Right now, Bart would have said anything to put Shelley Anderson and her children at ease.

He watched Lila make a beeline back to her office, and then turned toward the boy and offered his hand. "And you are…?"

"Josh." One word, sullenly given. Limp handshake.

"Fine jacket you have. My great-granddaughter plays baseball, too."

Now, *that* got the boy's attention. His hazel eyes came alive.

"But she's a girl!"

"That she is, boyo. She's a girl on second base."

Bart let Josh mull that over while he turned to the beautiful little girl hiding behind her mother's legs with her thumb in her mouth. He walked to Shelley Anderson's side and bent down until his knee protested. "And who's this little princess?"

A pair of chocolate-brown eyes, as big and round as any he'd ever seen, peeked up at him. Bart glanced up at the mother, but her attention was solely on her daughter.

"Are you Esmeralda Hossenfeffer?" asked Bart with a wink as he looked at the little girl again.

A tiny giggle emerged from behind the child's thumb. A sweet sound.

"Are you Isabella Farmer-in-the-della?" The gentle teasing came easily to him, a man surrounded by family, where five grandchildren and one great-grandchild had filled his daily life from the moment they'd been born.

The thumb popped out of the girl's rosebud mouth, and she shook her head fast.

"Are you—?"

"I'm Emily Joy Anderson!"

Bart snapped his fingers. "That's just what I thought all the time," he said, pleased to see the spirit hiding inside the child. He extended his hand to Emily, and she took it before disappearing behind her mother again.

Bart centered his attention on Shelley Anderson, who sported a lovely smile as she hugged her daughter. "You have two beautiful children, Mrs. Anderson," he said.

Her smile widened and she nodded. "I certainly do. They're beautiful, they're smart and, well, they're just the best." She kissed them each on top of their heads.

Josh made a face. "No mushy stuff."

"Sorry," said Shelley in a light, musical tone.

Bart chuckled under his breath. The woman wasn't sorry at all. No shadows darkened her eyes now; no frowns marred her smooth forehead. And he silently applauded. It was a pleasure to see some confidence overtake the worry he'd seen on her face earlier.

He led the little family to his sunny office and invited them to sit down. He was ready to learn all he could about Shelley Anderson and her children. Not because he was an old gossip with time on his hands. Not at all. In fact, his meeting with this family carried great responsibility.

For twenty-five years, Bartholomew Quinn had been charged with leasing a particular waterfront property on a sliding financial scale when appropriate. He answered to the William Adams Trust, named for the founder of Pilgrim Cove, about his choice of tenants. And so far, he hadn't missed a step in identifying those who needed a bit of fiscal help along with a respite from daily life. Sea View House provided the answer for folks recovering from emotional exhaustion no matter the reason.

The instincts of a lifetime had awakened when Shelley Anderson had called for the appointment. Now they crackled along every nerve. Sea View House was certainly what she needed; he hoped it was what she deserved.

CHAPTER TWO

THE OLD ROGUE HADN'T missed a trick. Bartholomew Quinn, with his leonine head of white hair and his twinkling blue eyes, had learned all about her—about the divorce, about her job, about the children—in twenty minutes. Shelley glanced at her watch. Correction. Fifteen.

She recognized the Irish in him—she was half Irish herself—and credited his success in drawing her out to both the traditional gift of gab and a long-ago kiss to the Blarney stone.

Of course, Bart Quinn had something she wanted very much. A house on the ocean at an affordable rental. A temporary sanctuary where she and the kids could come to terms with their lives and find some peace. For that possibility, she'd compromise her natural reticence in a heartbeat.

"Teaching is a noble profession," said Bart, "that doesn't pay well."

Shelley chuckled ruefully and nodded. "I haven't used the word 'noble' myself, but I've always viewed the shaping of young minds as important work regardless of salary."

"Even kindergarten?"

"Especially kindergarten!" Shelley could feel her blood heat up. She'd had this discussion in the past with people who thought she was wasting her mind and her time on the babies of the school system. She'd grown used to defending her choice, but was disgruntled every time she had to. She'd expected better of Bart Quinn.

"Those children are lucky to have you, Shelley Anderson. I bet you're a fine teacher."

Well, all right! Shelley looked at Bart's teasing expression, and felt herself relax. She'd been on target about him after all. A miracle, when she didn't trust her own judgment about men anymore. Not even about older gents.

"Mom, can we go?" Josh's voice held a distinctive whine, and Shelley stifled a groan as she glanced at him on the leather office couch and recognized his all-too-familiar sullen expression. The car magazine that Bart had provided hadn't held Josh's attention very long.

A noisy commotion at the doorway prevented her from answering her son. Two youngsters, a boy and a girl, darted into the room and scrambled toward Bart, Lila right behind them.

"Hi, Papa Bart," the children said simultaneously, the girl crawling onto the older man's lap and kissing him. Her blond hair was pulled back into a ponytail; her grin would no doubt leave a trail of broken hearts in the future.

"Sorry, Granddad," said Lila. "Just wanted to tell you I'm taking them to their game. They insisted on seeing you first."

"Surprise visits just break my heart," said Bart, winking at Shelley and returning the little girl's kiss. "This angel is Lila's daughter, Katie. She's my great-granddaughter. Looks just like me, wouldn't you say?"

Shelley almost giggled herself. The patriarch obviously loved center stage as much as he loved those children.

"And this young man is my grandson by proxy, by the name of Casey Parker. Parker Plumbing's just across the street. His grandpa and dad couldn't run the place without him."

The boy's eyes shone with delight, and he nodded vigorously. "Looks like these powerhouses are ready to hit one out of the park," continued Bart, his voice as serious as an announcer's.

The kids giggled, but Shelley's eyes were on her own son, who was sitting at the edge of the couch now. Transformed. His eyes shone with interest. He leaned forward, looking ready to join the other children.

"You play for Ted Williams, too?" asked Josh.

Bart's two young visitors turned as one unit toward Josh, the backs of their red jackets visible to Shelley for the first time. The words Ted Williams Little League were written there in big letters.

"Yup," answered Katie.

"It's the only l-l-league in t-town," said Casey, a wide grin on his face.

"My jacket's blue," replied Josh, standing up and turning around to show them the name of the revered baseball hero.

"Ted Williams?" chorused the pair. Now three puzzled faces turned to Shelley.

"The color of your jacket depends where you live," she said.

Katie recovered first. "So, are you moving here?" she asked with a hand on her hip. "I'll tell the coach to put you on our team and you'll get a red one."

Casey nodded in agreement. "Everybody p-p-plays!"

Bart's voice saved Shelley from replying. "We've also got a summer league. Starts in June, right after school lets out."

Shelley's heart danced a jig as she heard the Realtor's words. As she looked at her son's happier face and the friendly children in the room, she knew Bart Quinn would somehow make it possible for her to rent a place. She exhaled in relief, not realizing until that moment how much she'd been counting on a summer at the beach.

She wanted to shout with happiness, but had to be content with a smile for Mr. Quinn. She was about to speak to him when she heard her daughter's voice for the first time since Lila and the children had appeared.

"But, Mommy, if we stay here all summer, how will Daddy find us?"

Deep silence filled the room after Emily's question. Shelley crossed to where her daughter was sitting and squatted in front of her.

"That's simple. We're going to tell Daddy exactly where we are. With the address and directions and everything. He'll find us and visit with you and Josh. Don't worry." She wished she believed the words herself. If only Carl would stick to his promises, the kids would feel more secure.

Emily dimpled up at her, for the moment happy again. Maybe this time Shelley had said the right thing.

Lila's voice penetrated her musings, and Shelley rose to her feet. The other woman was gathering her charges to take them to their game.

"Nice meeting you, Mrs. Anderson. And you too, kiddos." She turned to her grandfather. "Taking them to Sea View House?"

Bart Quinn nodded. "You bet your sweet petutie I am. It's perfect for them."

"It *is* perfect for some, isn't it?" replied Lila, her words slowing as she spoke.

Shelley wondered at the sudden change in Lila's voice, a wistfulness, perhaps a yearning. But she had no time to brood. Bart was urging her, Josh and Emily to follow him to his vehicle.

"With both of us out, tell Jane she's on her own," Bart said to Lila when they reached the exit. "The phones are all hers."

"Will do. For someone new to the business, she's having a great season. I'm glad we hired her."

Bart grunted. "The old intuition still works."

Lila's blue eyes sparkled with laughter, as she patted her grandfather on the arm. "The old everything still works on this guy. Anyway, hope to see you again, Mrs. Anderson."

"Same here. Please call me Shelley."

Lila smiled, then glanced at Bart. "She'll fit right in, I think." She faced Shelley again. "We're very informal around here. Can't be otherwise, living next to the ocean in a place where everyone knows everything about you."

"But I'll only be around for two months."

"Doesn't matter. In two weeks you'll feel like you've lived here forever. All it takes is a breakfast at the Diner on the Dunes, a dinner at the Lobster Pot and, most important, an evening at Neptune's Park." Lila pivoted to Emily and Josh. "You're going to love that place. Ferris wheels and roller coasters, and fun houses, and bumper cars…you are going to have a great time."

Shelley watched her children's eyes grow bigger and rounder with every word Lila spoke. Finally the woman looked at her watch and made a running exit with her two charges. "Can't be late for the game."

"Thanks," said Shelley to Lila's retreating back, before looking at Bart Quinn again. "Your granddaughter is terrific."

"That she is. She's happy today and it does my heart good. Seems to be getting a bit easier in recent times, less pretending…but…" The old man shook his head, silent and pensive. "Well, now," he said, a moment later, "are you ready to visit the house?"

"Absolutely," replied Shelley, more than willing to change the topic of conversation. Lila's troubles belonged to Lila, just as hers belonged to her. No one seemed able to escape disappointment or sadness in life, and she couldn't do anything about that. The only action she could take was to cope with her own problems as best she could.

Shelley motioned for the children to join her, and in less than two minutes, they all bundled into Bart Quinn's ten-year-old black Lincoln Town Car. He was almost as proud of that car as he was of his grandkids. "The trunk's so big," he bragged, "I could pack my whole Main Street office in it!"

The man loved life. He laughed often. Shelley wished she laughed more herself. She wished her fairy-tale life—with handsome husband and two children—had had a happy ending. She wished… she wished… She was a fool to wish. What was the old saying? If wishes were horses, beggars would ride? She looked around her. Well, she was riding in a Lincoln, wasn't she?

They drove back along Main Street where the usual variety of businesses was located. Near Bart's office were a diner, a bank and a barbershop called the Cove Clippers. They passed Parker Plumbing and Hardware and turned left on Outlook Drive.

Bart drove straight down the street where more houses stood, and Shelley could soon see the ocean straight ahead in the near distance. She could smell it, too.

"Almost there," began Bart. "It's a special house, you know. People who live there for even a short while, go away happier."

And leprechauns live under toadstools. "Are you sure it's the house?" asked Shelley. "Or is it merely being on vacation that helps?"

"Well, young lady, I wouldn't want to say for sure, but Laura McCloud, who lives there now, has no complaints. And she hasn't taken a swim even once! But lately, she smiles all the time, especially when she looks at Matt Parker."

Whoa! Information overload. Too many names with no faces.

"Are you saying the house is already rented?"

"Only until next month. Laura's lease ends the week before Memorial Day. You and the children can spend the holiday weekend here if you'd like. And then come back in June as soon as convenient."

"That's more than I expected, Mr. Quinn. You really can pull rabbits out of the hat."

Bart Quinn guffawed, turned left on Beach Street and pointed toward a big house on the first corner lot. "Here's the old girl."

Shelley stared. Sea View House was huge. Two and a half stories, a big sloping roof, gray weathered wooden shingles, a saltbox style from the early days of colonial New England. A wide porch ran the width of the house, and a white picket fence bordered the yard.

"Wow!" she said. She'd imagined a tiny cottage. "Far grander than anything I expected."

"But you'll not be leasing it all," said Bart, pulling the car into the driveway. "Did I forget to mention that? You'll have the first floor, known around here as the Captain's Quarters. It's plenty roomy. In fact, with three bedrooms, it can accommodate your little family and any visitors you may get."

The children climbed out of the big car before Shelley did and headed up the driveway toward the back of the house.

"Hang on a minute, kids," called Shelley, scrambling after them. The sea was their backyard neighbor. She'd prefer to introduce her children to that particular neighbor and make sure they viewed the ocean's power and vastness with respect.

"Go after them," said Bart. "Laura's not home now, so I'll find my way in and meet you on the back porch. But take your time. Have a grand adventure."

The breeze blew steadily as Shelley, Josh and Emily made their way up the driveway, through a grassy backyard and then onto the sand. Today the air was cool enough without needing the ocean breeze for relief. But Shelley knew that in July and August, the wind would be a blessing.

Shelley studied the back of the house. The covered porch on this side was large, too, with wide steps leading up to it from the yard. A couple of rocking chairs stood empty, and Shelley could imagine herself sitting on them at the end of the day, listening to the sounds of the Atlantic.

The bright sun shone down as she, Emily and Josh walked closer to the shore. When she looked out to sea, the vast blue sky blended with the blue-green of the ocean to form an inseparable horizon. "Look out there, kids. Look at it." She raised her arm, pointing out over the ocean. Then she twirled in a circle on the sand. Miles of beach in each direction, and dead ahead, the magnificent Atlantic.

"But no one's here, Mommy," said Emily. "It's just us."

"That's because it's still too cold to go swimming. But just you wait. In the summer, there'll be loads of kids to play with."

She turned to her silent son. "Think you'll enjoy spending the summer here?"

He cocked his head, eyes narrowing. "We can't hide, Mommy. Daddy's going to find us, you know. He's smart."

Shelley cupped her son's troubled face in her hands and tilted it until he looked straight at her. "We're *not* running away from Daddy, Josh. We're not hiding. He'll know where we are all the time. I promise you that." Whether Carl chose to visit was another story. Shelley didn't voice her doubts aloud.

She sighed deeply. Emily had thought her dad would get lost finding them, and Josh thought they were hiding from him. Her two children had put their own spins on her idea, but both had the same fear. Loss of a father. Too bad their philandering, superbusy father didn't deserve such loyalty.

The image of Carl and his blond associate locked in a tight embrace was never far from her mind. A naive, unsuspecting wife didn't forget shock or betrayal easily.

"Let's walk to the waterline," said Shelley, putting a hand in each of her children's. She'd rent the house in any case, but she'd really hoped for a buy-in from the kids. "Let's get the feeling of what's it like near the ocean. Maybe we'll find a lobster!"

"Oh, Mom," sighed Josh. "You need a trap to get lobster. You need to go out in deep water."

Josh kept talking as they walked, and soon the children were busy searching for shells in the hard sand. Gradually their excitement built as they exclaimed over each discovery. Little by little, Shelley felt her body relax. The three Andersons were going to spend the summer at the beach. She, for one, couldn't wait.

And neither could Bart Quinn. She ushered the children to the back porch and through the door that led to the kitchen. The Realtor sat at a square Parsons table studying a calendar. Foot-wide gray planked flooring seemed to flow from the porches throughout the house. Tied-back Cape Cod curtains allowed daylight in through the windows, but the eastern exposure would insure a cool kitchen at the end of long summer days.

"Laura knew we'd be visiting and left the house neat and clean. So, let's take a walk through." Bart Quinn suited action to words and rose from the table.

"I want to sleep with Mommy in this house," said Emily.

"You can do that, little lady," replied Bart. "There's a big bed in the master bedroom."

"Goody."

The apartment was everything Bart had promised and Shelley had hoped for. Three lovely bedrooms, one of which seemed to be serving as an office now, an entry hall with a living room to one side and a separate dining room to the other. Large, but comfortable and informal, they were rooms to be used every day, not just for company. Chintz covered the couches and chairs, and braided area rugs lay on the planked floors.

"Cozy," said Shelley as she looked around. Not so big that she'd be cleaning all the time, but big enough for them to have space. In fact... "Josh! Emily! I have a great idea." She waited until they were in front of her. "How about we ask Nana and Poppy to stay with us for a few weeks?"

Her children's eyes shone. A natural grin crossed Josh's face. "Yeah," he said. "That would be good. Then we wouldn't be alone."

Her heart dropped. Again disappointment filled her. When would she get used to knowing that her son didn't feel secure with having just one parent around? Or more probably, he didn't feel secure with *her* as the only parent. His grandparents would reinforce his own sense of normalcy and security.

She glanced at Bart Quinn. Nothing passed his notice. She'd already learned that, and what she saw now confirmed her theory. Kindness and understanding.

"Buck up, boyo," said Bart, focusing his eyes on Josh. "You'll have so much to do and so many new friends to play with, you won't have time to be lonely or alone...unless you want to be."

Without waiting for Josh to reply, he turned his attention to Shelley. "As a matter of fact," he continued, "you won't be the only adult at Sea View House, either."

"What do you mean?" asked Shelley, realizing Bart wasn't including her parents in his announcement.

"I started to tell you earlier, but somehow got sidetracked. The upstairs has already been rented for the summer. A professor from California who just accepted a job at Harvard," explained Bart Quinn. "Poor man lost his wife not too long ago. Still has a grief in his heart."

"The upstairs?" asked Shelley, taken by surprise, and not absorbing the other details.

"We call it the Crow's Nest around here. When the current William Adams renovated the place, he built two separate apartments, with separate entrances, so that his idea for providing an affordable rental property would be practical. We charge market price for some tenants, which helps the trust to maintain the house. No one in town but the board of directors and me knows who's who."

"I'm not a charity case, Mr. Quinn. I can support my family just fine."

"And who's saying you can't?" replied Bart, a definite Irish brogue lacing his voice. "Saints preserve us! Surely not I." He pointed to the front windows overlooking the shady, tree-lined street and then pointed to the back ones, where they could see the waters of the Atlantic cresting in small steady waves. "What price do we put on that?"

Quinn paused, but Shelly knew he didn't expect an answer.

"Sea View House is not about money, my dear. Sea View House levels the playing field. Financial problems shouldn't make personal hard times harder. That's what my friend William Adams believes, as have all the generations in his family before him. Many people have benefited from their philosophy. Ordinary people, just like you and me, who need a bit of a vacation, who need to carve a bit of time to regain their equilibrium."

Shelley understood his message all too well. Hadn't she come to Pilgrim Cove searching for just that type of reprieve? Searching for time and space to come to terms, to help herself and her children? Hoping she could afford the luxury of it? She hadn't realized, however, that people like William Adams existed in real life.

"Time is a gift," she murmured.

"Aye, it's that. And what could be more precious?"

Shelley looked hard at her children. Bart Quinn struck a chord. What could be more precious than an endless summer with Josh and Emily?

Confident once more, she reached into her purse for a pen. "Where's the lease, Mr. Quinn? I'm ready to sign."

AN HOUR LATER, Bart Quinn stood at his office window watching Shelley Anderson drive down Main Street on her way back to Boston. But she'd return at the end of next month for the Memorial Day weekend and then again in mid-June for the summer.

He was more than satisfied with his choice of tenant. Mrs. Anderson and her children were exactly the kind of people the William Adams Trust wanted to invest in, which was very reassuring, since he had to answer to the board for each tenant he selected. The summer provided twice the challenge since there were always several candidates then. Everyone wanted a vacation at the shore.

The current lessee, Laura McCloud, had rented off-season. The house had been vacant in March, and although Bart was under no obligation to rent it, Laura had proved to be a wonderful choice.

Shelley Anderson, too, would be another feather in his cap. Her kids were more important than her pride about the adjusted rent. Yes, indeed, Shelley Anderson was just the kind of tenant they sought.

Bart rubbed his hands together. The professor was paying full freight; the kindergarten teacher was reaping the benefits. They both needed a summer in Pilgrim Cove. Sea View House was a perfect match for each. And all arranged by Bartholomew Quinn.

He reached for his sweater and walked to his office door. Jane Fisher could handle the last hours of the day. "I'll be at the Lobster Pot with my daughters," he told the new employee as he left the building. "My work for today is finished, and a bowl of their prize-winning clam chowder is my reward."

"Mr. Quinn, you're always at the Lobster Pot at the end of the day!" said Jane.

"And why not?" replied Bart. "My two daughters own it, and my family hangs out there. Maggie and Thea would call the police if I didn't show up!"

"Then go, go, go." The woman made sweeping motions with her hands before reaching for the ringing phone.

"I'm on my way. And you close up on time. Your own daughters will be waiting and they're a lot younger than my two."

She waved him away and started chatting with the caller. Asking questions, taking notes.

Bart watched for a moment, nodded and then walked out the door. Yes, indeed. He could still pick 'em. With a jaunty step, he almost danced to his car.

Memorial Day weekend promised to start the season with a whoosh. Not only would Sea View House have two lovely people, but the town would also celebrate the marriage of longtime residents Rick O'Brien, retired chief of police, and Dee Barnes, manager of the Diner on the Dunes. And none other than Bart Quinn was standing up as best man for the chief.

After opening the car door, Bart paused, the key jingling in his hand. Summer in Pilgrim Cove looked more than promising. Heck! Summer be damned! He loved the town in every season. Life in Bart's stomping grounds was never dull.

ON THE MONDAY before the Memorial Day weekend, Daniel Stone pulled away from the Quinn Real Estate and Property Management office, the keys to the second-floor apartment of Sea View House in his pocket.

"We got hoodwinked, Jess," he said to the golden retriever sitting next to him on the front seat of his SUV. "The old man never said anything about a woman and two children sharing a house with us. And it's too late to move. Everything else on the beach is rented."

The dog thumped her tail in reply, without taking her eyes from the passing scenes outside the window of the moving vehicle.

"Not concerned about an invasion of privacy, are you?" asked Dan as he scratched his loyal friend behind her ears. Jess crooned with pleasure and for a moment, Daniel's heart was light, his mind on nothing but the moment. An ocean breeze, a lovable dog, a car ride. Sweet and innocent.

He turned onto Beach Street and pulled into the driveway of the big corner house. "The hell with it, Jess. We'll just ignore the neighbors and go about our business. We may be starting over on the East Coast, but that doesn't mean we want a lot of people in our lives. Especially not a woman whose hair—now what did Bart Quinn say? Oh, yeah— had 'red dancing lights in it.' Why would we care? You and I know that no one can ever replace Nikki."

The dog whined at the sound of the beloved name, and Dan almost joined her in chorus. After two years, he still choked whenever he thought about his wife. His beautiful wife, who'd cried with happiness at hearing the news of her pregnancy three months before the accident. A pregnancy they'd both thought would never happen.

He'd tried to teach himself to be strong, but he'd learned by now that grief couldn't be banished. At least, not by him. Not when he thought about his Nikki—joyful woman, childhood sweetheart, best friend. She would have been a wonderful mother. He blinked hard. He'd loved her from the moment he'd met her in junior high.

Damn that bus! Damn that rain! She hadn't had a prayer of surviving. They'd all known it, but they'd prayed anyway. Of course, neither she nor the too-small infant had survived. In the beginning, Daniel hadn't thought his in-laws would, either. Nikki was their first-born. Their bright, beautiful girl. Her death had devastated them as much as it had him.

In the end, however, they'd had each other for comfort. They had other children, grandchildren and the promise of more. And, like his own parents, they'd worried about him, too. Included him in family events. But, at the end of the day, it was Daniel who was truly alone, his pain a constant companion.

"And now, Jess, we're three thousand miles away from home so there won't be reminders everywhere we go." Except for the memories in his own head. A person couldn't escape those.

He opened the car door and let the dog jump out. Nikki's dog, really. He didn't doubt for a moment Jess's ability to grieve, either. She knew Nikki was not coming back, and had attached herself to Daniel as though afraid to lose him, as well. Or maybe to protect him from harm.

"Okay, Jess. Time to unload." He unlocked the side door to the house, his private entrance to the Crow's Nest, grabbed a suitcase from the car and started up the inside staircase.

The door at the top of the stairs opened directly into a large, bright kitchen with sliding doors leading to a deck at the back of the house. The deck had been the deciding factor for Daniel. He could sit out there enjoying the sights and sounds of the beach.

Enjoying an unimpeded view of the ocean. Watching everything and everyone to his heart's content while still maintaining his privacy.

He carried the first suitcase into the big bedroom, then went downstairs for more items. He grabbed Jess's water bowl, took fishing rods, a baseball glove and a surfboard and stashed them in the tiny bedroom along with a carton of law books. Out of the car came a bag of paperbacks—all thriller reads. Pure escape. Perfect for the summer. His laptop, printer and supplies went into his large bedroom, which contained an oversize desk and chair.

When Dan's vehicle was empty and his possessions stored, he stepped from room to room and nodded. The Crow's Nest was a fully functional, compact apartment—perfect as a temporary home for a single man, with or without canine. Curtains bordered the windows; oval rugs covered the bedroom floors. That was the extent of the decorating. Plain and uncomplicated. Just as he hoped his new life on the East Coast—both here and later in Boston—was going to be.

He wanted nothing more than calm, uncomplicated days. A summer at the beach should provide him with just that. Except... Mr. Bartholomew Quinn had probably ruined that expectation. Why couldn't the Realtor have rented the downstairs to a quiet retired couple?

CHAPTER THREE

SHE SHOULD HAVE WAITED until Saturday morning to make the trip to Pilgrim Cove with the kids. The Friday-night holiday-weekend traffic had been horrific getting out of Boston, and a normal two-hour trip had lasted six—especially with dinner and more bathroom breaks than a human bladder could possibly need. In reality, using the rest rooms had become an excuse for stretching their legs.

And now Shelley was approaching Sea View House at almost eleven o'clock at night and had to bother her upstairs neighbor for the key to her apartment. That's what Bart Quinn had suggested when she'd called him on her cell phone two hours earlier to say she'd be arriving much later than anticipated.

"I'll leave the key with Daniel Stone," Bart had said. "He's home most evenings, so it'll be convenient for everyone. Especially me!" And then Bart had invited her and the children to breakfast the next morning at the Diner on the Dunes, a popular eatery near his office, which he'd said was very easy to find.

How could she argue about anything when Bart was being so helpful and she was the one at fault? But she felt awful about disturbing the professor tonight. Surely, an older gentleman would want to retire early, probably had a routine he followed, and because of her would now feel obligated to stay up late. Annoying her closest neighbor was not the best way to start the summer!

Shelley sighed as she turned onto Outlook Drive and headed toward Beach Street. Nothing she could do about it now, but she'd try to make it up to Professor Stone with a homemade peach pie or, better yet, a home-cooked dinner. Bart had said the man was a widower. Maybe he'd enjoy one of her soft-as-butter Yankee pot-roast meals, or one of her Italian specialties, or... Recipes shuffled through her mind like a deck of cards in the hands of a Las Vegas dealer. She felt herself relax. One problem solved.

She signaled left on Beach Street and realized she'd have to park in front of the house. Professor Stone's big car, or whatever his vehicle was called, sat in the driveway. If she pulled in behind him, he wouldn't be able to leave until she did. They'd have to work something out very soon about using the driveway, because on-street parking was limited in the summer due to the large numbers of beach goers.

Shelley pulled to a stop in front of Sea View House and glanced up at the second floor, glad to see lights on inside. Then she released her seat belt and twisted around to look at Josh and Emily asleep in the back. Still in their own safety belts, they'd somehow managed to lean toward each other, fingers touching across the pillow between them. A true picture-perfect moment. Her heart filled as she studied them. Beautiful. Innocent. Confused.

She quietly opened her door, stepped out of the car and, on impulse, lifted her eyes to the vast star-studded heavens. "Dear God," she breathed, her hands clutching the door's edge, "please grant me the wisdom to help make my children happy again. That's all. Amen." Short and simple, but fervent, and with as deep a yearning as any mother's prayer ever uttered. She felt a tear escape the corner of her eye and wiped it away with an impatient stroke. Darn! She should have prayed for courage and strength!

She closed the door gently, walked to the back of her car and opened the trunk. If God helped those who helped themselves, then she'd better get busy! She grabbed the first suitcase.

FROM HIS BEDROOM, where he lay propped against the pillows catching up with the adventures of Jack Ryan, Daniel heard the soft click of a car door through his open window. He glanced at his watch, then checked the street. Jess stood on her hind legs, front paws on the sill, looking out next to him. Yeah, Toyota Camry. Woman standing by the open door. His neighbor had finally arrived, just as Bart said she would.

He was about to go downstairs and hand over the keys, when in the combined light of the moon and front-yard pole lamp, he saw her look at the sky, then dab her face. Damn! Forget his intentions. He wasn't going anywhere near a crying woman. He turned from the window, walked to the kitchen and downed a glass of water. Jess stood at the kitchen door, whining to go out. Nature wasn't calling; adventure was.

"Hang on a minute, girl." Daniel stepped to the front window again and checked his neighbor's actions. Good. The woman—what was her name? Susan? Sheila?—was unpacking the trunk. Safe enough. He grabbed the keys to the downstairs apartment from the kitchen table, opened the door and jogged down the flight, Jessie at his heels.

He turned left when he reached the driveway and continued to the front of the house. The woman was on the concrete path halfway to the porch, the large duffel bag in her arms bigger than she was in every direction. Maybe her short straight hair and her slender neck just made her seem delicate. From his six-foot vantage point, she looked…small.

"Need some help?" he asked, good manners overcoming his need to toss her the keys and beat a hasty retreat.

She screamed, twirled, and the bag dropped to the ground. Her wide-open eyes reflected their terror. Her hands fisted at her sides. The dog barked once and trotted toward her.

Daniel stopped in his tracks. "Heel, Jessie." The golden came right to his side, sat and looked up at him. "Good girl." He patted her with automatic movements, but kept looking at the petrified woman.

"It's all right," he said. "I'm Daniel Stone, your upstairs neighbor, and this is Jessie. As gentle as they come. I'm sorry you were startled."

She said nothing. Just stared.

"Look," said Dan, holding out his hand, keys dangling. "These belong to you." Great. Just great. He'd be sharing his summer with a lunatic. He'd murder Bart Quinn the next time he saw him.

The woman's eyes narrowed. She glanced toward the car and back at him without moving her head. He wondered *how* she did that. He already understood the *why*. She was protecting her kids. So maybe she wasn't crazy.

"Didn't Bart Quinn tell you I'd have the keys?" Scintillating conversation. Daniel didn't know what else to say or do, except get a cell phone for her to call Quinn. And that's what this plan had been all about in the first place. Saving Bartholomew Quinn from having to be up so late.

"You're the professor?" Her voice, laced with incredulity, squeaked at the end of her question.

He nodded.

And then she started to laugh. And couldn't stop. She flopped onto the duffel bag, holding her stomach. "The—the professor?"

Certifiable. The laugh was wholesome, lyrical, but the lady was definitely certifiable.

"I'm sorry," she finally said. "But I expected an elderly man. I had the whole scenario in my head. White hair, maybe a walking stick..." She fell suddenly silent, and looked at him with compassion, before pushing herself to her feet.

Daniel knew exactly what she was thinking. Bart Quinn had undoubtedly told her about Nikki. Not about the pregnancy. Bart only knew what Dan had chosen to tell, and Dan had drawn the line at that revelation.

She walked to him and offered her hand. "I'm Shelley Anderson, who's just learned that Harvard professors can have only—" she squinted at him "—a few strands of gray."

He took her hand in his. It *was* small. Small, soft but firm when she grasped his palm. Her eyes were dark brown, darker than his. "And I'm Daniel Stone, who can tell Bart he was right."

She tilted her head in question.

"My downstairs neighbor has strands of sparkling red in her hair."

To her left, a car door slammed, distracting her, and suddenly two children appeared and started running toward their mother. Shelley eyed the dog and took a giant step back, allowing more room for her youngsters, preventing them from crowding the dog.

Jessie's tail wagged in quick-march tempo, sweeping the ground where she sat. She started to rise, her attention on the young newcomers. Dan knelt down and patted her. "Stay," he whispered. The dog loved children, but Dan could tell that Mrs. Anderson was apprehensive. All he wanted was a peaceful summer, not trouble with the kids downstairs, or their attractive but questionably sane mother.

But trouble stared at him from the scowling face of a brown-haired boy. A boy who'd stepped in front of his mom as soon as he saw Daniel. He could have just as easily been wearing a sign saying Keep Away From My Mother.

The little girl, on the other hand, leaned against her mom's leg and sucked contentedly on her thumb, her eyes half-closed.

"Who's he?" asked the boy.

"Josh!" Disapproval rang in the woman's voice. "No need to be rude. This is Professor Stone, our upstairs neighbor."

The kid's expression didn't change, his mom's words bouncing off him like arrows bouncing off an armored knight. Nothing was getting past the boy. Certainly not the upstairs neighbor.

"And these are my children, Joshua and Emily, who definitely need to be asleep." She glanced at Josh, then at Dan with an apologetic smile.

She was fooling herself if she thought Josh's attitude came from lack of sleep. Dan shrugged. Not his business!

"I've still got these," said Dan, holding out the set

of keys. He looked at Jessie. "Stay." Then he walked toward his neighbors and handed Shelley the key ring.

"Thanks," she said, looking at him, then the dog. "I guess you'd better introduce us."

"An excellent idea." Finally, something sensible out of her mouth! He studied the youngsters. Both sets of eyes were on Jessie, who was as alert as ever. Sitting tall and waiting.

"Come on, Jess," invited Dan, motioning the golden to his side. He swore the dog actually grinned. "This is my friend Jess," he began, directing his speech toward the children. "She loves to swim and she loves to play, and she loves…to be loved." Dan scratched Jess behind the ears, patting her the entire time while the dog crooned in ecstasy. "She's a golden retriever, and she's six years old."

"Ooh. I'm six years old, too."

Dan looked at Emily, who looked back at him, her eyes as round as the moon in the night sky. Seemed she surprised herself by speaking up. "Six years old?" Dan said. "Well, isn't that something?"

"She's big." The child stared at Jess. "Bigger than me."

Daniel didn't need to be a Harvard professor to understand what she was telling him. He knelt next to the dog. "She is big, Emily, but very, very gentle. She loves people. Especially children."

The girl looked up at her mother.

Shelley smiled. "Let's go say hello to Jess." She

turned to her son. "You, too, Josh. The dog needs to know you, so she knows you belong here, at Sea View House."

Within seconds, the youngsters were petting his dog and lavishing attention on her. Jessie was in doggie heaven, returning their affection, licking them both as though they were the most important people in the world. But it was Joshua Anderson who captured Daniel's attention. His eyes sparkled, and he giggled. Every time Jess snuggled her snout under the boy's arm and licked him, he laughed again. The child was finally acting like a regular kid. Not that Dan knew a lot about child development.

"Maybe they need a dog."

Shelley Anderson spoke aloud, but when Daniel glanced at her, she was staring into space, talking to herself. Okay. He'd met the neighbors. Delivered the keys. Introduced Jessie. His missions were accomplished. Time for him to say good-night.

"So, if you're all set now," Dan began, "then Jess and I will get out of your way."

She refocused on him and nodded, then turned to stare at her car. At the duffel bag. At the house. Then back at the car. She faced him again. "We're fine. We can handle it." Her tone was brittle, her eyes tired, but she forced a smile and stood taller, as though recharging her energy reserves. "Thanks for the keys," she said. "Good night." Then she yawned twice.

The woman was not fine. And neither was her little family.

Fortunately, they weren't his problem.

But he hoisted the duffel bag and carried it to the porch. Then he walked to the car and grabbed two suitcases from the trunk. The sooner the Andersons were inside their apartment, the sooner everyone in Sea View House could get some sleep.

"I can handle it," repeated Shelley, snatching a grocery bag.

He didn't know if she could or couldn't and didn't care. Dan deposited the last of his bundles on the porch, satisfied that every large item had been dealt with. Then he turned to Shelley once more. "You'll all want to sleep late tomorrow." He nodded at Emily, who lay across the duffel bag, Jess by her side. "Unfortunately, I'm meeting some friends for breakfast. Hope I don't disturb you when I leave."

"No problem," she replied. "Actually, we've got a breakfast date, too. With Bart Quinn at the diner."

Bart! He nodded, grateful for the heads up. He'd breakfast with Bart and the other ROMEOs during the week instead. Spending more time with the Anderson family was not high on his priority list.

THREE IN A BED. Shelley and both kids. It worked for the first night at Sea View House, although they were all so exhausted, they could have fallen asleep on a concrete floor. Shelley yawned and groped across Emily for the wristwatch on the night table. She managed to knock it to the floor. Through half-closed eyes, she glanced around the room. Pale gray light filtered between the window blinds and hinted at the coming morning. But it was still early. She stretched and closed her lids completely, ready to doze off. But Josh rolled over, his knee connecting with her hip. She slid aside, tried to straighten his leg, but her son instantly found a different angle, restless in his sleep. A characteristic acquired in the past year.

She studied his beloved sweet face, his little-boy mouth pursed while he slept, and wished she could kiss his worries away. Children should be allowed to have childhoods! Instead, Josh had wanted to protect her last night from their upstairs neighbor.

Tears formed in the corners of her eyes. Was the cost of divorce too high? She leaned over and kissed Josh gently on the forehead. Should she have tried to compromise? She slipped out of bed and found her way to the bathroom, then to the kitchen.

Pale sunlight permeated the curtains and shone directly through the glass panes on the door. Suddenly, Shelley felt her spirits lift. She turned the door bolt and stepped onto the porch.

At high tide, the Atlantic's foam-topped breakers hit the shore in a steady rhythm. To the left and right, an expanse of clean sand stretched as far as she could see. Nothing disturbed the scene. In the quiet of the morning, she stood alone in the world, in that place, at that moment.

And then, the picture changed. From the left, a man and a large dog entered her vision, jogging along the hard-packed sand close to the water. He wore a gray sweat suit and running shoes, and began to strip as he reached the vicinity of Sea View House.

Shelley didn't move. Her hands tightened on the porch railing. She couldn't help noticing his dark wavy hair, the wide shoulders, the ease of movement. Daniel Stone didn't resemble any professor she'd ever had in college!

His eyes were trained on the ocean and the dog romping in front of him. She was staring at his broad back, now bare to the sun. Shelley watched him raise his arms over his head then out to the side, stretching and then shaking them. Triceps, lats, and smaller muscles stood out in relief with each movement. Her respiration rate increased; shallow, short breaths kept her going. When Daniel reached for his waistband, she stopped breathing completely. And didn't blink.

Speedo! He wore a Speedo underneath. A tight, brief suit for some serious swimming. Shelley rocked on her feet, not knowing whether to feel disappointment or relief as the twosome entered the water. Disappointment won. Not so surprising when she realized how restless she felt inside. Aroused. And damp. Being a voyeur had turned her on! She shook her head in disgust. Was she so sex starved that the sight of a half-naked stranger could have such an effect?

She paused in her thoughts. Could be the answer

was yes. Her appetite in that important area of life hadn't been satisfied in almost two years. With all her other worries, she'd barely noticed, or pushed it aside when she had. Why, for heaven's sake, had her sexuality chosen to reawaken itself now?

She turned to go back inside, but the professor and his dog were headed farther into the ocean, and she couldn't look away. His broad back tapered into a narrow waist, followed by a tight rear end. His long legs consisted of well-defined muscles, period. No flab anywhere on him. The man looked better than good.

Then he and Jessie dived into the water and began to swim parallel to the shore. They continued about a quarter mile, then reversed direction. Within minutes, Shelley realized that she was watching a genuine athlete at work.

His strokes were strong and steady; she wondered if he had more stamina than the dog, and got her answer when Jessie paddled to shore, shook herself off and ran along the beach in tandem to Daniel's progress. Did the man think he was doing laps in a backyard swimming pool?

On that thought, the scenario changed unexpectedly. Daniel rolled on his side, then onto his stomach, then rolled over again, drifting with the current. His arms and legs weren't moving. Jessie immediately leaped into the foam, aiming directly for the man. Shelley tensed as she watched the two. Was Daniel in trouble? Damn! How could she help? She glanced quickly around the open porch. No equipment. Where were ropes kept? Inflatable raft? A tube? She had no idea. She looked out at the water again. Man and dog were still riding the current.

Heart pounding, she ran down the three steps to the backyard and headed toward the water as fast as she could. She kept her sights on them among the small waves and saw Jessie using her head to butt Daniel toward shore. Shelley doubled her efforts. Surely she could help Jessie bring Daniel onto the sand. As she watched, the pair finally reached shallower water, and Daniel stood up. He leaned over Jessie, lavishing praise and hugs on her. Looking and sounding as healthy and as in control as an Olympic swimmer.

Shelley stood immobilized. Panting. In shock. Having a hard time grasping what had just happened. And then it hit with the force of a monsoon. "You son of a bi—" she glanced at Jess, who really was one, then back at Daniel "—raccoon. How dare you! How could you! You scared the living daylights out of me."

HE'D BEEN CORRECT last night about two items. The woman downstairs was as crazy as a loon. And her hair did have red sparkles. Lots more of them in the morning sunshine than were visible in the pale moonlight.

She was still yelling at him, however, and instinct suggested he take the path of least resistance. He kept his mouth shut and let her explode.

"This is the Atlantic Ocean, you idiot, not a wading pool."

It was no hardship to watch her chocolate-brown eyes heat as her anger exploded at him. But then he felt like a heel. Her anger masked real fear. She'd been scared.

He put his hand up in a stop motion, hoping she'd cool down. No such luck. He waited and waited, until she finally wore herself out. But then she turned her back and started walking to the house.

"Hang on a sec," he called.

"Not interested," she replied, continuing on her way. "Play your games with someone else."

"Saving lives at the shore is not a game."

She twirled to face him. "*You're* saying that? As far as I can see, you broke the first rule."

He cocked his head.

"Never swim alone." This time she met his gaze and didn't look away. Her big eyes held the passion of her convictions. And for the first time, Dan saw a strength that made him rethink his first impression of her.

"I wasn't alone." He nodded at Jessie, who'd sat herself at his side, seemingly following the conversation of the two humans. "She's been trained for water rescue—usually freshwater—and I put her through practice a couple of times a week." He decided to go the extra mile. "I'm sorry you were so frightened."

He watched as her gaze shifted from him to the

dog and back to him again. He watched her expressions change as she processed the new information. Finally, she leaned closer to Jessie and scratched her under the chin. "You didn't mean to scare me, did you, sweetheart? You're quite a wonderful animal, aren't you?"

Jessie licked her face and vocalized her agreement with a whimper. Shelley threw back her head, allowing her laughter to harmonize with Jessie.

Gamine smile, a champagne-bubble laugh, shining eyes filled with humor and a heart-shaped face that could empty a man's mind of all rational thought. In a flash, Dan pulled on his sweatpants to hide his obvious response. He felt alive again after a long time, but he didn't need to announce it to the world.

CHAPTER FOUR

ALMOST TWO HOURS LATER, under a bright morning sun, Shelley loaded her kids into the car and headed toward the Diner on the Dunes, which was not on the beach at all. Instead, the eatery was located on Dunes Street. Her stomach rumbled, and she was happy to recall that the diner was Bart Quinn's favorite breakfast hangout. The food had to be good!

She pulled into a crowded parking lot. Looked like Saturday breakfasts were popular with everyone in the town. After finding a spot, Shelley led the children to the front entrance of the single-story white clapboard building. She raised her eyes and saw round windows near the roofline, framed in steel like the portholes of a ship. Cute.

As she was about to push open the door, she noticed a bright red-and-white sign above the entrance. Home Of The ROMEOs. ROMEOs? Her imagination ignited. Maybe a motorcycle gang? Or a group of star-crossed lovers drowning their sorrows in a pot of coffee? Or maybe simply the name of the owners?

The aroma of fresh coffee had her salivating as soon as she stepped inside. The hostess greeted them immediately and took them to a large round corner booth in the back that at first glance seemed totally occupied by men. Men with white hair. Men with gray hair. Men with no hair. Men with sharp eyes trained on Shelley.

"There you are," boomed Bart, rising from his seat to welcome her. He turned toward the others, who were now smiling. "This is Shelley Anderson, and these two are Joshua Anderson and Emily Anderson. They'll be spending the summer in Pilgrim Cove at Sea View House."

Bart's friends all spoke at once. Words of welcome and best wishes. Friendly men.

"Breakfast with this bunch is a ritual for all new tenants of Sea View House," said Bart as Shelley and the children sat down. "We want you to know your neighbors."

Shelley smiled. Bart was a kind person.

"I'd like to introduce the ROMEOs," said the Realtor.

Shelley nodded at him. "The ROMEOs! I was wondering about that." She looked around the table. "Not a motorcycle gang?"

She couldn't tell which man chuckled the hardest, or rapped the table the loudest, but one gent had a tear rolling down his face.

Bart—still laughing—pointed at the reserved sign, which was surrounded by coffee mugs in the middle of the table. The word ROMEOs appeared across the center. Shelley pulled the sign toward her, and saw, in smaller lettering beneath the title, Retired Old Men Eating Out. ROMEO.

Now it was she who couldn't stop laughing. "I don't see any old men here!"

"You picked another winner, Bart!" said the man closest to Shelley, with the wavy salt-and-pepper hair. "First, my soon-to-be daughter-in-law, Laura McCloud, and now Shelley Anderson. We've got a banner year going so far." The speaker offered his hand. "I'm Sam Parker. Semiretired. Parker Plumbing and Hardware on Main Street. Welcome to Pilgrim Cove."

"You've already met Sam's grandson Casey at the office," said Bart, looking at Joshua. "Remember?"

Josh nodded.

"And Katie, too," piped up Emily. "She plays baseball."

Every ROMEO looked as proud as if Katie belonged to each of them, but Shelley was intrigued by her own daughter. Had Katie's baseball playing made an impression on Emily? She had no time to dwell on the subject, however, because the other men started to introduce themselves. Shelly shook hands with each in turn.

"Ralph Bigelow, retired from the light and power company. Any electrical problems at the house, you call me."

"Lou Goodman, former librarian at the high school. I hate the word *retired* so now I volunteer at the public library." He looked at the kids. "We've got a terrific children's department. And when Laura McCloud reads to the kids, the stories come alive."

"Max Rosen," said the man next to Lou Goodman. "Call me Doc—everyone does. I sold my Boston medical practice and now I'm semiretired. I cover the ER at our local hospital a few days a month and I'm on call for Sea View House."

"And for any of his friends who have an ache, pain or worry," mumbled Bart.

"And I'm Joe Cavelli," said the final member of the troop. "My son's married to Bart's younger daughter, Thea. She and her sister, Maggie, own and operate the Lobster Pot. The best restaurant in New England." Joe reached into his pocket and pulled out a card. "These old coots," he began, nodding at his companions, "think you're going to remember all this information. But you won't. This will help."

He handed Shelley a larger than normal business card. On one side was printed "ROMEOs." On the other was a listing of each name, phone number and specialty.

"According to this list, there are a couple of you missing today," she said. "Mike Lyons, environmental conservation, and Rick 'Chief' O'Brien, retired police chief. So…let's see…there are eight of you."

She paused and looked at each of them. "Thanks. This is great. I feel like I'm surrounded by a squad of fairy godmothers...er...fathers."

"Just as long as you don't feel surrounded by a bunch of Mad Hatters," said Lou Goodman, the librarian.

Shelley chuckled and shook her head. "I didn't for a moment think that. Just nice people."

A lot of coughing and shuffling. "Okay, no more compliments for you gentlemen!" said Shelley. They looked more relaxed immediately.

"Mommy, I'm hungry."

"Perfect timing," said a young waitress, pad in hand, standing next to the table ready to take their orders. She looked at Shelley and nodded at the ROMEOs. "I know what these guys get. Dee told me a million times. But what will you and the kids have?"

"Pancakes," said Josh without hesitation. "Sausage on the side." He looked at Shelley. "That's Dad's favorite breakfast when we go out in Boston."

Shelley nodded. "That's fine, honey. Whatever you want."

Inwardly, she sighed. Her son didn't even like sausage! She turned to Emily. "How about you, Em? French toast?"

Emily nodded, looked at the waitress, then pulled Shelley closer to her. She whispered, "Ask her if it's like yours. Real good."

Shelley kissed her daughter's cheek and squeezed her. "I'm sure it's very good, sweetie."

"What? The French toast?" asked Bart, who then started to laugh again. "If Dee was here today, she'd give you her recipe. But right now, she has other things on her mind. Like getting married tomorrow!"

The waitress took off with their order, and Shelley learned about the courtship of Dee Barnes and Rick O'Brien, who'd be culminating their five-year relationship with a wedding.

"And we've got another wedding coming up next month, as well," said Bart, looking at his friend, Sam Parker, who then looked at Shelley.

"He means my boy, Matthew, and Laura McCloud, who I mentioned before. Third weekend of June. Evening ceremony on the beach near Sea View House. Laura wants it there and Matt's not objecting. She thinks living at Sea View House brought her luck. Personally, I think it's a bunch of rubbish. People make their own luck. But—" Sam looked off in the distance "—they're very much in love. My grandsons are crazy about her, and that's all that counts."

Shelley looked around the table. Lovable curmudgeons. All of them. "Seems that something's always happening in Pilgrim Cove."

"True enough," said Bart, "especially with the tenants at Sea View House." He winked. "You never know."

As if on cue, the waitress returned. "I have a message for you, Mr. Quinn. From Daniel Stone. Said to tell you he's running late. Don't hold breakfast for him. He'll catch you during the week."

So the professor's breakfast friends were the ROMEOs! Shelley started to chuckle. The chuckle evolved into a full-throated laugh. Daniel Stone was as wide-awake as she was. He wasn't running late. He was just running. From her!

"Darn that boy!" said Bart.

Shelley heard the disappointment in the Realtor's voice, saw it on his face and was a little startled. "What's wrong?"

"I wanted to officially introduce you to Daniel Stone, so you'd know he's an upright fellow. A man you can trust as your closest neighbor."

"Right," said Sam Parker, as three other men nodded their agreement. "We've all met him. And he's as fine a man as they come."

Nice of them to be concerned, but not necessary. "Not to worry, gentlemen." Shelley leaned toward the center of the table as if to share a secret. "I trust Jessie. She wouldn't be as sweet as she is if she weren't being treated well by her…hmm…fine man. And besides…" She paused for effect as silence reigned over the table. "Daniel carried my heavy suitcases to the door last night," she teased in a stage whisper.

"Ahh." A veritable men's chorus. Nodding heads.

Then each ROMEO leaned back in his seat with a contented grin.

"And the summer's just beginning," said Bart with a twinkle in his eye. "Who knows what can happen?"

The man had no subtlety, but his heart was in the right place. However, nothing was going to happen between Shelley and the man upstairs, who hadn't been able to get away from her fast enough last night or this morning. He'd pulled on those sweatpants quickly, nodded at her and continued walking the dog along the shoreline away from Sea View House.

And as for her, forget it. She had other priorities. Shelley glanced at Josh and Emily, who had cleaned their plates quite well and were starting to fidget. Daniel Stone may have been able to jump-start her internal-combustion engine, but she had no desire for a major overhaul. Not even for the summer. This summer, her attention would be firmly on Emily and Josh.

"Is the amusement park I noticed near the beach open yet?" Shelley asked.

Josh straightened in his seat when he heard the question.

"Neptune's Park? Sure is," replied Bart. "The owners have been setting up for days. The season starts this weekend. Every year, it's the same routine. The park stays open till midnight on the weekends. So you kids are in luck."

"Midnight?" said Josh, his face lighting up. "Awesome!"

Shelley reached over and squeezed him close. "You're awesome," she said, giving him a quick kiss on the cheek, and urging both children to their feet before Josh could protest her show of affection.

She turned to Bart and his cohorts, thanking them for the unique experience of breakfast with a band of do-gooders.

"Some would call us nosey parkers! But we don't care. What we do care about is Pilgrim Cove, so we put a lot of effort into making it a wholesome yet progressive town," the librarian said.

"Come around when my folks visit," invited Shelley with an unfamiliar enthusiasm. "All of you. Wives, too. Cocktails and dinner. Hmm…let's see how I can tempt you. How about a stuffed butter-flied leg of lamb grilled to juicy perfection? Rose-mary potatoes and a salad with walnuts and Gorgonzola cheese topped with a raspberry vinai-grette dressing."

She had their attention, but she, herself, was get-ting more excited. "Please," she said, "I'd love to cook for you. I haven't done anything big in so long, I'm almost breaking out in hives from the depriva-tion."

"Holy lobster pot!" said Bart. "If my daughters heard that menu, they'd grab you for their restau-rant."

Shelley grinned. "Thanks, but no thanks. I'm an

at-home kind of cook. Saturday-night entertaining.
And big Sunday family dinners with friends, too…"
Her voice trailed off. That's the way her life used to
be when she and Carl were married. With her cook-
ing skills and her love of entertaining, she'd turned
out to be a bigger asset to him than he'd ever realized in the beginning. What irony that her talents
had backfired! In the end, the domestic goddess
came in second to the attorney goddess. Not that
Shelley had known there had been a contest.

Ancient history now. Time to move on. Figura-
tively and literally. "Let's go, kids. We've got a lot
to do before we hit Neptune's Park." She looked at
the men. "Thanks again for the breakfast and even
more for the welcome." She eyed her offspring and
was relieved when they voiced their thanks, too.

As she and the children walked through the diner,
she heard Bart say, "She's perfect. Pretty, talented,
stronger than she knows. She sparkles. And she's the
perfect one to bring the lonely professor back to
life."

Shelley almost smashed the door open. She'd
give those matchmaking, meddling old men dried
prunes for dessert!

LATER THAT MORNING, with her car loaded with groceries, Shelley pulled into the driveway of Sea View
House behind Daniel Stone's vehicle. No time to
stand on ceremony about parking spots when she'd

be much closer to her back door, which opened directly into the kitchen.

"If you both help me real quick, we'll have time to go exploring on the beach."

"I thought we were going to Neptune's Park," said Josh, disappointment in his voice.

"We will. Later on."

"But…"

"Look at your sister, Josh. She's falling asleep."

"No, I'm not, Mommy." Emily smiled, then sighed and closed her eyes.

Shelley eyed her son. "Looks like I'm depending on you for help…or, you can take a nap, too."

The look of horror on his face made Shelley laugh. "I guess I'll help," he said, reaching for a bag of groceries.

"I knew I could count on you."

They each carried two bags into the house and returned to the car for the third time. Josh reached for the last bag of supplies from the trunk, and Shelley opened Emily's door.

"Woof."

Coming in from the beach, Jessie outpaced her owner and headed straight for Josh, licking his face and whining.

Josh twirled toward Shelley. "Mom! She's happy to see me."

"I can tell." Yup, she'd get him a dog after the summer when they returned home. Maybe a golden retriever, just like Jessie.

To her surprise, the dog left Josh and trotted to her in greeting. Sniffed and looked up at Shelley. Then whined.

"Well, hello to you, too." Shelley petted her and looked toward her owner just as he called the dog back.

"Sorry," said Daniel. "The breed is sometimes too friendly."

"I don't think that's possible. What could be bad about a friendly dog?" Shelley smiled at him and saw his brown eyes slowly darken.

"Uh, you need some help today?" Daniel walked toward the trunk of her car.

"We're fine," said Josh, slipping in front of the man and hoisting the groceries. "I'll put these inside, Mom. Then I'll be right back."

"And I'm sorry about that," said Shelley, nodding toward her son before turning to Daniel. "He's... ah..."

"Mom-my!" The word was a cry.

"That's Emily, nap interrupted." Shelley, glad of the distraction, walked quickly to release her daughter from the seat belt. Scooping her up, she returned to her neighbor.

"Your son," Daniel continued quietly, as Josh rejoined them, "is trying to protect you...from me."

"That's 'cause we're divorced." Emily's quiet, matter-of-fact voice resonated in the clear air. "And Daddy said Josh should look out for us 'cause Daddy doesn't live with us anymore."

No wonder Josh had developed an attitude in the past few months! She'd murder Carl for throwing that piece of responsibility at an eight-year-old boy.

"Shut up, Emily!" Josh looked at his sister, the all too familiar scowl once again visible.

"Josh! That's enough." Shelley carefully placed Emily on her feet and reached for her son. "Joshie, look at me."

He slowly brought his eyes to her level as she squatted in front of him. "Looking out for us is not your job, son. It's mine. I'm a very smart lady, Josh, and I'm perfectly capable of taking care of us." She held his gaze and hoped the sincerity she planted in her voice came through. "You know what your job is?"

He shook his head slightly, the scowl gone, but the forehead still creased.

"Your job is to play baseball. To go to school and do your best. Your job is to be a good friend to Emily." She paused to catch a breath. "Josh. Your job is to be a boy. To be eight years old. Later on, you'll be a spectacular man. But not now. Getting older is like climbing steps one at a time until you get to the top of the staircase. Little by little. Do you understand?"

She waited for his response, aware of his effort to absorb so much, but knowing her job wasn't finished yet. She needed to remove more of the burden he was carrying.

When he nodded, she continued, "There's a

chance, Josh, that you and Emily might not have understood what Daddy was saying. Maybe he said something like, 'take care of yourself.' And you thought he meant to take care of everybody."

Josh looked thoughtful. Then he cocked his head. "Maybe." He reached out and touched her face. "Do you think so? Maybe he said something else?"

She met his earnest gaze. "I can practically guarantee it. Don't you think Daddy knows the difference between being eight years old and thirty-eight years old? He's been both, you know, and he's good with math!"

And then her son laughed, his face suddenly brighter than the afternoon sun in the clear blue sky over Pilgrim Beach. Tears pressed against Shelley's eyes. Tears of relief. She needed a minute to compose herself. "Please take Emily inside for me, Josh. She needs more of a nap. And put the milk in the fridge right away."

"Sure, Mom." The kids disappeared. She heard the door slam shut, and felt a tear roll down her cheek as she gathered her remaining strength to stand up.

"Here you go. Hold on." Daniel's voice. She'd forgotten about him and, at the moment, didn't care that he'd witnessed her conversation with Josh. She moved her head and with her peripheral vision, saw his hand reaching toward her.

It was a large hand. A masculine hand. Broad fingers, clean, blunt nails and skin tanned from his

California sun. She glanced up. He stood at ease in his navy jersey and shorts. Just waiting. She saw the question on his face and looked down again. His open palm faced her now. She placed her hand in his, and felt the quiet strength and support this man offered as she rose from near the ground.

"Good job," he murmured as she shook the stiffness from her legs.

"Thanks," she replied. "But don't be too impressed. I had no clue...the words sort of just fell out of my mouth." She turned away, new thoughts tumbling over themselves and resolving into speech. "The truth is, I'd like to shake that man to his senses! What kind of a father puts such a heavy burden on a child?"

Daniel shrugged. "Hey. I don't know the guy, but if I had to guess, I'd say he's not thinking of the consequences to Josh at all. Maybe he simply wants a way to keep track of you and what goes on in your home. Josh is the way."

Shelley stepped back from Daniel and didn't reply. Was this really a control issue? She thought about her postdivorce relationship with Carl. A constant push-pull with him about everything. Second-guessing herself and her own decisions. Feeling guilty. Worrying all the time. Was Carl doing that to her? Undermining her confidence? And was she allowing him to?

She leaned against the car and glanced up at her neighbor. "You're not a divorce lawyer, are you?"

She joked, but her laugh fell flat as the possibility reared its head.

Although he seemed startled by the question, Daniel shook his head. "No, I'm not a divorce lawyer. Unfortunately, I've seen several friends go through the painful process, their common sense flying out the window. The East Coast doesn't have the franchise on separation and divorce!"

She smiled easily now at his attempt at humor. "I need to go inside. But thanks for your help."

He shrugged. "I didn't do anything. You handled it all." Suddenly, Daniel looked toward the ocean, his gaze becoming dreamy, as if going to a far-away place. "Nikki and I missed out on kids…we almost had…but we were very happy anyway… very happy…." A moment passed, and Shelley barely breathed, sensing that he rarely spoke about his wife. Then Daniel shook his head as if recalling himself to the present. He looked at her. Hard. "So I'm not sure it means anything if I say…I think you're a good mother."

He immediately motioned to the dog and disappeared through the side entrance before Shelley could thank him again. She stared at the closed door. Her upstairs neighbor was embarrassed! The California professor—a beach boy with the broad shoulders and body to die for—was one big hunk of shyness.

She walked toward her back entry, her mind retracing all her interactions with him. Each time, he'd watched, waited and listened. And then he'd replied or taken action. Last night, he'd seen what needed to be done and had done it. This morning on the beach, he'd stood patiently while she ranted and raved at him, and then he'd quietly explained about practicing lifesaving techniques.

A man of quiet strength. No constant chatter and commotion. No bluster. No need to be center stage.

By the time she opened the kitchen door, she realized what she was doing. She was comparing a man she'd known for fifteen years with one she'd known for fifteen minutes. Unfortunately, her children's father was coming up short.

IN THE END, they all took naps that afternoon. Shelley rolled over in her bed, opened her eyes and stretched. Sitting up, she listened for evidence of activity, but the house was quiet. She leaned back against her pillow, eyelids closing again, wanting to steal another minute before getting out of bed.

A sense of well-being filled her. Maybe the nap had helped. Maybe the credit belonged to the fresh air and being at the ocean. Or maybe it was the compliment from her upstairs neighbor. "I think you're a good mother." A phrase worth more than gold to her. She *was* a good mother. Always had been.

The doubts had infiltrated recently because of all the changes in their lives. The family structure had changed. Emotions had run high. Conflict and confusion had reigned for a while.

But today, a new acquaintance had said, "I think you're a good mother." The compliment was enough to make a gal hop out of bed and gather those children for a trip to Neptune's Park.

Shelley stepped to the threshold of Emily's room and smiled at the two children still sound asleep on the double bed. Josh was sprawled across the foot, apparently having given up the fight while waiting for Emily to fall asleep. Emily was tucked under the top sheet, head on her pillow, Raggedy Ann under her arm.

The room itself had once been used as an office, and Emily had claimed it immediately. As the child had explained to her mother, she needed the big desk for all her "arts and crats" stuff. Shelley agreed wholeheartedly. A place for Emily's supplies would keep them both sane.

Shelley knew, however, that the projects themselves would be created smack-dab in the middle of the kitchen. Although Joshua preferred the privacy of his bedroom for his works-in-progress—"Emily touches everything!"—Emily chose to be near her mom.

Tiptoeing to the bed, Shelley placed a butterfly kiss on each child's forehead and began to nuzzle them awake.

Sweet hugs from Emily. A jaw-cracking yawn from Josh. But in seconds, both children were up, washed and ready to go.

Shelley opened the kitchen door, stepped onto the

back porch and promptly shivered. The pale light of the setting sun behind them cast shadows on the water as evening drew near.

"What, Mom?" said Josh.

"The sun's going down and we all need jackets and long pants. Summer's not quite here yet."

"But we'll be late," protested Josh, heading toward the steps.

"No such thing as late at Neptune's Park," said Shelley. "Remember? Open until midnight."

Josh's eyes grew bigger. "Are we really staying out that long?"

Shelley shrugged and smiled. "Maybe. We'll see."

Josh grabbed his sister's hand. "C'mon, Emily. Let's change and get our jackets."

Shelley grinned. It all came down to motivation. She doubted they'd be out past nine o'clock, but even if they were, so what? It was a holiday weekend, they were on vacation and tonight was a night for fun. She pulled a sweatshirt over her jeans, put money and keys in her pocket and called her children.

"Let's walk. It's only about a half mile away. I think you're both old enough and strong enough to do it."

Ten minutes later, Shelley realized that dozens— maybe hundreds—of other people had had the same idea. "Stay together, kids," she said, offering a hand to each. In pairs or small groups, Pilgrim Cove residents of all ages were converging at the amusement park. "Look at the Ferris wheel, Mom. That's first."

Shelley did look and her stomach flip-flopped. The ride was at least seventy feet high. Then Emily pulled at her hand. "Look. A merry-go-round. Horses." Her stomach settled. She could handle a carousel.

"Let's kind of work up to the Ferris wheel, Josh. How about the bumper cars?"

Josh nodded. "There's lots of rides here, Mom." Excitement laced his voice. "And it's open all summer. We can come here every night. This is great."

"Slow down, sport," said Shelley. "I'm not a millionaire. Let's just have a good time tonight."

She guided them to the ticket booth and reached into her pocket for her cash. "Look at that," she said, pointing to a sign. "Aren't we lucky? It's half price on opening night."

"Then buy lots of tickets!"

She did. And spent the next hour riding the roller coaster three times, the whip twice, with Emily in the middle, and the musical carousel, which her daughter loved the most. Josh overcame his chagrin at having to cater to his sister and mounted a smiling painted Arabian without complaint.

"There's the bumper cars," said Josh when the tame ride was over. "Let's go."

"This ride is your treat," said Shelley. "Emily's too small to drive her own car. We'll stand here and watch you." She gave him the tickets and found a place behind the rail, a minute later watched him happily smashing into his neighbors' vehicles.

"Mommy, look," said Emily. "There's Jessie and her man." Emily darted into the crowd before Shelley could see where her daughter had spotted Daniel and Jessie. Shelley raced in pursuit, but couldn't catch up with the child, who easily zigzagged around all obstacles between her and her objective. "Jess-ee. Jess-ee." Emily's little-girl voice got the dog's attention, and the golden greeted her with kisses, nuzzles and wagging tail. Pure love.

Heart pounding at Emily's quick action, Shelley arrived at the spot. "Emily! Don't you ever run off like that again. You could get lost with all these people around." Shelley reached to hug her child, but Emily's arms were fastened around Jessie's neck.

"She's fine, Shelley. Just fine." Daniel Stone's voice was compassionate, his eyes warm as he looked down at her from his position on the other side of Jessie.

Shelley rose and noted for the first time that he'd put Jessie on a leash. "Emily is fine *this* time," she replied. "But what about *next* time?"

He nodded. "Point taken."

"Maybe I should follow your example with Jess," said Shelley, nodding at the leash. She grinned up at him. "Not a bad idea. A harness would be even better."

He replied with a slight smile, but remained quiet

as he studied her, his eyes first alight with humor, then darkening as he continued to study her.

"What...?" she began. And then felt herself blush under his scrutiny. Recognized the moment his gaze heated, and felt her heart start to thump in response.

Breathe. She tried. She couldn't. Instead, she blinked. And as suddenly as it had appeared, the heat in Daniel's eyes was gone. Had she imagined it? She didn't think so. Her thoughts were interrupted when she heard "Mom! Mom!" Only her child's voice had the power to penetrate her foggy mind.

Shelley pivoted and waved to her son, who was peering in all directions. Josh ran toward her. "Didn't you see me driving, Mom?" He stopped short when he saw Daniel. His eyes narrowed as he looked from Daniel to Shelley. He said nothing, however, until he studied Jess. "You've got her neck in a fat leather collar," he said in an accusatory tone. He raced five steps to the dog and gave her a hug. "Won't it choke her?"

Shelley smothered a laugh. If anything, Josh was choking the dog.

"Does she look unhappy to you, Josh?" asked Daniel.

The dog was dancing on her hind legs, licking Josh as though he were her new best friend. "No. She's happy. She's always happy to see me."

Daniel nodded. "I can tell."

Josh looked up at Jessie's owner. "Are you and Jessie staying upstairs all summer?"

"That's the plan."

Shelley chuckled at the expressions flitting across her son's face, a curious mixture of distrust and delight assigned respectively to the man and the dog. She glanced at Daniel. He winked at her, and his grin said it all.

"Sorry about that, Josh," said Daniel. "Can't have one without the other."

Emily tugged at her and pointed. "Mommy. Look who's coming. Casey and Katie."

Shelley followed Emily's gaze, and sure enough, Bart Quinn, Sam Parker and another man she hadn't met, plus the children, were approaching, the kids leading the way.

"Wow! Is that your dog?" asked Katie, running up to Josh and Jessie, Casey right behind her.

"She's b-beautiful." Casey stopped a foot from the dog and allowed Jess to sniff him.

"This is Jessie," said Josh, standing tall, his arm possessively around the canine. "She's a girl golden retriever and she likes kids."

"Good," said Casey. "Th-that's the best kind of dog."

"Wow," repeated Katie, patting Jessie all over and getting slurped for her efforts. "Are you lucky!"

"Well, Jessie lives at Sea View House, but she's not exactly mine." Josh glanced at Daniel. "That's Professor Stone. He lives upstairs and Jessie's really his."

Two pairs of eyes turned to Daniel.

"Hi," he said.

"Hi," they replied in unison, examining Daniel

for a long moment, longer than an introduction usually required. They looked at each other, nodded, then studied Daniel again.

Shelley grinned inwardly as she watched. Those kids were up to something.

"Papa Bart, maybe *he* can do it," said Katie.

"Maybe yes. Maybe no," replied her great-grandfather. "Only one way to find out, lassie. Ask him."

Katie stepped in front of Daniel. "Do you like baseball, Mr. Stone?"

"Sure." Daniel glanced from the child to Bart. The older man just smiled, his eyes twinkling.

Then Casey spoke up. "You got any kids?" he asked.

Forehead creased, Daniel turned his attention to the boy. "It's just Jessie and me."

"B-but, do you *like* kids?" The boy's earnest expression had Shelley paying close attention to both Casey and Daniel.

Daniel started to smile. "Sure, I do. I like baseball, kids and apple pie. Anything else you want to know?"

"Yeah. We need a new c-coach. D-Dad can't do it. We're all getting m-married! Right in the middle of the season."

Between Daniel's bewilderment, Casey's earnestness and Katie's precociousness, Shelley couldn't contain her mirth. And neither could any of the ROMEOs in attendance. A chorus of adult laughter punctuated the evening air. Everyone joined in…except Daniel, whose complete attention centered on her once more.

"Nice sound," he said. "But not nice to laugh at me." His exaggerated pout had her giggling again.

"Wh-what's so funny?" asked a wide-eyed Casey, his expression totally innocent.

Shelley couldn't stop laughing. The child was adorable and funny. At least to her. She plopped herself on a nearby bench, enjoying the release her laughter gave her. She felt wonderful.

Her own children stared at her as though she'd morphed into a complete stranger. "I'll tell you what, kids," she said when she caught her breath, "how about I volunteer to coach the team."

CHAPTER FIVE

DANIEL WASN'T the only one jolted into silence. Seven pairs of eyes joined his in studying the woman now relaxing on the bench. Happy. Carefree. Lovely.

He glanced at Josh, the only person in the group who'd know the truth about his mother's skills. Let the kid argue. Dan had no intention of igniting any politically incorrect flames.

"But, Mom! You don't know how to play baseball." Josh's voice held a note of genuine anguish, and Dan hoped the boy could either back up his assessment or be proved wrong.

"Sure, I do," replied Shelley. "Don't I always go to your games and cheer at the right times?"

Dan groaned silently. Josh was noisier.

"C'mon, Josh," said Shelley, a smile still on her face. "How hard could it be? Three strikes and you're out! The umpires judge the balls and strikes, not me. And what I don't know, I'll learn. This summer is for fun. A time for new adventures as a family. We'll all do new things, including me."

Nice speech, but the kid wasn't buying it. In fact, the boy was looking at him, a struggle between need and distrust on his face. For the first time since he'd met Josh, the boy's protective streak toward his mother revealed a definite crack, at least for the moment. The kid just wanted to play ball. Long summer days loomed ahead. As far as Dan was concerned, Josh's desire was perfectly normal.

"Ahem." Bart coughed with feeling.

Dan glanced at the older man. A blind person could have read the message on his face. *Do it.* His eyes were compassionate but demanding. His expression encouraging.

But Dan hesitated. Light-years passed while he considered his options. When he'd first arrived in Pilgrim Cove, somehow he and Bart had spoken of loves lost. Somehow? Later Dan realized that Bartholomew Quinn had a way of making a person talk. But to his credit, Bart had also shared. In fact, he'd confided that his Rosemary still nestled in his heart, keeping him company every day, just as Nikki kept Daniel company. But the similarities ended there. Bart, the extrovert, had been able to shift into Drive, while Daniel, more reserved, was still stuck in Park. Or perhaps Reverse.

Since Nikki's death, he'd managed to function at the university, meeting all obligations with students, staff and administration with professionalism. He managed to eat, sleep and visit his family. And Nikki's family. He forced himself to make conversation and to meet his responsibilities everywhere. So why was it so hard for a person of his intellect and achievement to actually jump in and begin living again? He knew the answer, simply didn't like it.

Because living was a matter of the heart. Not the mind. And his heart was out of commission.

But now Bart was reminding him of his new resolve. The point of his move to the East Coast. New job. New people. New sights and sounds. With no reminders. He wanted to lift his spirits. He wanted to participate…safely…in life again. What could be safer than a boy's baseball league?

He studied his attractive downstairs neighbor once again as she leaned back on the bench. Divorced. And totally relaxed, at least for the moment. He hadn't seen her so at ease before. And now she'd jumped in and volunteered for a job she'd never done in her life and didn't know how to do. He glanced at Josh's unhappy face…poor kid!

Then he winked at the boy and looked at the mother. "How'd you like an assistant coach, Coach? Someone who could…ah…help with practices and maybe give you some tips?"

She actually looked startled at the idea, but had no time to answer before Bart Quinn's approval floated in the air.

"A perfect solution." Bart motioned to the larger of his friends. "Chief, I think you've met Daniel, but come meet Shelley Anderson and her children."

Dan watched the introduction, one part of his

mind hoping Shelley wasn't annoyed about his offer, and the other part of his mind amazed that Rick O'Brien, the retired police chief who was getting married in the morning, still had the time and desire to wander around an amusement park. Must have an understanding bride or a bad case of nerves.

The former chief's voice boomed when he greeted Shelley, and Daniel had his answer. Nerves. Rick O'Brien's tone had been well modulated earlier in the week. The ex-cop was as jittery as any groom of any age, anywhere in the world. Dan smiled in commiseration, remembering when he… and then wished he hadn't.

He heard the former chief welcome Shelley to Pilgrim Cove, as if he were the mayor of the town. The ROMEOs all sounded the same when discussing the community. What a bunch! But they did carry their self-imposed responsibility with honor and they always followed through.

"I know every street, every business and just about every person in this town, Mrs. Anderson," said Rick. "If you need anything, or need to know anything, just ask. I'm usually at the diner every morning about eight with my buddies."

"Call me Shelley, please. And these are Josh and Emily."

Daniel watched Rick examine each child. Watched him memorize them. Once a cop, always a cop. He'd worked with many police officers almost a lifetime ago as a law intern in the district attorney's office. Mostly good experiences, he thought as he shook Rick O'Brien's hand. "Good luck tomorrow. If she's the right one, it's worth everything. Including the attack on your stomach right now."

The former chief slapped him good-naturedly on the shoulder. "No problem there. I've loved that woman for years. Dee's the right one. The only one."

Interesting. Wasn't this a second marriage for both the bride and groom?

To SHELLEY, the holiday weekend sped by in what seemed like a minute, and in no time, she was back at work in her kindergarten classroom. Since she'd left Pilgrim Cove, images of Daniel Stone had sprung into her mind regularly, sometimes hovering there like a visitor on an extended stay. As she straightened up her desk the first Wednesday afternoon back at work, his slow grin and warm brown eyes remained with her. So did his broad back and shoulders. She liked the way he cocked his head and paid full attention when listening to someone speak, even when the speaker was eight years old.

She didn't know much about his background—what his field was or what had precipitated his move to Boston—but she knew enough to feel comfortable sharing the house with him. She didn't need the additional endorsements of Jessie and the ROMEOs to reinforce her impression.

The night at Neptune's Park had improved their neighborly relationship. After Dan volunteered to coach the team with her, Josh had actually invited him to ride the Ferris wheel. What a reward! Afterward, the entire group had munched hot dogs together, and Bart insisted on treating everyone to ice cream. If the weekend was an indication of the summer ahead, Shelley was convinced she'd made a wonderful decision.

From the school, Shelley drove directly to the local supermarket. Her mom was picking up the kids that afternoon, and her dad would join them at the house later. It was their year-old Wednesday routine. While Shelley shopped, her mom cooked dinner. It's what Ellen Duffy wanted to do and Shelley didn't argue. Now that Ellen worked only part-time, she enjoyed fussing over her grandchildren in the middle of the week.

Shelley hummed to the music on the radio, mentally organizing the chores and packing that needed to be done before she and the children could move to Sea View House for the summer. Her parents would join them for the remainder of June and return for some weekends during the season. The kids were excited about sharing the house with Nana and Poppy. Finally, life was moving forward smoothly. Shelley's hum changed into a private karaoke sing-along. Off-key as usual, but she didn't care. For the moment, she was happy and she sang.

She almost didn't hear the ring of her cell phone.

She pressed the button to connect the call just as she pulled into the parking lot of the grocery store.

"Hello," she said.

"Shelley. It's Carl. Where are you?"

I'm fine, Carl. Thanks for asking. "I'm pulling into the Food Club parking lot. Why?"

"We need to talk. Something important's come up, and I need you to listen and concentrate."

Shelley's stomach tightened. She knew that tone of voice, that edge of excitement. He wanted to drag her into something.

She rolled down her window an inch, then shut off the engine. "Your life is your own now. You don't need to discuss anything with me."

"On the contrary. This news definitely affects you. In fact, I'd like to take you to dinner and discuss it."

Dinner? With Carl? "I don't think so, Carl. I'm sitting in the privacy of my car. No children around. No adults around. Let's talk now."

She heard his big sigh at the other end. "Shelley, at the risk of making you angry, I have to insist. My news is something good, but it's bigger than you can imagine. And it will affect a lot of people—definitely the kids and possibly you."

"What do you mean? Definitely the kids? Haven't they had enough changes in their lives?" She hated the way her voice shook and took a deep breath. "You're scaring me, Carl," she said more quietly, "and I don't like it."

"Then have dinner with me tomorrow night," he cajoled softly, "and you won't be scared. Like I said, Shelley, the news is good. The biggest thing that's ever happened to me."

Shelley's mind whirled. She'd be better off knowing what all this was about so she could plan. She'd probably have to deflect whatever it was. Having dinner somewhere with Carl was easier than having him coming to the house and creating general havoc with the kids.

"If I can get a sitter, I'll meet you at seven. Concord Cafeteria."

"Cafeteria! Come on, Shel. I'll take you out for a real dinner. I want us to enjoy ourselves. And celebrate."

Nice words. A couple of years too late. "This isn't a date, Carl. The Concord is near your office, and the food doesn't matter."

He sighed again. "For crying out loud! Okay. I won't argue. But take a cab into town and I'll drive you home. I know you hate driving in the city."

"My driving's not a problem. I'll confirm tomorrow. Bye."

She disconnected and collapsed into herself. Her hands shook; her legs felt weak. She didn't like surprises emanating from Carl. Especially when he was being thoughtful of her. Wanting to take her out for a nice dinner. Wanting to drive her home. No, thanks.

Carl could be very charming. And very loving.

After all, she'd loved him once. Totally. He'd been her whole world then. And some people—like her parents—might think she was too suspicious now. She closed her eyes and rested her head against the back of the seat. A sacred trust had been broken. A betrayal so painful that the damage still lingered.

And now, she'd bet a week's vacation that Carl wanted more from her than just an opinion. She knew him too well. He was trying to soften her up because he wanted something that she wouldn't want to give.

CARL WAS WAITING for her at the front door of the cafeteria, and Shelley had to admit that he looked great. A handsome man, he'd filled out over the years since their marriage, all muscle, as he'd pursued a regular exercise program. His green eyes lit up when he spotted her, the intensity followed by a quick expression of relief. Interesting, Shelley thought, that he'd have a touch of anxiety about whether she'd show up.

"You look wonderful, Shel," said Carl, kissing her quickly on the cheek.

Wonderful? After a day spent with twenty five-year-olds? "I've still got finger paint under my nails and 'Where is Thumbkin?' in my brain. Let's go inside." She met his gaze and reached for the door handle, but not fast enough to miss the flash of admiration in his expression.

"Sometimes," he murmured, grabbing the door from her, "I think I hardly knew you."

But he had known her. He'd known the Shelley she'd been when she was nineteen years old. Hell, he'd influenced her growth into a young wife and mother. But he didn't know the woman she was becoming now. In fact, Shelley was in the process of discovering that woman herself.

"You knew me, Carl. We've known each other for fifteen years including a ten-year marriage. And you can take total credit if you don't recognize me now," she said, leading them to the stack of trays and silverware inside the self-serve restaurant.

"Point taken," he replied, handing her a tray. "Let's figure out what's good here tonight."

She followed his lead into innocuous conversation, and in a few moments, followed him as he selected a booth in a quiet area along the back wall of the cafeteria. She preferred the privacy, too.

"So, tell me about the kids," said Carl. "You know I think you're a wonderful mother, but are you really going through with the crazy beach-house idea?" He smiled with warmth and his eyes twinkled. She couldn't take offense.

"Actually," she said, "it's a wonderful idea. The children have already made some friends. Josh is signed up for a summer baseball league. And Emily has two pails of seashells in her collection already."

"You'll make sure they don't get burned and that there's a lifeguard on duty at all times?" The concern in his voice was genuine. The concern of a loving father.

Shelley relaxed and nodded. "Of course I'll take care of them. And you're invited to visit at any time, Carl. Just call first. I can spare you a hamburger."

He threw his head back and laughed. And Shelley saw the side of him that she'd once loved. Between his good looks, charm and intelligence, he had the charisma that most people only read about. And tonight, her little joke had made him laugh.

"We're still very good together, Shel," said Carl, lifting his can of soda in a toast to her.

She nodded in acknowledgment, then added, "But not good enough."

Carl became quiet. She felt him studying her before he glanced at his soda. His thumb traced around the rim over and over. Then he focused on her again, his eyes never leaving her face. "The party wants me to run for the congressional seat in our district, Shelley. A substitute candidate for John Reilly, who passed away from a heart attack last week. You know he was up for reelection."

Shelley nodded.

"Because of circumstances," continued Carl, "I don't have to go through a primary. I *am* the candidate. I've been in deep talks with the leaders, and I'm going to do it."

Shelley's eyes widened. "You weren't kidding when you said 'big news,' were you?"

He shook his head. "I've been aiming for a political career all along. You know that."

She did know. He'd always been a political animal, but his career hadn't been on her mind lately. She'd been more concerned about her own.

"I've taken on a number of cases in the public interest over the years," said Carl, "but this last one— the water pollution one—has made me almost a household name."

Shelley sat back and examined this man she was once married to. He was on his way up. "Well, congratulations and good luck." She paused a moment, her thoughts whirling. "Oh, my. Your parents must be thrilled. They've always had big dreams for you. First a congressman, then a senator. Maybe the White House next?"

He shrugged. "Can't know the future. But my parents are excited, pulling out all the stops with their connections. And I was hoping," he said in a quiet voice, "that you'd be excited, too."

All she really wanted to know was how his decision would affect their kids. "I wish you only the best, Carl. And I am excited for you. But the truth is, I think you care about water pollution about as much as I care about football."

Good grief! He looked as though she'd really hurt his feelings. "Am I wrong, Carl? I'll apologize if I am."

He reached for her hand and pressed it gently. "Every issue is important on this campaign. It's going to be a big campaign, Shel, and I'm going to need the kids with me part of the time."

She tilted her head in question while his fingers

clasped hers in his palm. So familiar a touch. "I can understand that."

"I knew you would," he replied with a smile. The sweet kind. "We had a lot of good years together, and I was hoping to count on your support."

"With the children? Of course. The kids are yours, too. And neither of us wants to air our dirty linen in public."

"Thank you." He raised her hand to his lips and kissed her palm.

She disengaged. "That wasn't necessary."

"But safer than if I kissed your beautiful mouth."

Stunned by the unexpected remark, Shelley stared at her ex-husband. "What's going on, Carl? I don't need your compliments or personal attention."

His eyes darkened with a sexual heat. "Don't you?" he asked softly. "We had ten good years, Shelley. Very good years. We could have more."

She rose to leave.

"Hang on a moment, Shel," said Carl. "Hear me out."

Her mind ran at warp speed. For the second time in two days, she reminded herself that she needed to know everything if she was going to plan a defense. She sat down again.

"I made a mistake in our marriage," said Carl. "And I admit that." His voice was sincere, his eyes imploring. "I want you to know how sorry I am. And if you'd consider a reconciliation…I swear you'll never have reason to complain again."

A what? Shocked into silence, Shelley couldn't speak, couldn't move, couldn't think. Carl seemed to take her silence as encouragement.

"Think of the kids, Shelley. They'd be so happy if we got back together. And your parents would be overjoyed."

She had to give him credit for that one. Her parents had remained loyal to her on the surface, but in their hearts, they'd never believed the divorce was Carl's fault. They'd blamed her for his dissatisfaction. If her husband was looking elsewhere, she should have done something about it. Yes, her parents would be thrilled, right along with the children.

"And, Shelley, if I get elected, you'd have a voice in state education programs. Influence priorities and reform."

"What?"

"You sure would," said Carl, nodding his head for emphasis. "Teaching in the public schools would give you tremendous credibility. Here you are, working with the youngest, most vulnerable children. People will listen to your ideas. You're not some ivory-tower theorist. You're in the trenches with the kids." He reached for both her hands. "You've always been crazy about children, Shelley. And now, you can make a difference."

It was too much to absorb. "I need time to think," she said, getting up from her seat.

"Of course you do," said Carl, rising also. "Think

hard, Shelley. Think what's best for Josh and Emily. We can become a family again. Give the kids what we both know they really want."

What about what I want? "I'll be in touch," she said, walking toward the door on shaky legs.

"Good. But don't take too long." He was only a step behind her. "Basically, I'm a family man, Shelley. You know that." He tapped her shoulder and she turned around. "My life's been crazy lately, and I hate missing my dates with the kids. I want them with me."

MAYBE SHE SHOULD HAVE taken a taxi after all. Her hands shook so hard, her ignition key wouldn't go into its slot. She grasped the steering wheel and took a few breaths until she felt a measure of control returning.

Carl knew her well. Knew how to push every one of her buttons. Her yearning for family, her concern for children, her parents' happiness at seeing their daughter secure once more and, most important of all, the happiness of her children.

She pulled out of the parking spot and merged with traffic, heading toward the outskirts of the city. She couldn't wait to get home.

Pilgrim Cove popped into her head. That's where she wanted to be. Her new summer home, at least for this summer. She could walk Pilgrim Beach for miles and just allow her thoughts to flow. An image of Daniel Stone superimposed itself over the imaginary sand and water in her mind. And suddenly, she smiled. Daniel was a nice guy. His dark eyes held steady, his demeanor calm when he looked at her. He was a solid, nonthreatening presence in her world. Her heart returned to a normal beat.

Just what was best for the children? Carl loved them. That wasn't an issue. And they wanted him in their lives every day. No question that Carl had his good points. An excellent provider, he was a partner in one of Boston's most prestigious law firms. He was intelligent, interesting and very attractive. And he'd loved her once, the way any woman in the world wanted to be loved.

When she finally pulled into her driveway and garage, she could hardly remember making the trip. She shuddered at the implications. It was scary to know she'd been traveling on automatic pilot at night.

Sleep was a long time coming. Carl's words "I want them with me" kept going around in her head. Were they simply expressing a yearning, or were they a threat to fight for full custody if she didn't go along with his plan?

Don't borrow trouble. She tossed on her pillow, then glanced at the bedside clock and groaned— 1:00 a.m. How would she ever get up in the morning and arrive at work on time? It was a rhetorical question. She'd just do it. Push herself out of bed and start the day whether she felt like it or not. That's what working moms did. And if she and Carl were a couple, what would happen? His career would definitely come first.

Shelley jumped out of bed and paced. She was avoiding the crux of the issue. Careers counted. Children counted. Family counted. All that was true.

But what really counted in a marriage was the trust between a husband and wife. Could she trust Carl again? Or was she being naive? As naive as the inexperienced college girl he'd called "his Madonna" years ago, when he'd spotted her working at the campus bookstore?

She didn't know. But now, she was able to fall asleep. She'd identified the root of her unease.

"T.G.I.F.," SAID SHELLEY to her co-worker the next afternoon as they hurried to their cars in the school's parking lot.

"You can say that again. I'm ready for summer! And so are my third-graders."

"And so am I," added Shelley as the other teacher slipped into her own car. Shelley's statement was half-true. Although she was mentally ready for summer break, she certainly wasn't physically ready and was eager to use the weekend for chores. Lots to do before she and the kids left for Sea View House. And only one week to accomplish everything.

They'd leave the following Saturday morning, the day after school officially closed, and still have three weeks of June, all of July and at least half of

August. Her parents would join them on Saturday afternoon, making the two-hour trip in their own vehicle. Shelley wasn't quite certain, but she thought she was possibly even more excited than Josh and Emily.

She waved her friend off and was about to open her own car door, when a shiny silver Lexus pulled into the vacant spot left by the third-grade teacher.

Good God! She knew that car. It seemed Carl hadn't waited long to send in reinforcements. Shelley watched until her former mother-in-law stood outside the luxury vehicle. Barbara Anderson looked as elegant as ever, her blond hair stylishly cut and in place. Her beige linen suit was paired with low-heeled pumps and gold jewelry.

She looked like a woman who understood and was comfortable with her station in life. While Shelley knew that to be true, she also knew that Barbara Anderson possessed as sharp a brain as her husband's and son's, and had established a successful marketing consulting business on her own. She was the perfect parent to foster a campaign for an ambitious politician. On the domestic side, she was also the grandmother of Shelley's children.

Barbara smiled in greeting and extended a hand and a brief hug. "You're looking wonderful, Shelley. As pretty as ever. And I love the short hair. Very smart."

Shelley chuckled. "Very easy to take care of, Barbara. The secret of my success." She said nothing more, just waited for the older woman to speak. Barbara, however, seemed to have a hard time getting started. She clasped and unclasped her fingers, a very uncharacteristic gesture for the self-assured woman.

Finally, Shelley reached for Barbara's hands and smiled. "Are you the entire cavalry, or has Carl also sent some backup?"

To her surprise, Barbara pulled away and stood very straight, not meeting Shelley's eye. "Carl doesn't know I've come to see you. But of course, I do know that you had dinner together last night."

"That's right. We did." Shelley's voice held no inflection. What passed between her and Carl was no one else's business. Her own parents didn't know about the meeting.

But now Barbara seemed to have found her strength. Her gaze held Shelley's. "I know you met Carl for dinner," she repeated, "and I know what you discussed. I'm here to ask you…even beg you…to remarry my son."

CHAPTER SIX

BARBARA'S REQUEST completed the one-two punch to Shelley's stomach that Carl had begun the night before. Beg? Her former mother-in-law was definitely not the begging type. Tiny drops of perspiration broke out all over Shelley's body, and she took a deep breath, girding herself for confrontation— something she'd thought was a thing of the past.

"I don't like feeling railroaded, Barbara. If you've spoken with Carl, then you know I told him I needed time to think."

"And that's just why I'm here. To help you think." Barbara's expression was eager, her eyes bright.

"Excuse me?" replied Shelley, trying to maintain her composure, yet lighten the tone of the conversation. "I haven't donated my brain to science yet."

A fleeting smile crossed the other woman's face. "I should have added the word 'clearly.' You're young, Shelley, still relatively inexperienced. I just want to make sure you're thinking clearly."

Shelley opened the car door and threw her purse inside, wishing she could drive off right then. "I haven't made any decisions yet, and I'm certainly not rushing this one." If she had come to a conclusion, she would have informed Carl first. Not Barbara. She was no longer the impressionable undergrad in awe of Carl's wealthy, ambitious family. In the past two years, she'd worked hard to develop her own identity.

"You and Carl were a wonderful couple," said Barbara, totally animated now. "I always thought you'd be a twosome forever."

Shelley had thought the same, but didn't want to go down that road at the moment. "Sometimes, life doesn't work out the way you plan."

"But yours can! Don't you see it, Shelley? With Carl in office, you'd have a life much better than you'd ever dreamed. The children would have two parents every day, and you'd never have to work again. Think of all the advantages. The prestige, the security, the influence.

"Look, darling," continued Barbara in a hushed voice, stepping closer to Shelley as if to share a confidence. "Look at my life. I'm lacking for nothing. Walter has been more than a good provider. And if he…has a wandering eye every so often…so be it."

Nausea hit Shelley with a vengeance, and she had to swallow hard. She swayed toward the car and grasped the open door for support. "I don't need to know this, Barbara. Your marriage is your business."

"Don't be dense, Shelley. It's your business now,

too. You grew up in a blue-collar family, just like I did. But I went from blue-collar to blue blood. You were almost there, and you can still have it."

The woman paused for breath. Her eyes shone with conviction. "Come on, Shelley. Do you really want to be a schoolteacher all your life? Walt and I have a good marriage. I love him and he loves me. But he's not perfect. There's not a man alive who is. So I pretend not to know. Who cares in the end?"

Shelley sank into the driver's seat and concentrated on her breathing before replying to Carl's mother. She finally looked up. "I guess we're different people, Barbara, because…to answer your question…it seems that I care. I care very much."

"Then you're still a naive little girl." With her tone noticeably cooler, Barbara's pale complexion turned paper-white. "And Carl? What about Carl? What about his congressional race?"

An important question, but Carl's decision to run for office was not Shelley's responsibility. "Trust is hard to rebuild," she said gently. "Your son has a way to go yet."

"Shelley! Please! Please think about all the good you've had together. This is an opportunity of a lifetime for him. And you know he's worked damn hard for it. We all did. He didn't inherit a legacy like the Kennedy kids or the Bush children."

"I do know that," replied Shelley. "But this situation isn't simply a career decision for me. It's a personal one."

Barbara's expression softened a fraction. "Sometimes the two come together. And sometimes you have to seize the opportunity. You and Carl could have a second chance. The children would be so happy. A fabulous life."

Shelley looked pointedly at her watch. "I'm running late to get those very children. Why don't you come home with me for a visit with them?"

But the other woman shook her head. "Sorry. Too much to do. I really stole a piece of my day to see you. I hope it wasn't wasted." A question lingered in her voice, as she waited for a reply.

Shelley stared at Carl's mother, trying to choose her words carefully. "Let's say our conversation was very enlightening, but I'm making no promises. I don't know the ending of the Carl-and-Shelley story yet, but I do know this—you are my children's grandmother, and my door is always open to you regardless of Carl's and my situation."

Barbara didn't twitch a muscle, and Shelley pressed on. "Being Grandma is also an opportunity of a lifetime. I sincerely hope you don't waste it."

First, Barbara looked shocked, then she shook her head slightly, a tiny smile on her face. "The lioness roars. Good for you. Maybe my son didn't appreciate what he had during his years with you— but he will…."

Talk about enlightenment. Shelley waved to Carl's mother and backed out of her spot. Couldn't leave the place fast enough. She felt a web beginning to tighten around her, all the strands emanating from Carl and his family. It would only get worse. Now, they'd see her as the one who got away, and Carl would pursue her to satisfy his need to win on all fronts.

Too much to think about. She couldn't wait to get back to Pilgrim Cove.

FOREVER AND A DAY. That's how long it had seemed for the next Saturday to come around. The closer it came, the more Shelley had wanted to be back at Sea View House. Now, she glanced at the dashboard clock. With any luck, she'd be pulling up in front of the house in about fifteen minutes.

Visions of the big, gray saltbox had bolstered her energy and kept her going through all the details of departing Boston for the summer. Stopping newspaper delivery, redirecting mail delivery, supervising Josh's and Emily's packing, organizing her own selections. But worth all the effort to be back in Pilgrim Cove.

Strange to feel that way when so far she'd only spent one long weekend in the town. But what a weekend! The ROMEOs. Bart Quinn. The clean sand and sparkling ocean right outside her back door. A beautiful dog. An amusement park. But most of all, her thoughts always returned to the quiet man upstairs. Daniel Stone.

Did that mean she wasn't considering Carl's proposal seriously? Or did it mean she'd unconsciously made up her mind? Or did it mean nothing more than she was a healthy single woman who was ready to start living a full life again? Of course, it could merely mean she needed and appreciated a new adult friendship. Someone who didn't know her as part of the Carl-and-Shelley duo. And that was a good enough reason to look forward to seeing Daniel. Maybe she'd see him today after her crew had settled in.

"Mom, are you sure Daddy knows how to get here?"

Hadn't she had this conversation with Josh a dozen times already? "I'm absolutely sure. Didn't he tell you himself last night on the phone?"

"Yeah. But when's he gonna come? What if— what if he gets lost or…something?"

Something. The word was whispered because Josh didn't want to think about "or something." The possibility that Carl wouldn't find time to visit. "I can guarantee your dad will be visiting you in Pilgrim Cove." *Even if the reason has more to do with me.*

Carl had called twice during her last week at home. He'd wanted to take her out again, but she'd put him off, telling him she was buried in preparations for the summer away from home.

"Then rest up," he'd said, explaining that she'd be very busy once the campaign was in full swing— if everything went the way he'd hoped it would.

She'd avoided answering. Instead, she offered

him an invitation to visit Pilgrim Cove, reminding him to call in advance so she and the kids would be sure to be home. Between baseball games, Pilgrim Beach, Neptune's Park, regular errands and activities, she couldn't be certain they'd be at Sea View House if he just showed up.

Echoes of his grumbling response remained in her mind as she turned right on Outlook Drive, heading toward Beach Street. Seemed Carl didn't appreciate boundaries unless he set them. Choosing to pick her battles, she'd overlooked the grumbling. The man was under a lot of pressure these days. But she wouldn't dispense with the boundaries.

"Mom?" said Emily in a soft voice tinged with concern. "Do you think Jessie will remember me?"

Finally, an easy question to answer! "She sure will. No doubt about it. That Jessie is one smart dog."

"Do you think she knows I'm coming?" Emily's voice held awe. In her mirror, Shelley saw her daughter's face aglow with wonder at the possibility.

"Don't be a dork!" said Josh to his sister. "The dog's not *that* smart."

"I'm not a dork," Emily managed to say before she began to cry.

Easy? Was anything ever easy? Shelley turned onto Beach Street and pulled into Sea View House's driveway. An empty driveway. Seemed the man upstairs wasn't upstairs, and disappointment rolled through her, surprising her with its intensity. Had she been looking forward to Daniel's company that much?

The answer scared her. Consciously or unconsciously, she had been counting on seeing him again. Now, that was something to think about. She'd barely absorbed the significance of that admission before a second realization hit. Carl's reappearance and request had changed her life again in the past week, and until that situation was resolved, she'd have to relegate Daniel to the status of a casual neighbor. If she could.

LATE THAT AFTERNOON, at almost five o'clock, Daniel Stone stood at the bridge of the commuter ferry heading back to Pilgrim Cove from Rowes Wharf in Boston. He turned his head from left to right trying to work out the knots that had formed while he was hunched over his books. Internet research was fine to a point; for Daniel's work, however, an extensive law library was needed such as the one at Harvard.

His biggest challenge at the university this year was to introduce a new ethics curriculum based on current business practices. The fallout from Enron and other major players in American business had precipitated a reexamination of standard curriculum and demanded revisions. What exactly were the lawyers' responsibilities if on the corporate staff or on retainer as part of a law firm? How should legal ethics, attorney-client privilege and social responsibility be balanced? With not only a doctor of law, but also a doctorate in philosophy, Daniel most enjoyed examining these types of complex issues using an interdisciplinary approach.

Between the university's library and his own apartment, he'd put in more than a full week's work as he synthesized material for the new course. Now he was tired and looking forward to being back at Sea View House and to a good meal at the Lobster Pot. Not good, he amended mentally, but great. Bart's daughters had proved themselves earlier in the week. In addition to the cuisine, Thea and Maggie were as outgoing as their dad and made Daniel feel very welcome.

He rolled his shoulders forward and back, continuing to stretch, as the Pilgrim Cove harbor in Pilgrim Bay took on shape and form. In addition to the ferry's commercial pier, dozens of pleasure boats bobbed gently at private docks. A familiar sight to a man raised near the water.

Almost there. Daniel rested his arms on the boat's railing and stared at the small waves. Tonight, he would have loved to come home to someone who cared about him. Nikki. He sighed in remembrance of how they'd often enjoy a glass of wine at the end of the day. Then they'd either go out for dinner, or sometimes throw ingredients together. "Not potluck," she'd say with a grin, "more like hodgepodge." He'd called it "Nikki's Gumbo" and didn't care at all how the meal turned out, as long as they had a good time fixing it.

He missed that. The times at the end of the day when they'd reconnected. He sighed and tried to massage his neck. No point going down that road. Soon, Jess would greet him at the door with the excitement of a puppy; they'd both stretch their legs with a run on the beach and then Daniel would go to the Lobster Pot. Alone. And tonight, feeling lonely.

Shelley Anderson's gamine grin and sparkling hair popped into his mind, and he felt an answering grin emerge on his own face. He'd bet she didn't have time to feel lonely. Not with those two lively kids. Of course, she might *want* some time alone at the end of the day. What adult in her situation wouldn't? He shook his head at the irony. Could be that neither of them was happy at the end of the day.

The boat docked. Daniel hefted his briefcase and laptop and walked down the ramp to his parked car, nodding to new acquaintances and stopping to greet folks he knew better. Sam Parker, Doc Rosen and his wife, Marsha, were waiting to board. Dressed in formal attire. Very unusual in Pilgrim Cove.

"Boston Symphony concert tonight," explained Sam. "We've got season's tickets." And Daniel remembered hearing that each one of the Parker family was musically gifted.

Doc looked at him and winked. "Going with Sam is a treat. We get a behind-the-scenes commentary on the composer, as well as a lesson in music appreciation."

"He's great," said Marsha. "He should be teaching this stuff in a classroom somewhere. The students would love it."

"Stop your jabbering and get on the boat," grumbled Sam with the familiarity of a longtime friend. "I never even went to college."

"So what?" replied Marsha, stepping onto the gangplank.

Daniel watched the three friends board the boat talking all the way. "Have a great time."

"We always do." Marsha Rosen turned around and bestowed a warm smile. "Starting right now with the ferry ride. It's fun."

Fun. He couldn't remember the last time he'd had any. Daniel smiled and waved goodbye. While the ferry was a novelty to him, it provided Pilgrim Cove residents with vital commuter service to Boston. Every half hour to and from the city until ten. Until midnight on Saturdays. Standing at the rail in the evening would be a romantic experience. With that thought came another vision of Shelley Anderson, and he picked up his pace as he went to his car.

Two vehicles filled the driveway at Sea View House when Daniel arrived home. Two? She must have company. He shrugged, trying to ignore his pang of disappointment. Just as well she was busy. He'd almost forgotten about the disaster of the one date he'd gone on since Nikki died. He'd been awkward with the woman and couldn't wait for the evening to end. It would be the same with Shelley. As long as Nikki kept tugging at him. He parked his car and went to the side door. Jessie's joyous welcome would have to be enough.

Five minutes later, Dan and a delighted Jessie jogged to the back of the house on their way to the beach. Dan immediately noticed the changes on the porch. A white patio table now occupied the center of the floor, and several webbed chairs were placed around it. Extra chairs were folded against the side of the house. Three people were sitting around the table, Shelley and an older couple. They didn't look happy.

FIRST, SHE'D STRANGLE her former mother-in-law. Then she'd contemplate doing the same to her own parents. Sitting outside in the late afternoon of a gorgeous June day should have been a relaxing experience. Instead, Shelley glared at the glass of lemonade she held, wishing it were a martini. Preferably a double.

Barbara Anderson had lost no time informing Ellen and Phil Duffy about her son's political plans when she realized Shelley's parents were spending three weeks with their daughter and grandchildren at the beach. The grandchildren who were also *her* grandchildren. "And," Barbara had added, "didn't *all* the grandparents feel that the children would be so happy with their mom and dad together again?"

Damn! Her parents were such easy marks! They'd always liked and admired her ex-husband, and now they were excited about his forthcoming campaign for Congress. They'd like nothing more than to witness the reunion of their daughter and former son-in-law. After all, every marriage goes through rocky times, and she and Carl could rebuild. Barbara Anderson knew how they felt and knew exactly how to build allies.

Shelley's nerves were stretched before the vacation began. "We're not saying you should marry him tomorrow, honey," began her dad, "but working on the campaign with Carl provides the perfect opportunity to become close again."

Shelley was about to reply, when from the corner of her eye, she saw Daniel and Jessie sprinting up the driveway toward the beach. She stood up immediately, called his name and walked toward him.

He looked good. Hair mussed enough to make her fingers itch. Body big and broad enough to make her imagine being wrapped in his arms, at least for a moment's respite. But his eyes were half-shut. Pain defined his expression. Either pain or fatigue.

"Headache?" she asked as she reached him.

He looked surprised at the question, then offered a smile. "Too much reading." He rubbed his temple. "Plus a stiff neck. It'll pass. How have you been?"

"You wouldn't believe it if I told you." She dismissed the question with a quick motion of her hand.

"Come meet my folks. And if you sit down for a minute, I can almost guarantee to relieve some of that pain."

She must have tempted him, because he followed her up the three steps to the open porch. Her parents were polite, even warm, until she motioned Daniel into a chair.

"I work my headache magic only for special people," she began, "and considering you're my closest neighbor and assistant coach...well, I've got to keep you in good shape." She stood behind him and pressed the tips of her fingers against his temples. "Just relax," she said quietly, "and let the tension go." She rotated the pressure and started the massage. Then noticed the look that passed between her parents.

"You know, dear," began Ellen, "Mr. Stone was on his way to the ocean. Maybe he'd prefer a swim to set him right."

Her mother's voice was full of concern, but she wasn't adept at invoking nuance well enough to make her real point without insult. Daniel obviously understood Ellen Duffy's message well enough. Under her hands, Shelley felt him start to rise. "Don't move," she whispered, before addressing her mother. "Daniel's a beautiful swimmer, and I'll let him escape in a few minutes, but not before the pain is eased. C'mon Mom, how many times have I done this for Dad?"

"And for Carl," said Ellen with purpose.

"That's right," replied Shelley in a steady voice. "Seems these type A personalities need a little help."

Dan made a sound somewhere between a laugh and a moan of pleasure. "This feels wonderful, but your theory is dead in the water. I work hard and I play hard," said Daniel, "but I wouldn't categorize myself as a type A. I like to relax as much as the next guy."

"Right," said Shelley. "And that's why you get headaches."

Daniel grunted, closed his eyes and tilted his head back. Shelley could see the effects of her massage start to appear. Lines across his brow and around his eyes were vanishing.

She worked quietly, aware of the disapproval emanating from her parents, but ignored it. Any decision she made regarding her future would be hers alone.

"It's awfully quiet around here," said Daniel. "Where are the kids?"

Shelley laughed. "Is that a complaint, Professor? We're enjoying the quiet. Emily's sleeping and Josh is on his computer playing a game…unless he's fallen asleep, too, which is a possibility."

Ellen Duffy stood up. "I think we should wake them up and get them ready to go to dinner." She disappeared into the house.

Shelley looked at her father. "Can you talk to her, Dad? She's on a mission, and all she's going to do is get my back up."

"She loves you, Shelley. Only wants what's best for you." Now, Philip rose from his chair and joined his wife inside the house.

"Well, I guess he told me," said Shelley. "And I guess I'll have to suck it up for the next three weeks until they're back in the city."

Daniel's hands reached and found hers. "The pain's almost a memory now, Shelley, and for that relief, I owe you." He stood and faced her, and she saw the concern in his expression. "Do you need a pair of unbiased ears?" he asked quietly. "I am a very experienced listener."

His offer was tempting, very tempting, but Shelley shook her head. "Not really, but thanks. No one but me can make this decision." She leaned down to pet the dog. "Take care of your owner, Jess. I think he's a very nice man." An understatement. *Nice* didn't cover his enormous appeal to her. Sexual and otherwise. Funny how it was the *otherwise* that claimed her attention now. His intelligence, humor and perception. His kindness. Getting to know Daniel Stone was similar to unraveling a mystery one clue at a time. She wanted to discover the next tidbit, whether or not doing so was a good idea.

WITH NO HEADACHE and feeling refreshed after his swim and shower, Daniel left Sea View House more than ready for a satisfying dinner at the Lobster Pot. No sounds came from the Captain's Quarters apartment downstairs when he left, but Shelley lingered in his mind.

She was a woman with a fistful of problems, or as she'd said, decisions, and frankly, he was glad she hadn't taken him up on his offer. She'd be too easy to care about. Too easy to get involved with. His goal at the beach was to prepare for the new semester, catch a little sun, swim and relax. Not to pick up women.

Then he laughed. He had to be the only male in the world above twelve years old to say the beach was *not* for picking up women. He shook his head at the absurdity and got into his SUV. He'd probably meet up with a couple of ROMEOs at the restaurant.

He parked and got out of his car. Then he inhaled the delicious aroma coming from the Lobster Pot. He headed for the front entrance, noticing the outdoor decks were attracting diners despite the cool evening temperatures. After a long New England winter, folks were hungry for more than food. They were hungry for outdoor living.

As soon as he entered the restaurant, he spotted Maggie Sullivan making her way to the entrance area. An attractive woman with honey-blond hair and snapping blue eyes, he could see the strong resemblance to her daughter, Lila. She greeted him like a long-lost friend, the perfect hostess, knowing how to make people feel at home.

"It's good to see you back here," said Maggie. "How's our town treating you?"

"Just fine, but I'm starving."

"Great! You came to the right place, Professor. Come on with me."

Daniel chuckled, realizing he was fated to be known as "the professor" for as long as he stayed in Pilgrim Cove. As he followed Maggie, he noticed Bart chatting with diners at a nearby table, then walk to another one to do the same. "What do you pay him to work the crowd, Maggie?" asked Daniel, nodding at Bart.

"Who? Dad? Are you kidding? He'd pay *me* to let him do it! And here he comes."

"Daniel! Good to see you." Bart turned toward his daughter. "I'll seat him, Maggie. Go take care of someone else."

Maggie grinned. "I was going to give him table 2 against the wall where it's quieter and he can eat in peace. But if you're going to take over…" She let the sentence trail off, and Bart lost no time waving her away.

"Come on, Danny-boy. I want to show you our latest addition to the decor."

Daniel grinned, having already spent an evening reading the decor that gave the Lobster Pot the down-home ambience it was known for. He glanced at the largest poster in the center of the main dining room, which proclaimed, "The Lobster Pot, where no lobster is a shrimp."

"I guess that's the logo you've adopted for the restaurant."

"It sure is. Maggie's been drawing cartoons for years, and Thea helps her invent the captions. But now look at the new caption they came up with in honor of Dee Barnes and the chief's long courtship."

Daniel followed Bart's gaze to a poster where an adorable caricature of Dee, with mermaid fins, was sitting pertly at the edge of a dock. Above the water in front of her, was a large fish arching in the air, a police cap on its head. The caption read After Her Five Year *Perch*, He Wanted To *Snapper* Up.

Chuckling, Dan turned to the proud father. "I guess that says it all."

"It does indeed. Years of friendship, five years of courtship and then in five minutes, a wedding! People waste time too often, they do, they do. It's a shame."

Was there something personal in his message? Daniel focused on Bart for a moment. His relationship with the older man had grown to be a comfortable, trusting one, with perhaps an overtone of family to it, as between an uncle and nephew.

"Are you trying to tell me something, Mr. Not-So-Subtle Quinn?"

"Who? Me?" Quinn's expression was priceless—the picture of innocence. Which meant guilty in Daniel's mind. But before he could reply, Bart was walking and talking again. Daniel followed in his wake, stopping only a moment later.

"And look who else is eating dinner at the Lobster Pot tonight! The rest of Sea View House. How

are you, Shelley? Emily? And I can't forget Joshua?
I hear you've both signed up for baseball."

The children nodded, wide-eyed. Daniel imagined that was the common reaction to Bart Quinn
from the youngest set. But he was curious about
Emily. "You, too, Emily?" he asked gently.

Emily nodded quickly. Her eyes shone. "T-ball,"
she whispered. "That's what kids my age play."

"Well, how about that? Good for you."

Daniel turned his attention to Shelley, watching
her introduce her parents to Bart.

"Three weeks, eh?" said the Realtor. "Then come
to breakfast at the Diner on the Dunes with me on
Monday. You'll meet so many good people, you'll
want to settle in every summer. Maybe retire here,
too, when the time's right."

Her parents' response to Quinn was very different from the response they'd given Dan. Smiles,
handshakes, warmth all around. Dan glanced at
Shelley and gave her a big smile himself.

"We've just ordered our meal," said Shelley.
"Would you like to join us, Daniel?"

CHAPTER SEVEN

THE LAUGHTER around the dinner table ceased, and the silence reverberated in Daniel's ears. The frozen expressions on the faces of Shelley's parents before they gathered their manners again told its own story. All eyes were on Daniel.

He didn't know the reason behind the Duffys' behavior, and he wouldn't join them for dinner, but now it was time to have a little fun. He rocked back on his heels and focused only on Shelley. "Thank you, darlin'." His voice was tender and warm, but loud enough for the others to hear. "I appreciate the invitation. You're a sweetheart to include me."

Her parents' eyes widened in identical expressions, while Shelley's blush started at her collarbone, traveled up her slender neck to her cheeks and finally to the roots of her shiny hair. Beautiful. He found himself staring at his lovely neighbor, and felt his own pulse take flight. Everyone else in the vicinity faded away for a moment...or an hour. He didn't know how much time elapsed until his peripheral vision picked up the confusion on their faces.

"Unfortunately, I'll have to take a rain check to-night," said Daniel as he refocused. "But I'll check in with you tomorrow. We still have a lot to discuss." He glanced at Mr. and Mrs. Duffy, and decided to cause another small ripple. "Has Shelley mentioned that we'll be working closely together all summer coaching Josh's team?"

He let the words sink in, watched their consternation grow. "Seems that accommodating all the children who want to play ball is a serious goal around here," he continued, "and some very persuasive people asked me to be Shelley's assistant." The Duffys didn't have to know that the persuaders were eight years old.

"Yeah," piped up Josh. "We wouldn't of had a team without the professor. Mom can't do it herself. Even though she's read about ten books so far."

"Thanks for the support, Josh." Shelley's voice was dry as ash when she looked at her son.

Dan choked back his laughter and turned to face Shelley again. "Ten books, huh? Very impressive."

Her eyes glowed with humor. "I'm no stranger to research, either, Professor!"

His spirits lifted. She had a way of keeping him off balance. He never knew what to expect each time they met, and he found himself liking the unknown.

"The season's on top of us, Coach," he continued. "Meetings and practices this week and next. I got the schedules while you were in Boston, but now that you're back, you're in charge."

He thought he saw her gulp, but she nodded briskly. He could easily picture her as one of the cheering moms in the bleachers, but coach? No matter, he'd pick up the slack. She'd volunteered for her son's sake, and Dan figured she'd read a hundred books before she'd let Josh down. She had grit.

Glancing around the table, he also figured she'd need a lot of it this summer. "Enjoy your dinner, folks. I'm sure I'll see all of you tomorrow," he said, nodding at Mr. and Mrs. Duffy before walking with Bart to the table at the back wall.

"What in tarnation was that all about?" asked Quinn.

"I was hoping you'd know. They disliked me on sight."

Bart's brow creased and he shook his head. "I've got no clue."

Now Daniel allowed himself to laugh out loud. "Well, Bartholomew Quinn, that's got to be a first for you!"

SHELLEY HUMMED with contentment as she gave her homemade potato salad a final mix before covering the bowl and placing it in the fridge alongside her coleslaw the following afternoon. Daniel had accepted her invitation for a barbecue supper later that day and she was glad. After her parents' less-than-cordial greetings, she hadn't been sure he would. Maybe he'd only accepted because Shelley and he really did need to discuss their coaching responsibilities.

She sighed with frustration thinking about her parents' attitude. Ordinarily, they were very gracious people, and if the situation with Carl hadn't existed, they would have been as friendly as could be toward Daniel.

To her great relief, when she'd addressed the issue with them that morning, they'd surprised her with smiles and assurances of cooperation. She'd shrugged her shoulders at their unexpected capitulation, simply relieved to have eliminated the problem, and begun rounding up the kids for a morning swim.

Not that they really swam. Emily tiptoed toward the water, wet her feet and ran away from the waves; Shelley dunked and ran after Emily. Josh, however, tried to keep afloat with a few strokes before jumping the waves. But they'd all had fun. *Fun.* Her original purpose in coming to Pilgrim Cove. She needed to remember that goal despite the pulls and demands of other people.

And now she needed to baste the steaks with the teriyaki marinade she'd concocted for the first family barbecue of the season.

At four o'clock that afternoon, the back porch seemed filled with people, just the way a Sunday dinner should be. Shelley piled plates and utensils in the middle of the table, family-style. Daniel and her folks were deep in conversation, and Shelley's humming evolved into quiet singing. She enjoyed hearing Dan's deep, well-modulated voice in the background. Jessie was there, too, lying beneath the table in the shade.

Shelley stood next to the grill, about to transfer the steaks to the flames, when from the corner of her eye she saw someone approach. She raised her head, stunned to see her ex-husband striding toward her from the driveway. He held his head high, wore a smile on his face and confidence in every step. His aviator sunglasses and designer polo added to the image.

"How's my family?" he called.

Screams of "Daddy, Daddy" filled the air as Josh and Emily ran to their father. Carl reached for them and carried one in each arm back to the porch.

Shelley glanced at her parents, who looked elated at Carl's arrival, and suddenly realized why they'd had an attitude adjustment since the prior evening. Ellen and Phil had known Carl would show up today. In fact, they'd probably made a phone call to suggest it.

She didn't know what to expect next, and when she turned toward Daniel, a frisson of anxiety passed through her. She breathed easier when she saw his smile. And when he winked at her, she relaxed and felt herself grin. Coward! Why had she been concerned? Carl had no hold over Daniel, and Daniel had no vested interest in the goings-on of the Anderson family. She also knew, however, that nothing would escape her neighbor's acute powers of observation. He'd probably be able to write a book by the time this day was over.

Carl's voice grabbed her attention again as he approached the Duffys, who sat at the table. "And how are my favorite in-laws?" He leaned over to kiss Ellen and lowered the kids to the ground in order to shake Phil's hand. "It's been too long," he continued, "but it doesn't have to be."

Carl was preaching to the choir, putting on an unnecessary performance, and Shelley tried to brace herself for whatever came. She didn't have to wait long. Carl turned from her parents, whipped off his shades and walked toward her with hungry eyes. No warning could have prepared her, however, for the full frontal kiss he planted on her mouth.

"Hmm. Tastes good," he said with a grin afterward.

"Back off," Shelley replied, reclaiming her space by stepping away from him. "If you want to win points, I suggest you pay attention to the children."

"I definitely intend to, after I introduce myself to your new neighbor."

"*I'll* introduce you," said Shelley quickly, recognizing the aggressive tone in Carl's voice. Once more, her stomach tensed.

She looked to where Daniel had been sitting at the table, and saw that he was now standing, casually leaning against the porch rail, one hand at his side, the other holding a beer. He looked as cool and relaxed as ever. His eyes twinkled when he met her gaze, and he surreptitiously nodded at Carl. He was sending her a message. Hot damn! He was laughing to himself. He had watched Carl's entire performance and was laughing!

She felt an unexpected giggle start to emerge and pressed her lips together, then immediately felt guilty about wanting to laugh, too. She was in no position to poke fun at her children's father. In fact, she was partly responsible for the pressure he was feeling right now, because of her indecision. But at least she didn't have to be concerned about Daniel.

DANIEL WISHED he could reach over to smooth the worry line from Shelley's brow. She took responsibility for the whole world on her shoulders. Hopefully, she'd soon realize that he could take care of himself. He had to admit, however, that she was a sweetheart for caring.

Dan remained leaning nonchalantly against the railing until Shelley and her ex-husband approached, side by side. Then he straightened to his full six feet, meeting the fair-haired man eye-to-eye.

"So, you're Shelley's upstairs neighbor," said the newcomer, putting his arm around Shelley as he spoke. "Carl Anderson," he said with a nod.

"Daniel Stone." Dan extended his hand, forcing the other man to relinquish his hold on Shelley to clasp it, or look diminished. Shelley stepped to the side, her expression inscrutable, which made Dan blink and examine her again. He'd never seen Shelley other than animated and easy to read.

The blond man's handshake was firm to a fault, his glance assessing. Daniel maintained his gaze. "That's right. I rent Sea View House, too. I'll be here all summer."

"You must have a great job." The words were not complimentary, and a tiny sneer marred Anderson's handsome face.

Daniel leaned back against the railing again and allowed a lazy grin to emerge. "Oh, I make out all right. And from what I've recently read, you have plans for this summer, too." He injected a note of admiration in his voice. "In fact, I guess you have plans for the entire year." Nothing like flattery to change the direction of a conversation.

Carl's eyes widened a fraction. "You follow politics?"

"I read the papers," replied Daniel. "The *Boston* papers. Your litigation's been good on environmental issues. If the voters care about that, you'll stand a decent chance. At least a fair chance. The incumbent passed away, so it's an open seat, isn't it?"

And that's all it took to neutralize Carl Anderson for the moment. The politician picked up the conversation and ran with it. Daniel glanced at Shelley's relieved face and wanted to cheer.

But an hour later, Daniel had to admit that when Carl was with his children, no one could fault the attention he gave them. Neither Emily nor Josh spared even a brief glance for Dan, which was understandable. But when they ignored Jessie, too,

Dan realized how much the kids had been starving for their dad's company. And that was too bad. He'd assumed that after two years of living apart, Shelley's divorce was definitely an event of the past, and the fallout had been contained.

Two years. He was a jerk! Why should Shelley's life have rebounded any more smoothly than his after two years? His eyes followed her as she went about the business of hostessing, and then he took a turn at the grill so she was free for other duties while the kids were with their dad. When Josh called her to join their game on the sand, Dan waved her on. "Everything's under control here. Go to your son."

"Thanks," she replied, heartfelt sincerity reverberating in the one little word.

He watched her join Carl and the children in their impromptu soccer game, glad that the kids would have good memories of the day.

"They are a lovely family, aren't they?" Ellen Duffy's voice broke into his thoughts. "In fact, they're a lovely couple. Don't you think so?"

Dan startled. "Pardon me?" he said, turning around to face Shelley's mother. "I was under the impression Shelley and Carl were divorced."

The woman looked away. "Well, yes. Yes, they are. But—" she faced him again "—we're all hoping their unfortunate split was a mistake that will soon be in the past."

A shock wave of disappointment rolled through

him, followed by a familiar echo of loss. He caught his breath as he felt a newly opened window closed again, and then lost his breath completely when he realized how affected he was by Ellen Duffy's revelation.

Despite the dimensions of his love for Nikki, he was still a warm-blooded, warm-hearted human male in the land of the living. And Ellen Duffy would never know what a favor she'd done for him.

HE NEEDED HER. Even though they lived in progressive times, the public preferred a candidate of Carl's age to be a stable family man before they sent him to Washington. Carl knew he brought other, equally important, qualities to the table—a substantive platform, high energy, creativity and an ability to build a coalition—not to mention the personal attributes his campaign manager considered strong assets such as good looks and a fit body. Voters noticed everything, and if a handsome face brought in votes, he'd keep on smiling.

But he needed Shelley for insurance. The divorce hadn't been his idea! He'd been content with their lives. But Shelley—so damn naive about real life and real marriages—still believed the fairy tales about total fidelity. His own parents, who were devoted to each other, had an understanding between them, and Carl didn't see anything wrong with that. Evidently his former in-laws didn't see too much wrong with it, either. In fact, they seemed ready to hold Shelley responsible for Carl's forays. He mentally shrugged. If guilt worked, he was all for it.

"Hey, Shelley. Let's take a time out. We need to talk."

He didn't like the cautious look she gave him, but she nodded and told the kids to wash up for supper.

"You're staying, Dad, right?" asked Josh, running toward him and wrapping his arms around Carl's waist.

Carl ruffled his son's hair. "You bet," he replied, conscience tugging at the tone of desperation in Josh's voice. "We'll be right there."

Josh and Emily ran off, and he turned toward Shelley. "Have you thought about our last conversation?"

"Of course I have," she replied, leading him toward the shore, farther from the house. "But I have no answer for you yet."

"You see how much our reunion would benefit the kids," he began.

"That's never been the question." Her eyes flashed. Her auburn hair crackled with a matching fire. Oh, yeah…she was a striking woman, and would look very good standing next to him again.

"It's been barely a week since we spoke," she continued. "Don't push."

He wasn't an idiot, and he backed off. Her message was loud and clear. But, man, she still didn't understand. An office romance was nothing. The real point was that he'd had no intention of *leaving* her for someone else.

"Shel, we could have a life you've only dreamed about."

Now sorrow filled her eyes, and she shook her head. "I've already had my dream. It just didn't last. This political career is *your* dream. If I go along for the ride, it'll be because of every other factor involved, *not* my ambitions. Hell," she murmured, "I'd be giving up on *ever* reclaiming my own dreams."

He understood what she meant. "I promise, Shel, you'll never have anything to worry about again."

She glanced at him assessingly. "I would hope not." Her voice trailed off, and he knew she had doubts.

"Then you *are* seriously considering my proposal?"

She winced. This time he couldn't blame her. Bad choice of words. But she met his gaze and nodded.

Relief filled him. He took her hand, kissed her palm and quickly led her back to the house. "How about dinner next Saturday night?"

"All right," she said slowly.

He faced the group on the porch. "Ellen, Phil. Would you like to join Shelley and me in Boston next week? Dinner at my place. For old times' sake and maybe new times', too."

He turned to Shelley. "Get a baby-sitter, or on second thought—" he looked at Daniel "—since you're such a good neighbor, how about volunteering?"

DANIEL HEARD Shelley gasp, but ignored her for the moment, while once again meeting the other man's gaze head-on. He allowed a smile to cross his face. "It would be my pleasure."

"Oh, no, Dan. I couldn't ask you to do that. I'll get a sitter."

He didn't press the point, seeing that Shelley was still unnerved by her ex's suggestion. In truth, Daniel had no particular plans for the next weekend, so staying with the kids was no hardship. He could take them to Neptune's Park and distract them while their mom was away.

"The offer remains open," he said to Shelley. "No problem."

"Thanks," she said in a quiet voice. "I'll let you know." She stared at him for a minute before bustling with the meal again. He figured she was serving the most marinated steak in the country.

It wasn't the delayed meal, however, that made Daniel feel uneasy. Shelley didn't look happy. And Daniel didn't trust Carl. But there was nothing he could do about any of it. Not his business.

But his heart was heavy. No question about that. And it was difficult remaining neutral while Carl Anderson successfully manipulated everyone in his orbit.

Dan watched the politician chat up his former in-laws after bringing them full plates of food. He watched him embrace Emily and Josh freely—a good thing—but when he started calling Shelley "sweetheart," Dan decided it was time to leave the party. Until he saw Shelley grimace and give her ex-husband a speaking look. Dan silently cheered, his heart much lighter. It seemed to him that Ellen Duffy's hopes for a reunion were not a sure thing.

LATE THE FOLLOWING Saturday afternoon, Shelley stood at the forward rail of the ferryboat heading into Boston. Her parents also chose to remain outside, sitting on a bench, and seemed to be enjoying the ride. None of them had ever been to Carl's new condo, but she had directions to give the cabdriver when they arrived in the city.

The half-hour ride over the water should have relaxed her, but she found herself gripping the rail until her knuckles turned white. *She had to make a decision and make it soon.*

Although the children didn't know what was really at stake, they'd sensed the excitement in their dad and became infected with it themselves. Normally, they'd complain about a new baby-sitter, but tonight they were more than willing to stay home with the teenager Shelley'd managed to find, a girl who lived only a block away. Actually, the mom seemed happier than the daughter about the girl's chance to earn some money, and reassured Shelley that she would be on call that evening herself. So now Shelley and her parents were on their way to spend an evening with Carl. And the kids knew it.

The boat docked; several cabs were lined up at the permanent taxi stand adjacent to the wharf.

"Let's go," said Shelley to her parents. "He's catering the food, so we won't be disturbing a master chef at work if we show up a little early." Of course, if they arrived early, they could also leave early. She indicated the bottle of Amaretto she'd brought as a gift. Carl's favorite liqueur. "We can always start the evening with this."

"I'll stick to beer. Thanks anyway," said Philip Duffy wrinkling his sixty-four-year-old nose.

Shelley laughed. "Josh looks just like you when he does that."

Her dad's face flushed with pleasure. "He's quite a boy, my grandson. All I want is for him to be happy."

"I know, I know," said Shelley holding the taxi door open for her parents and then getting in herself. Josh was a terrific kid who wanted a dad fulltime, and she was on the brink of a decision that would affect both her children for the rest of their lives.

The taxi driver knew the city well, and in fifteen minutes, they were deposited in front of a newly converted building housing luxury condominiums.

"No grass to mow here," said Shelley in a quiet tone, thinking about the lovely yard she had at her home only a few miles away.

"Carl has no time for that stuff now, Shel. Be reasonable."

"Are you sure you're not Carl's mother, Mom, instead of mine? I wasn't criticizing. Just observing."

Ellen's hug was reassuring. "Ah, Shelley. I just want the best for you. You can get used to living anywhere, as long as your family's together." Good old-fashioned values that Shelley believed in. But at what price?

No point in replying to her mom. They all knew the key to changing the status quo was in her hands. And Shelley would turn that key only *when* and *if* she thought the time was right.

Carl really seemed to want to make amends. True, he needed her badly, maybe so badly that his need would be a catalyst to change his behavior. People do make mistakes and then correct them. And he was the father of her children. She'd definitely bring an open mind to the evening.

"Carl said a doorman would let us in," said Ellen as they approached the entrance. "I don't see him, and I think we're a little early."

"Don't need the doorman," said Phil Duffy. "Someone's coming out now." He thanked the exiting residents and held the door for the two women. "Let's go."

"Lucky us," said Shelley, glancing around. "It's Apartment 5-B. And now we can find it ourselves."

The swiftness of the elevator ride made Shelley laugh. "It's fun, like the whip at the amusement park." Still chuckling, she got her bearings and led her parents toward Carl's apartment. The door opened as she approached.

A familiar, tall, leggy blonde was profiled in the doorway. "'Bye, sweetie. See you later. Much later. I just love living in this building." Her intimate chuckle left no doubt as to the purpose of the proposed rendezvous.

Shelley stood in the hallway, frozen, as though watching a performance unfold on stage. Somewhere, in the back of her mind, any hope she had for rebuilding her marriage evaporated forever. Gone in an instant like a dream unremembered.

The blonde turned, saw them. "Oh, my." She shook her head and tsked. "Carl," she called inside. "First aid is needed out here. And I don't think I can help." She walked passed Shelley, then paused. "It's déjà vu, isn't it? But if you can pretend I don't exist, you can still have it all. That's my best advice. And my best offer."

"Easy to be generous with advice," replied Shelley to the woman she now realized was Carl's longtime girlfriend, "when you know I won't take it." Carl's associate shrugged and continued toward the elevator.

Shelley looked at Carl, who stood on the threshold of the apartment. He started to speak, but Shelley put up her hand in a stop motion.

"Don't even try. But thanks for making my decision so easy. We won't be staying for dinner after all." She hefted the bottle of liqueur, tempted for a moment to chuck it at him, but turned to her parents instead. "We'll raise a glass to new beginnings when we get home. Are you with me?"

"Talk to her," interrupted Carl, looking at the Duf-fys. "She's kept my name. She's still an Anderson. And, Shelley, you're nuts if you think it's over. Any shrink will tell you that two parents are better than one."

Shelley shrugged and did a half turn, heading to-ward the elevator, her mom and dad keeping pace on either side of her.

Carl's voice followed them. "Don't be so high-and-mighty, Mrs. Shelley Anderson, who's got a guy living right upstairs at the beach. Very conve-nient for shacking up. But not good for my children. And, trust me, it won't look good in court."

AT FIRST, silence filled the taxi on the trip back to the pier. Shelley's parents sat on either side of her, each holding one of her hands. Several moments passed.

"I'm such an idiot…."

"I'm so sorry, Shelley…."

"He's a jackass…."

Shelley glanced first at her dad, then at her mom, then started to laugh. They both joined in, and for a moment, the car rang with good humor. But then Shelley found she couldn't stop. Tears ran down her face as she shook her head from side to side.

"I'm such an idiot," she repeated. "Fooled twice by the same guy. No judgment at all. About Carl or about any man. What in the world do I know about men? Carl was my first and only. And how am I going to teach Josh to be an honorable man? I'm thirty-four years old. You'd think I'd be wise by now."

"Shush, sweetheart, shush," said her mom, patting her hand. "Everything will be all right."

Shelley laughed again. Her mom sounded like every other mother in every generation. The way Shelley sounded when comforting her own children.

"Didn't you say you were coaching Josh's team?" asked her dad.

"Yes."

"The children are eight years old, so you'll teach them to play fair and that winning isn't everything."

"Carl thinks it is."

"Then Josh and Em are lucky to have you." Phil leaned over and placed a kiss on her cheek. "I'll be at every weekend game—cheering my daughter!"

Her parents' change of heart about the revival of her marriage was a relief to Shelley. Seeing Carl in action had obviously shaken them up. They'd only wanted the best for their daughter, and fifteen years of mostly happy memories were hard to erase especially when their daughter's future seemed so insecure.

"We haven't had dinner yet," said her dad, "and we still have a baby-sitter. How about stopping off at the Lobster Pot when we get back to Pilgrim Cove?"

"Why not?" said Shelley. Not that she was really

hungry, but if a good meal in a friendly environment could restore her parents' spirits a little, it was worth her time.

And the stop had been worthwhile. Thea's warm greeting put Shelley at ease as soon as she entered the restaurant. She consumed her entire dinner. Her folks did the same.

"Look at that," she said, pointing to their plates. "We must be feeling better."

"Are you sure you do?" asked Ellen.

"Yes. Yes, I do," Shelley replied. No question about that.

After leaving the Lobster Pot, she drove directly home and pulled into the driveway behind Daniel's vehicle. Which didn't necessarily mean he was home. He liked to take long walks especially in the early morning and late evening.

She automatically led her parents down the driveway and up the porch steps to the back door, the one that led directly to the kitchen, where so much of her daily life was focused. "I'll take the sitter home, and if you like, we can have another cup of tea when I come back."

But when she walked inside, the kitchen was empty. No evidence of a teenage girl's presence littered the table or chairs. The place was too clean, and Shelley didn't like it.

"I've got to check the kids."

CHAPTER EIGHT

SHELLEY MOVED swiftly toward the hallway, but came to an abrupt stop when Jessie appeared. The dog's tail wagged hard enough to lead a marching band as she trotted directly to Shelley.

"Jess? What's going on?" Shelley leaned down and rubbed the dog's neck, feeling her alarm lessen. If Jess was here, then Daniel had to be in the house, and that meant her children were safe.

"I hope you believe in 'All's well that ends well,'" came a deep voice nearby.

Shelley's attention shifted from dog to man. Daniel leaned casually against the archway separating the kitchen from the hall. One shoulder was propped on the door frame, one foot crossed over the other, his arms folded in front of his chest. His hair was longer than when they'd first met, and a thick chestnut curl hung awry on his forehead.

She wanted to touch him, to reach for that curl. But she couldn't move, couldn't think, especially when she saw the curiosity in his golden-brown eyes slowly change to warmth.

"I guess you survived," he said quietly. "Unscathed." Then he smiled.

She forgot about the kids and her parents. She simply stood and stared. The man looked good. Too good. And so different from Carl. *Carl.* A flash of pain pierced her stomach as she crashed back to reality.

"What happened here?" she asked. "Did the sitter have to leave?"

A thoughtful expression crossed his face. "Hmm...you might say that. I guess not every fourteen-year-old is committed to baby-sitting on a Saturday night. At least, not by herself."

"Oh, no," said Shelley. "Did she invite a pack of friends?" Images of every teen party movie she'd ever seen or heard about kaleidoscoped in her mind. "How bad...?"

He held up his hand. "Not to worry. It didn't get that far. I sorted everything out."

"Thank you so much, Daniel. I really owe you for this." Shelley heard her voice crack as the implications of the evening struck her.

If Carl heard about this baby-sitting fiasco, he could use it against her. After the threats he'd made that evening, she'd expect no less. And after watching him achieve goals for over ten years, she wouldn't underestimate his determination. He was a master at strategy when he wanted something.

"Are the kids in bed?" she finally asked.

"Sorry. Didn't know where to put them with your folks staying here." Daniel glanced at Phil and

Ellen, who'd been quiet until then. "So we popped some corn, then hung together in the living room and watched a movie. Emily conked out in ten minutes. Josh took a little longer. Come on. You can tuck them in where they belong."

In fact, Daniel had done a pretty good job of tucking them in on the sofa with a couple of throw quilts. One sleepy, tousled child lay at each end of the couch, and Jessie, alert but seemingly content, stretched out on the floor in front of them.

Shelley would have been just as content to remain standing there all night, absorbing the slice-of-life scene that could have been limned by Norman Rockwell. *A Portrait of Home* is what she'd call it.

Her heart exploded with love. For her children's sake, she'd fight an army if she had to. An army—or one Goliath. And yet she'd never considered herself a particularly brave person. Conscientious, yes. Capable, yes. But nonconfrontational, preferring to resolve the conflicts in her life amicably. Even through her divorce.

But as she studied the two innocents who depended on her, adrenaline rushed through her body. Her spine straightened, her hands fisted at her sides and she knew her peacemaking days were over.

"I can't thank you enough," she said to Dan, her voice thick over the lump in her throat. Her parents echoed their appreciation, then each one took a sleepy child to bed.

"Forget about it," he said, stepping closer to Shelley and lightly stroking her jaw with his knuckles. "What are friends for?"

His touch distracted her; speech deserted her. She nodded, her eyes not leaving his face. He leaned in. Her heart fluttered in anticipation, but his lips barely brushed hers before he lifted his head again. "Good night." He called for Jessie and was gone.

She stared after him, feeling bereft. She'd wanted more.

NOISY WITH EXCITEMENT, her children crowded around her in the kitchen the next morning. Children with hope in their eyes. They'd known she'd been with their dad the night before, and now they hoped for a miracle thanks to Carl's broad hints to them before he'd left the previous Sunday.

Shelley would be the one to take the hit again. She'd have to absorb their anger. Their pain. Their disappointment. She opened her arms and gathered them in.

"Let's go outside and let the morning sun warm us up."

She didn't leave room for debate, just pulled the kitchen door open, and they trotted after her to a chaise longue at the front of the large porch. Shelley pulled a child down on either side of her, an arm encircling each one.

"I love you guys so much," she began, kissing them on the forehead. "And it's because I love you so much that I have to tell you the truth—even though you won't like it." She took a breath, allow-ing a moment of silence so they could begin to ab-sorb her message.

"Didn't you have a good time with Daddy?" asked Emily. "Is he coming to play with us again today? Josh said you were on a date."

"Be quiet, Emily. You don't understand any-thing." Josh's head snapped back as he looked at Shelley. His hazel eyes, at first shining with hope, had turned bright with anger, before finally becom-ing dull. Dull and resigned.

"It didn't work out, did it?" he asked. "And Daddy's not coming back to live with us." He waited a heartbeat. "Is he?" A tiny ember of hope still lit his voice.

She doused it. "No, Josh. He's not. But he's wel-come to visit, and you both will visit him just like always."

Tears flowed from her son's eyes, but he pushed them away with his fists. "Then why—why did he say things would be different? He said…he promised!"

Shelley's breath stuck in her throat. Had Carl ac-tually promised?

"Oh, Joshie. I'm so sorry. We all know a prom-ise is special. Sacred." She hoisted Josh onto her lap facing her, one hand lightly resting on his soft cheek. "If he promised, your dad made a mistake. A big one. And I'm so sorry."

"But he shouldn't of…." Fresh tears found new paths down his face, and Shelley allowed a moment to pass before trying to ease the pain further. "You know, everyone makes mistakes at some time or other." Not for the sake of the father did she try to give an explanation, but for the sake of his son.

"But he shouldn't have lied! That's not fair!"

Her heart twisted with his pain while she hugged him. "He wanted to make you happy."

"But he didn't. I'm not happy."

"I know, sweetheart. And you're absolutely right. It *isn't* fair. Either to you or to your sister. But you know what's weird? Maybe Daddy's not a happy guy today, either. Maybe now Daddy's scared that *you* are going to be angry with *him*." She waited for that idea to sink in while her own thoughts ran along a different channel.

In reality, Carl was probably not thinking about the kids' happiness at all. If Emily and Josh were on his mind, it was with the thought of custody. Carl would rationalize that the next best thing to presenting himself as an ideal family man was presenting himself as a responsible parent. A concerned parent.

She reached for her kids. "Group-hug time." Emily joined Josh on her lap. "And we three will march on together just like we have been doing. Daddy can still visit you, and you can still visit him. How does that sound?"

Emily glanced at her big brother, and Shelley hid a smile. Her daughter took her lead from Josh most of the time and was doing it now. Josh was silent for a moment. Then in a quiet voice, he said, "Four would be better than three. And Daddy forgets to visit a lot. But I guess that's the way it is."

The sadness and resignation in the young voice tore Shelley's heart. But it wasn't until little Emily started patting her brother's arm in comfort that Shelley lost it. The sweet gesture destroyed every bit of composure she'd mustered, and quiet tears fell.

She rubbed them away. "How about I take this fabulous family of *three* to Neptune's Park later on? Nana and Poppy, too."

Emily's eyes sparkled and she held up her hand, fingers outstretched. "That's five, Mommy. See, three of us and one Nana and one Poppy." Emily pushed and pulled her fingers to match the addition.

"You're absolutely right, my brilliant daughter. No calculator needed for you." Shelley sighed in relief. Despite her sadness, Emily would be okay. Not only could she be distracted by a host of activities, but also she'd always tended to cling more to Shelley than to Carl anyway. As long she had her mother, she'd be fine. At least for now. And that's all Shelley could cope with at the moment.

But Josh worried her. "Want to invite Jessie and the professor with us tonight, Josh?"

His face lit up for a second, but then he shook his head. "Nah. We're only going to be friends for the summer. Better not get too used to them."

Stunned by his comment, Shelley couldn't speak. Her eight-year-old had started to build a wall around himself.

DANIEL STONE SAT on his deck directly above Shelley's, his morning paper still mostly unread, his coffee mostly untouched and his position as eavesdropper mostly uncomfortable. He could hear the conversation between Shelley and her children, and was awed by both her personal strength and her understanding of the kids' reactions.

When he'd first gone outside to start his day, he'd had no idea that anyone was on the downstairs porch at all. The quiet of the morning, however, allowed words to drift clearly on the air. When he realized how personal the conversation was, he picked up his paper and his coffee and moved inside. Jessie followed him.

He could still hear the children's voices, but could no longer decipher their words. Then the door banged shut and quiet reigned downstairs. He sighed in relief, picked up his newspaper again and stepped onto his deck. He put the Andersons out of his mind. Until he heard Shelley's voice coming directly from below where he sat near the front railing.

"He can't take them from me, Dad. We have an agreement and there's no reason for the judge to change it. Unless Carl buys him off."

Daniel sat in shocked silence. Buy the judge off? Did she really have to be concerned about that? He heard her speak again.

"Oh, my God. Maybe he could do that. He's got influence now, as well as money… But I'm their mother. The kids need me."

As if on cue, Emily's voice sounded. "Mommy."

"I'll see what she wants," Philip said.

Daniel heard the door close. He jumped out of his chair and looked over the edge of the wooden railing. Shelley stood facing the ocean, her head in her hands. He could see her shoulders rise and fall with every ragged breath.

"Good morning, neighbor," he called in a quiet voice.

She whirled, wiping her eyes and then shading them as she looked up. "Hello. I was just going inside. I'll catch you later." She looked toward the door.

"Hang on a sec," said Dan. "Maybe I can help."

She stood perfectly still. "You heard me just now, didn't you?"

"I'm sorry," he replied. "Voices travel."

She turned away, her arm sweeping toward the glistening blue ocean and quiet beach. "I thought I'd find peace here at Sea View House, but I guess our problems follow us wherever we go. It's really too bad. There shouldn't be heartache in the middle of such serene beauty."

"Don't be fooled," Dan replied. "Mother Nature can be just as savage as she is peaceful."

"Like our lives," she said. "A roller coaster. Either an uphill battle or a downhill, out-of-control event."

Daniel shrugged. "I can argue that, but not while watching you get a crick in your neck. My porch or yours?"

"Neither. I'm going inside. But thanks for offering to help. We're both teachers, Daniel, and neither of us is qualified to take on my ex-husband."

Startled, Dan remained quiet before saying, "Stay right there. I'm on my way." He jogged down the staircase, then rounded the corner of her porch until he and Shelley were facing one another, separated only by the wooden railing. Could it be that after all this time, she was unaware that he was a licensed attorney? "Uh, Shelley?"

"Yes?"

"I *am* a teacher—on staff at Harvard—but I'm also a trained litigator. An attorney. I teach law. Business law."

Her eyes widened in horror. "Another lawyer! I am such an idiot about men! You are just what I don't need in my life. Thanks for your offer of help, but no thanks, Professor. I'll handle the situation myself."

"Hey. I'm on your side, Shelley. Remember that when the going gets rough. If you change your mind, I'm here."

Her arms akimbo, she finally stilled. "Maybe you're right. Maybe I should remember that sharks fight until one wins. I just don't know yet which one of you has the sharper teeth."

He winced. "Low blow."

"Maybe it just struck home."

She couldn't be more wrong, but Daniel said nothing. He watched her walk back inside knowing she was frightened about a custody challenge and was lashing out. He could take the insult, both to himself and to his profession, but maybe it was just as well she had no interest in him. He might be willing to begin exploring a new social life, but he wasn't ready for a roller-coaster ride.

LAST NIGHT SHE'D WANTED to kiss him, and today she'd treated Daniel like a pariah. Ten minutes after she'd left him on the porch, Shelley closed her eyes in disgust. She owed him an apology. She shouldn't have painted all lawyers with the same brush.

She'd liked him well enough a month ago, the night of their first meeting, when Jess had scared the wits out of her. Liked Daniel well enough to think about him a lot. Then she'd tucked those thoughts away while she considered Carl's plan. What a mistake! Despite the pressures from his mother and her parents, and—she had to admit—her children, she should never have considered reconciliation for a minute. Whatever love and personal respect she'd had for Carl were gone.

She'd go forward from here, steering clear of personal relationships, and concentrating only on

Josh and Emily. She'd face any custody battle if or when Carl instigated one. One thing she knew for sure. Nobody was going to take her children away.

Thoughts of the kids made her mind leap to the baseball season. She'd partner with Daniel on Josh's team as if it were a business arrangement, which it was, sort of. In fact, they had an organizational meeting scheduled for Wednesday evening. She'd invite him to go with her and apologize for today's outburst. And then they'd just be neighbors and volunteer partners for the rest of the summer. She felt herself relax, pleased with her plan.

In *theory*, it was a great idea, Shelley mused on Tuesday evening. In *fact*, she'd seen Daniel only at a distance since Sunday morning. He and Jessie took to the beach before sunrise and after sunset and stayed outdoors forever, or so it seemed to her. In between, there was no sign of the professor at all. Of course, her life was pretty busy, too, and their paths hadn't crossed. Her last resort would be to tape a note on his door if he wasn't home now.

She left through the kitchen, walked around to Daniel's entrance and rang the bell. The outside light came on immediately, and then Daniel appeared at the top of the stairs.

"Hey, Shelley. Come on up. If you can stand it."

She understood his meaning as soon as she walked in. The small apartment was a mess. Papers everywhere. Two computers—one PC and one lap-top—both on.

"I should have had a research assistant," he said. "But, stupidly, I turned the offer down."

"Don't trust anyone else?" she asked.

"No… Wanted to be sure I had enough work to keep my mind occupied."

"Oh," she said, for the first time examining Daniel rather than the apartment.

Deliciously disheveled. Scruffy, mussed and looking sexy enough to attract a harem if he'd wanted to. His powerful shoulders strained against the fabric of his dark T-shirt, and Shelley's fingers strained against the desire to stroke his broad chest. Not in the plan, she reminded herself.

"Uh, what are you working on?" she asked.

His eyes twinkled, the corner of his mouth turned up. "Ethics. A curriculum in legal ethics that will help turn great whites into small guppies fit for a home aquarium."

"Ouch!" she said, feeling the heat rise to her face, not only because of the shark reference—a subtle reminder of the insult she'd hurled at him—but also because of her more shocking thoughts, which weren't insulting at all! "That's one of the reasons I'm here, Daniel. To apologize."

He waved her words aside with a gesture. "Accepted. You had other matters on your mind."

"And I still do," she admitted, meeting his gaze. "But I had no call to take it out on you and your profession. How about joining us for dinner tomorrow night, and afterwards I'll take us to the Little League meeting."

"I accept with pleasure," he replied immediately. "I've inhaled those aromas from your place a time or two, and now I'm salivating."

Her mind raced for a meal requiring short preparation time yet providing a selection he probably wouldn't prepare for himself. "How about grilled salmon, steamed asparagus and small roasted potatoes? Or, if you don't like fish…"

He held up his hand. "Fish is great. But tell me the truth, do your kids eat a meal like that?"

She grinned. "I hate to admit how many PB&J sandwiches have supplemented their dinner over the years. They think dinner is always an experiment in my house and they're the guinea pigs."

He leaned closer to her and whispered dramatically, "Could they be right?"

His fragrance of musk and masculinity slammed her senses, stimulating memories she wanted to banish. Her insides tightened. Dear God, she had to get out of his apartment before she made a fool of herself.

"Sure, they're guinea pigs," she replied in a husky voice, surprised she was able to remember the question. "See you tomorrow about five-thirty." She ran from the Crow's Nest as though flames were licking her heels, and barely heard him say, "I'll bring dessert."

WHIPPED-CREAM ÉCLAIRS for dessert. As he took the box of sweets from his vehicle, Daniel thought of a few other places he'd like to cover with whipped cream besides flaky pastry shells. But Shelley didn't quite trust him. And without a connection forged by trust, or at least respect, having sex would be just that. Strictly a physical release. He needed more. Not love. Certainly not love as in "till death do us part." Been there, done that. But…now…finally, he needed something! Something beyond a quick dip in the pool.

Ironically, Shelley wanted him. He knew it. He could read desire easily enough, and her swift departure last night only confirmed it. In the end, she'd done him a favor, because he'd responded to her with the same intensity.

He walked around the back. Shelley's kids were playing on the deck, their grandparents setting the outside table, and he knew dinner would be free of any tension, sexual or otherwise. Now that he was no longer a threat to their daughter's future in Washington, D.C., Ellen and Phil had been treating him just fine. Like good neighbors.

As for the children, well, Jessie was the key there. Jessie…and the fact that he and Shelley had saved the baseball team. That was the story according to Casey Parker and his cousin, Katie, and Josh absolutely believed it. More significantly, however, the boy had seemed to place his dad and Daniel on separate tracks. Maybe he'd taken the cue from his grandparents. Maybe he'd figured it out himself when he'd said, "Daddy forgets to visit a lot. But I guess that's the way it is."

A lot for a kid to handle, but he'd put his money on Josh. That was one terrific boy.

"Evening, everyone," said Daniel, climbing the three steps to the deck. He waved at the Duffys, then turned to the children with a wink. "Shall I invite Jess to join us?"

Their animated response reminded him to chat with Shelley about getting them a pup of their own. "Be right back," he said, heading for his own doorway. When he returned with the dog, Jess made a beeline for the kids.

Dan opened the door and saw Shelley standing over the stove, doing something to the contents of a pot. Her face was rosy, her lips softly smiling, and she was humming under her breath.

"You're beautiful." The words traveled from inside his head and popped out of his mouth.

She twirled toward him, her look of astonishment comical. "It's my kitchen-glamour look. Welcome."

He held up the carton. "Needs refrigeration." *And so do I.*

TWO HOURS LATER, during the meeting at Town Hall, he promised himself a cold shower as soon as he returned to Sea View House. The business part of the meeting had just concluded, and now he and Shelley were being introduced as the new coaches for the Parker Plumbing Team of eight-year-olds. The applause was vigorous as they were handed bags of equipment, rule books, game schedules and tons of advice.

Daniel glanced at Shelley and knew she was forcing a smile. Could be she didn't relish being the center of attention—nor did he, for that matter—or, could be the reality of coaching just hit her head-on. The percentage of moms at the meeting was small.

He bent his head to hers. "It's an equal-opportunity league, Shelley," he whispered, "not just for children, but for coaches, too. You'll be fine."

Worried brown eyes looked back at him. "Oh, the gender thing doesn't bother me. It's the practices. How am I going to hit flyballs for them to catch?"

He laughed out loud and impulsively gave her a hug. "Sweetheart, we'll do the best we can."

Surprise and warmth replaced her concerned expression, but before she could reply, Matthew Parker, Casey's dad, walked up to them with his hand extended.

"Thank you, Shelley. Thank you, Daniel. Everyone thanks you for taking over the team this year. Especially my son, who wants to disown me except he also wants Laura as a mom, as well as a new cool house to live in before school starts again."

"We're glad to do it," said Shelley. "Ready, willing and able. Don't worry about a thing."

The Harlequin Reader Service® — Here's how it works:

Accepting your 2 free books and gift places you under no obligation to buy anything. You may keep the books and gift and return the shipping statement marked "cancel." If you do not cancel, about a month later we'll send you 6 additional books and bill you just $4.69 each in the U.S., or $5.24 each in Canada, plus 25¢ shipping & handling per book and applicable taxes if any.* That's the complete price and — compared to cover prices of $5.50 each in the U.S. and $6.50 each in Canada — it's quite a bargain! You may cancel at any time, but if you choose to continue, every month we'll send you 6 more books, which you may either purchase at the discount price or return to us and cancel your subscription. *Terms and prices subject to change without notice. Sales tax applicable in N.Y. Canadian residents will be charged applicable provincial taxes and GST. Credit or debit balances in a customer's account(s) may be offset by any other outstanding balance owed by or to the customer.

If offer card is missing write to: Harlequin Reader Service, 3010 Walden Ave., P.O. Box 1867, Buffalo NY 14240-1867

NO POSTAGE
NECESSARY
IF MAILED
IN THE
UNITED STATES

BUSINESS REPLY MAIL
FIRST-CLASS MAIL   PERMIT NO. 717-003   BUFFALO, NY

POSTAGE WILL BE PAID BY ADDRESSEE

HARLEQUIN READER SERVICE
3010 WALDEN AVE
PO BOX 1867
BUFFALO NY 14240-9952

GET FREE BOOKS and a FREE GIFT WHEN YOU PLAY THE...

Lucky 7

SLOT MACHINE GAME!

Just scratch off the silver box with a coin. Then check below to see the gifts you get!

YES!

I have scratched off the silver box. Please send me the 2 free Harlequin Superromance® books and gift for which I qualify. I understand I am under no obligation to purchase any books, as explained on the back of this card.

336 HDL D2AS   **135 HDL D33Y**

FIRST NAME	LAST NAME

ADDRESS

APT.#	CITY

STATE/PROV.	ZIP/POSTAL CODE

7	7	7	**Worth TWO FREE BOOKS plus a BONUS Mystery Gift!**
🍒	🍒	🍒	**Worth TWO FREE BOOKS!**
♣	♣	♣	**Worth ONE FREE BOOK!**
🔔	🔔	🍒	**TRY AGAIN!**

www.eHarlequin.com

(H-SR-08/04)

DETACH AND MAIL CARD TODAY!

Daniel swallowed his laughter and nodded.

"How's Sea View House these days?" asked Matt, still shaking Daniel's hand. "My favorite place in this whole town. That's where I found Laura and fell in love with her." His arm dropped to his side, and he stared over Daniel's shoulder with an unfocused gaze.

Daniel glanced at Shelley and rolled his eyes. He saw her swallow a chuckle.

"We walked the beach for miles," continued Matt. "Laura wanted to get back into shape after her bout with breast cancer and chemo and the grief over losing her mom. But we discovered a bonus on our walks. At night," he said softly, "you can see every star in the heavens…." His voice trailed off.

"Thank God he's getting married in three days," said Ralph Bigelow, one of the ROMEOs, as well as a coach of the older boys. "It'll put him out of his misery."

Daniel silently seconded the opinion.

"For a plumber, you're talking mushy, real mushy," said another coach.

"Yeah, yeah," replied Matt with a laugh. "And I'm expecting you all to be at the ceremony. The announcement was in the paper. The whole town's invited for champagne and fireworks on the beach this Saturday night. We'll be setting up along the shore near Sea View House." He looked at Shelley and Daniel, and slowly his smitten expression changed into one of horror. "Oh, she'll kill me. I forgot to ask you about using your driveway. She wants to walk onto the beach from Sea View House."

Daniel glanced at Shelley's glowing face. The answer the groom was hoping for was written right there. "Of course," he said, as though there could be any other response. "We'd be…uh… honored."

"Thanks," said Matt. "Couldn't choose any other location. We've already got the permit, and Big Ralph here is in charge of the pyrotechnics."

"And we thought fireworks celebrated *independence*!" said retired police chief Rick O'Brien.

"Look who's talking!" replied Matt. "You and Dee are married—what?—less than a month! And you're looking mighty fine, Chief. Mighty fine."

The Pilgrim Covers were still joking about marriage and weddings when Daniel and Shelley left the meeting and loaded the team's paraphernalia into her car.

"The way Matt Parker talks, you'd *never* know he and Laura are going to have a lovely reception at the Wayside Inn after the ceremony on the beach," said Shelley as she handed Daniel a copy of the team's schedule after he closed the trunk.

"Matt's mind is on Laura. Period." Dan understood the phenomenon. "He could eat mud afterward and not care. Or notice. As long as he has her."

Shelley's silence hung in the air. "You sound as if you're no stranger to the feeling, and yet…despite everyone's good intentions, I don't believe it lasts." She shrugged her shoulders. "I guess I'm a little cynical about the subject of monogamy right now." She turned away from him and walked to the driver's side of the car.

So *that* had been the reason for the breakup. He'd suspected infidelity, but had had no evidence to confirm it. "Not all men are unfaithful, Shel," Dan said in a gentle tone after he got into the car. "Don't let Carl destroy your belief in a future. A good future, filled with love."

"Not to worry, my friend. I'll move forward," Shelley replied, turning her head to look at him. "And I'll be satisfied—in every way. But on my terms." Her raised brow and unblinking stare reinforced her message. "No more promises for a lifetime."

He didn't believe her. The words made sense, but they didn't suit. Not Shelley. Not the woman for whom home and family were everything. Shelley Anderson was not the type to play musical beds. And he'd prove it right now.

"Since you're *not* looking for the commitment of a lifetime, how about a commitment to one short summer?"

CHAPTER NINE

SHE TOOK a breath. "Thought you'd never ask." Her heart pounded, but her voice was steady— very low, but steady. Dan's suggestion made some sense. Short-term relationship. No strings attached. Healthy for them both. She was physically attracted to him. No doubt about that.

Then why, suddenly, were her hands shaking so badly she couldn't fit the key into the ignition? Three times she tried to push the metal into its slot without success. When she glanced at him, he eyed her jingling key ring and started to laugh. Laugh!

"For God's sake, Shelley, you're not going to jump into my bed on a whim. You're a kindergarten teacher, for crying out loud. Kindergarten teachers don't go around sleeping with every Tom, Dick and Harry!"

Her glance morphed into a glare. "What century are you living in? And you, from California! That's where the action is, isn't it? Where it all starts."

"Don't let Hollywood's reputation fool you. Life's the same in California as in Anytown,

U.S.A.," replied Daniel, reaching for her keys and slipping the correct one into the ignition. "And that's because people are people wherever you go. The good, the bad and the—"

"—snuggly," said Shelley automatically.

"The what?"

Lord, had she actually said that? She must sound like an idiot. All Dan's fault. With clear conscience, she assigned the blame and led with her chin. "The snuggly. The good, the bad and the snuggly. When Josh or Emily get a case of the uglies, we try to change it into snugglies—you know, with hugs and kisses and stuff. And," she continued very slowly, "if you dare laugh at me, you are definitely walking home."

He laughed. Hard. "We're only a mile away, Shel," he said between breaths. "I can handle the walk, but you could never handle an affair. At least not now. Listen to yourself! People who do 'snuggly' don't do one-night stands or even one-month stands. Maybe—" his voice gentled "—not even for a summer."

Unexpectedly, she felt her lips tremble. "Then I guess I'll be alone for a very long time. Maybe forever." She had trouble getting the words out and couldn't stop the quiver. She put the car in motion, and silence descended for the short ride until she pulled into their driveway and parked.

"Shel?"

His gentle voice lured her, and she shifted to face

him. His hand rose and cupped her cheek. "You will not live alone for the rest of your life, Shelley. Believe me. Women like you and Nikki have too much love to give. Warm and nurturing spirits. Trust me when I say your ex-husband is a schmuck! And that word is now used all over the country, not just on the coasts."

She didn't know whether to laugh or cry, but she was touched by his words, by the use of his wife's name. And she was also human enough to appreciate his opinion of Carl.

"You know something, Daniel? This may scare you, but right now, you're not only my upstairs neighbor and my coaching partner, but you're quickly becoming a wonderful friend. Maybe the best friend I have!"

His eyes darkened and he leaned toward her, but she had no time to prepare for his kiss. A wonderful kiss—warm, firm and unhurried. "I'm flattered," he whispered, finally releasing her. "And not scared at all."

SHE BURNED the pancakes the next morning, proving her mind was not on the task. Both Josh and Emily pinched their noses closed and she couldn't blame them. "Okay, another batch coming up."

The doorbell rang, and Shelley looked at the kids. "How about some cereal today with bananas?"

"Yes! It's faster."

Shelley shrugged, then chuckled as she walked to the front of the house.

When she opened the door, a lovely blond woman stood there with a young boy on either side. One was Casey. Before Shelley could speak, the woman held out a hand.

"Hi. I'm Laura McCloud and these are my boys, Brian and Casey."

"Is J-Josh home?" piped up Casey.

Shelley nodded. "In the kitchen. Have you guys eaten breakfast yet?"

Laura looked startled, and turned to the kids. "Uh...did we eat today?"

Identical grins, identical shakes of the head. "We figured you'd take us to the diner," said Brian, the older of the brothers.

"How about settling for cereal with my kids instead. They're just starting and there's plenty. Eat on the porch if you want. Have a breakfast picnic."

The boys ran off, and Laura's expression held relief. "Thanks a lot. I don't know if I'm coming or going lately. But I wanted to stop by and thank you for the use of the driveway, and for taking over the team for Matt."

Shelley ushered the woman in. "Our pleasure."

Laura's eyes scanned the room, then moved upward toward the Crow's Nest. A sweet smile crossed her face. "You know, I've heard a lot about the summer tenants. Is the place all you had hoped it would be?" She began studying the room, slowly, as if memorizing every piece of furniture, every nook and cranny.

"Hmm…" murmured Shelley, deciding Laura really wasn't expecting an answer.

"This place," continued Laura, "this house made all the difference in my life. At first, it was my sanctuary, a hidey-hole where I could lick my wounds, and then a world opened to me that I'd given up on. Like a miracle." Her clear voice reflected her wonder. She reached for Shelley's hand. "That's why the ceremony had to be near Sea View House. At the water's edge. I knew that from the beginning. But only a few days ago, I realized I needed an aisle. Thanks again so much."

Shelley had to blink away tears…and she'd never met this woman before! But she recognized truth when she heard it. She squeezed Laura's hand. "I'm going to decorate your aisle. Leave it to me."

When Laura began to protest, Shelley laughed, knowing that she, her mom and even Emily would work wonders with crepe paper and ribbons.

"How will you walk on the sand?" asked Shelley.

"No problem. I'm wearing white running shoes!"

"What a great idea!" Shelley met Laura's eye and both women began to giggle.

"Just nerves," gasped Laura.

Shelley nodded. "Bridal jitters."

"But I am very happy."

"Yes," agreed Shelley, her voice now quiet. "Just as you should be. And from what I saw last night, Matt is just as happy."

Laura nodded, but her smile faded. "Only one

person's absence will mar the event. Matt's brother, Jason. He left Pilgrim Cove eight years ago after his twin was killed on the night of their senior prom. I guess he blames himself, but the folks here are heartbroken over his absence. Not only Sam and Matt, but Lila, too."

"Lila?" asked Shelley.

Laura nodded. "I don't think Jason even knows about Katie."

Shelley's eyes opened wide. "Oh…."

"Yes. A miracle is waiting for him here. But I guess we can't expect two miracles in one season."

TWO EVENINGS LATER, Shelley, Daniel, Emily, Josh and the Duffys stood among the guests toasting the bride and groom after their personal vows had been spoken. The new Mrs. Parker wore a simply cut gown that hinted at the curves of her body. The straight lines of the dress were offset by her thick wavy hair, now layered and formed into natural curls. Shelley nodded. The style suited her perfectly.

Bart Quinn escorted the bride as though she were made of glass. Sam Parker blinked constantly as he looked at his son and his new daughter-in-law. But Shelley studied the boys. Brian and Casey were almost totally focused on their new mom. They obviously adored her. Anyone could see the happiness shining in their eyes.

"New beginnings," she murmured to Daniel, who stood next to her.

"Which are followed by endings." His words were barely distinguishable, almost choked.

Startled, Shelley turned toward Dan. He stared out at the horizon. He didn't blink, but he swallowed hard, his Adam's apple bobbing up and down.

Shelley squeezed his hand. She knew he was thinking about Nikki. His faraway expression gave him away. Apparently, neither of them was ready to commit to another partner. Even on a short-term basis.

DANIEL STOOD in his kitchen early the next morning staring at the accumulation of his work. The curriculum would be unique. No standard texts for this course—until he wrote one. In the meantime, his chosen primary sources were organized into piles across the table.

He was so deep in thought, that at first Jessie's barking seemed to come from far off, although she was on the deck outside the kitchen with the sliding door open. Dan knew his dog as well as a parent knew a child, and her anxiety registered just as she dashed to him barking nonstop. When she ran back to the deck, Dan was at her heels. He looked out toward the beach, toward the water, his heart beating in double time. And then it almost stopped.

Someone was being tossed by the rough breakers in the morning's high tide. The weather had changed, and the day was overcast, the beach deserted. Too early for lifeguards anyway. The wind gusted in his face, and it was hard to see from where he stood, but he was almost sure the swimmer was a child.

"Let's go!"

He and the golden scrambled down the outside stairs, ran to the back side of the house and continued to the shoreline, which was closer than usual because of the high tide. But Dan still strained to see the swimmer. There! Out there, a head appeared above the water. And then it was gone. Sucked under. From the corner of his eye, he saw Josh playing with a kite on the sand near the house. So it had to be Emily. "Tell your mom to call Doc Rosen. Now!" he ordered without taking his eyes from the ocean. "Bring blankets."

He tossed his shirt as he ran, giant-stepping into the surf and not stopping until he could dive where he'd last seen Emily. But where the hell was she? He was chest high and felt the undertow try to pull him down. He stood his ground, but knew a little child like Emily couldn't.

Jess swam toward the right and Daniel followed her. He'd trust the dog's instincts over a human's any day of the week. Then he spotted Emily again, her long hair plastered like seaweed against her face. He swam toward her with the outgoing tide, then inhaled deeply and dived beneath, trying to estimate where she'd be pulled down again. He opened his eyes, desperate for a glimpse, but without the sun to brighten the underwater murkiness, he was out of luck.

He felt the outbound tide push him, just as something smashed against his body. Emily! He had judged distance correctly. He grabbed a leg, then her waist and hauled her out, raising her over his head while digging his toes into the sea bottom for stability. He gulped a breath of air a nanosecond before another breaker submerged him. But it didn't touch Emily!

When that wave passed behind him, he shifted the child into his arms and jogged toward shore as quickly as possible to keep ahead of the next breaker. Damn, the kid had been pulled far out! He scanned for Jess and saw her a quarter mile away trotting slowly back along the waterline. She'd performed as she'd been trained, and she'd get a thousand treats later.

But now, he turned Emily facedown in his arms while striving for the safety of the shore. One arm encircled her bottom, while one hand fisted on her belly. He'd begin rescue breathing when he got to dry land, but now he thrust the side of his fist into her stomach in the Heimlich maneuver adapted for a child. "Cough for me, baby. Come on, cough!"

Nothing. Her lips were blue tinged, and he started to curse. He pressed again, harder. "Now, baby, now. Cough!"

Water dribbled from her mouth. Finally, on dry sand, he laid her flat on her back, tilted her head backward with one hand and lifted her chin with the other to open her airway. He scrunched down, put his ear against her mouth to listen for her breathing and felt a shiver run through her body. She rolled slightly to her side, and then let go a fountain of ocean all over his face.

"Atta girl, Em. Come on. Give me more." And she did, three more times. She gasped. And breathed. Daniel watched every rise and fall of her chest, inhaling along with her. "Cough again. Good girl, Emily. Good girl."

Then she started to cry, little kitten sounds. One thin arm reached for him. She crawled onto his lap, laid her head on his chest and rested there, so tiny against his big frame.

He held her close, and from deep inside him, Daniel cried silent tears. *He hadn't lost this child.* He kissed the top of Emily's head over and over, and rocked her and gave thanks for being in the right place at the right time.

"I love you, my Daniel p'fessor." She spoke into his chest.

And now he laughed. Laughter through tears. "And I love you, my Emily first-grader."

She shook her head and yawned. "Second-grader." Her eyes closed. She slept.

He felt her relax, felt her full body weight against him, then felt his own muscles loosen up. Emily and he were both fine.

Dan sighed deeply. Little by little, pieces of the outside world impinged on his consciousness. An unnatural stillness surrounded him, as though the world were off-kilter. As though he and Emily were being watched under a magnifying glass. He took another deep breath and finally raised his eyes.

First, he saw a semicircle of legs—mostly bare and attached to different bodies—but then, like a homing pigeon, his eyes found Shelley. Skin the color of alabaster, eyes wide and unblinking with tears running silently down her cheeks to the sand. She clutched a pink quilt so hard, her knuckles shone white, and a moaning sound came from her throat.

She looked close to being in shock, and he wanted to wrap his arms around her, too, but that option was out at the moment. So he tried the reverse. "Don't faint on me, Shelley Anderson," he snapped. "Emily's okay."

She blinked. "No. No. I won't faint. I'm strong." Her choked words said otherwise, but she knelt beside him and her child, and with careful, slow motions tucked the blanket around them both.

His index finger stroked her cheek. "We're fine," he whispered. "Everything's okay." Her dark eyes met his, and in them, he saw sorrow. Pain. Guilt. And overriding those emotions was fear. But he murmured reassurances and watched her. She wanted to believe him! He squeezed her hand. "I promise, everything's fine." A myriad of voices overhead joined his. Shelley's parents were both talking at once, thanking him over and over. Several neighbors were heaping congratulations on him. He could have done without all of that.

Fortunately, Jess appeared then and lost no time nosing her way into the little group, sniffing hard. The small crowd, in unison, took a step back and watched Jess tug the blanket from Emily and start licking her face, hands and any part of the child she could reach. As she worked, she whined.

"She's okay, Jess," said Dan, rubbing the scruff of her neck, the words coming from him automatically now. "Emily's fine. You did it girl, you did it again."

Dan had learned long ago not to question how much Jessie understood and remembered. Her natural instincts had been honed for rescue, and Dan knew she wouldn't calm down until she realized they'd been successful with Emily. A few years ago, Jess had been half-crazed when they'd rescued her adored Nikki from the water.

The dog succeeded in her efforts, and Emily's eyes opened. "Jessie!" She hugged the golden. Then she saw Shelley and held up her arms. "Mommy!"

Shelley grabbed her daughter with lightning speed, and held her in her lap, squeezing her so hard, the child protested. Jessie sat squarely on her haunches and smiled her golden-retriever smile. And Daniel leaned back on his elbows, enjoying the mother-and-daughter reunion.

"So, I guess it's all over but the shouting," said a man's voice from above.

Daniel jumped to his feet and shook Max Rosen's hand. "Thanks for coming, Doc. But it's not over until you say so. Always a chance of infection from the brine."

"Let's check her out at the house," said the doctor. "And while I'm at it, I'll check you, too."

Daniel reached for Emily, but Shelley wouldn't let go. He helped Shelley to her feet instead. Now she looked at him square in the eye.

"'Thank you' seems so inadequate," she said quietly. "There's no way I could ever thank you enough."

"Then don't try," he said, giving her a gentle hug. "Sometimes words aren't necessary."

She smiled at him with such warmth, he almost believed it was something more. Almost. But he knew better. He'd saved her child's life. Of course she'd confuse deep appreciation with affection.

The neighbors drifted away then, but not before offering their help and support. Daniel watched Shelley step closer to the doctor, saw Max peer at Emily and make the child laugh. Good. He hoped the experience would soon be a vague memory. But some rules would be changing around Sea View House this summer for the children's sake. Which reminded him…where was Josh through all this?

Just then, he saw Shelley pause, turn, then call for her son. He followed her gaze. The boy didn't answer even though he stood only ten feet away from his mother. Instead, Josh's eyes were glued to Dan, his expression guarded while he watched Daniel's every move. He held something blue in his hand.

"I'll bring Josh back," Dan called to Shelley and the grandparents. "You folks and the doc take care of Emily." Shelley waved her acknowledgment and turned toward the house, Emily still in her arms. Phil and Ellen Duffy followed without a word.

Dan meandered over to Joshua. Emily may have had all the attention, and justly so, but that didn't mean her brother wasn't having a hard time, too. "Hi, sport," said Dan, reaching out a hand to ruffle the boy's hair.

"Here," said Josh, handing Daniel the blue shirt he'd thrown off earlier. "I found it for you."

"Thanks a lot. I can use it. The wind's kicking up again." Dan put the shirt back on while Josh watched. "We had a lot of excitement here today, didn't we?"

"Yeah." Josh hung his head and looked aside. "Are you mad at me?"

"Mad? Are you kidding? You did everything right, everything I asked you to do. Your mom, the doctor, the blanket. You did a great job." Still, the boy wouldn't look at him, stared at the ground instead.

"But I was supposed to watch her. I'm older." His voice cracked, and his shoulders heaved.

"You may be older, son, but you're not a grown-up," said Dan. "And only grown-ups can be responsible for children at the beach."

Josh peeked quickly at him. "Only grown-ups?"

"Absolutely," said Daniel. "That's the rule."

With a relieved expression, Josh looked up at Dan. "You're sure?" he asked, his mouth forming a tentative smile.

Dan nodded. "Positively."

In an instant, Josh wrapped his arms around Dan's waist and rested against him, just as his sister had.

Dan's fingers ruffled the boy's hair, and his hands rubbed his back. He leaned down and whispered, "You're one heck of a great kid. And Emily's lucky to have you as a brother."

Josh shrugged. "Well, I'm glad you saved her. Even if she is a pest sometimes."

Dan stifled a laugh. Josh was back to normal.

SHELLEY COULDN'T SETTLE down for the rest of the day. She cleaned; she cooked; she played with the kids. When Emily took a nap midafternoon, Shelley stood over her bed, checking for a spiked temperature as Doc Rosen had advised. And every time her eyes rested on her daughter, they filled with tears. Lucky. They were so lucky that Daniel and Jess had acted quickly. But what if they hadn't noticed? She shivered and consciously put her mind on dinner. A big Italian meat sauce with pasta. The perfect comfort food. Garlic bread wouldn't hurt, either.

Daniel would join them that evening. And Jess. But Shelley's mind shifted right back to Daniel.

There really was no way to thank him for saving Emily's life, but she'd given him a standing invitation to dinner for the rest of the summer. Such a small payment for such a huge debt.

She stood at the stove now, browning sausages and meatballs, while Josh sat at the kitchen table playing with a deck of cards. "Are we going to leave Pilgrim Cove now?" asked Josh.

"Leave? Do you think we should?" replied Shelley, shifting her gaze from the stove to her son.

Josh shook his head hard from side to side. "Nope. I like it here, but...the professor says we need new rules."

"Oh?"

"Yeah. And I made up a rule for sisters. No collecting seashells without a mother."

"Excellent rule, Josh." Shelley stepped to the table and kissed him. "In fact, it's perfect. Kids shouldn't be on the beach without a parent."

"That's what Daniel said, only...uh...I think he meant *little* kids. Not me."

Shelley hid a grin. "Daniel seems to have said a lot to you."

"He's cool, Mom." Josh's enthusiasm caught Shelley by surprise. "You know something?" the boy continued. "He's a hero. A superhero. He saved Emily. Him and Jess." He nodded with satisfaction. "They're a superteam. I bet he has superpowers."

She rolled her eyes at him. "Josh. You and your grandparents are too much." Philip and Ellen also thought the man could do anything, even walk on water, rather than swim in it! In fact, they were at the supermarket now buying pistachio ice cream for Dan—her mom had found out his favorite flavor—and the fanciest dog treats they could find for Jess.

"But, Mom. Daniel can swim! Like a shark. Or a dolphin. And he's saved people before. Not just Emily. He's like Aquaman."

"You are just full of information today." She glanced at her son. "How would *you* like to swim like a dolphin? Here's Mommy's new rule. Swimming lessons for both you and your sister. And when you're bigger, lifesaving lessons."

Josh nodded. "Good idea. Then soon, I can join the superteam."

She was saved from replying when her parents walked through the door, their arms loaded with shopping bags.

"Wow!" said Shelley. "I didn't need so much."

Her dad's eyes twinkled. "Oh, it's not all for us." Phil Duffy reached into a bag and started pulling out a silver bowl, dog toys, a box of kibble and a gigantic box of treats. "And an extra pound of chopped meat—for you know who."

"I guess I do," said Shelley, shaking her head.

"Now, Shelley," said her mom, "we need to simmer this meat, drain the fat and mix it with the dry food. Then Dan won't argue about feeding Jess table food. And Jess will have a great meal."

"You guys are really something. Did you buy

Dan a silver crown or a solid-gold bathing suit?" she asked with a grin.

"If he wants one, we'll buy it," replied her dad. "Anything at all."

Shelley put her hand up. "Not only won't he want anything like that, he'll be embarrassed if we try to shower him with gifts. He's very kind and giving. And quiet. He won't like a fuss."

The phone rang, and she picked it up. Lou Goodman, the retired librarian, had heard about Emily and was checking up. She'd barely hung up the phone when it rang again. Big Ralph, retired electrician and coach of the senior boys, was on the line checking up on Emily.

Shelley turned to her father. "You get the next few. Looks like the ROMEOs have all heard about the adventure."

Her dad nodded. "This whole summer is turning into an adventure. And I thought Mom and I were just here to keep you company with the kids."

"I agree with Dad," said Ellen. "This is a nice place. Nice people. And those old men are still kicking up their heels. I like that." And Ellen reached up and kissed her husband on the cheek. "Just like my old man right here."

Phil's arm came around her, and he kissed her back before looking at Shelley. "You know I robbed the cradle, don't you? Just look at my bride."

Shelley looked. Her mom's eyes shone, and her cheeks were tinged rosy. Her dad stared adoringly at his wife, and Shelley's heart lurched. She hadn't seen this open affection in too long. The playfulness and teasing had been lost under the stress of Shelley's situation.

"You're both looking wonderful. And that's the way it's going to be from now on!"

"I'll drink to that," said Phil, glancing around the room, "in about thirty minutes. Let's get this stuff put away."

DAN BATHED Jess with plain water to get rid of the salt and sand, toweled her dry and brushed her thick coat for half an hour. Then he took a hot shower himself. He looked forward to a quiet dinner with Shelley and her family, and truly hoped no one would make a fuss over the morning's events.

When he opened Shelley's kitchen door an hour later, he almost ran back upstairs despite the delicious garlicky aroma that made his stomach growl in anticipation. Shelley was at the counter tossing a salad in the biggest bowl he'd ever seen, but the house was full of people, full of noisy chatter.

Beyond Shelley, in the dining room and in the hall, he could see Bart talking to Rick and Dee O'Brien. And Sam Parker was there, and Doc and Marsha Rosen. He heard children's voices in the background. Brian and Casey Parker must have come with Sam and were probably with Emily and Josh at the moment. Without a doubt, everyone had come calling just to check up on Shelley's family after the close call they'd had that morning.

"A quiet evening would be better for her," he whispered to Shelley. And for him.

She patted his arm. "Shh. Not necessarily. They came to see Emily and you—and they're staying for dinner. I think my folks must have run into them in town."

Her voice was happy. Her face was happy. She was in her element. "You look radiant," he said, and chuckled when she blushed.

Then he looked around the room. "Your kitchen is like Nikki's studio. Color everywhere. Creation everywhere. Shapes. Textures. Oils, watercolors and clay. But different aromas—that's for sure. No turpentine here." He smiled at her and felt peaceful.

"Tell me about Nikki," said Shelley in a quiet tone of voice.

A month ago, he would have told her to mind her own business. A month ago, he couldn't have spoken about Nikki without a shard of pain rubbing against his vocal cords. Somehow, now, it was easier.

"Well, she couldn't cook. Not even a nickel's worth. But she had a passion for her work. She was damn good, too." He waved his arm at Shelley's preparations. "Like you."

The warmth of her smile almost melted him. "A few years ago," he continued, suddenly having the urge to share, "I pulled her out of the water, too. She was an excellent swimmer, but we were on a boat, and the weather changed quickly. Somehow she slipped, fell and hit her head." He saw Shelley's compassion. "It always happens so damn fast. One minute, she's there. The next...I almost couldn't find her...." He blinked hard.

"But you did," said Shelley, pressing his hand. "And you did it again today. That's who you are, Daniel. One of the good guys." Her big brown eyes shimmered with satisfaction; her mouth curved with gentle humor. "And I'll bet you loved Nikki the way every woman wants to be loved. Completely. With all your heart, and with loyalty and respect?"

"Of course I did. Since junior high. I think she knew it." Amazing how relaxed he was talking to this woman who wasn't Nikki.

"I needed to hear that, Daniel. Thank you."

"You're welcome," he replied automatically. Then he looked at her and understood what she meant.

"Your ex is an idiot, Shelley. Only a colossal idiot would let you go. Like I said before, a real jerk."

Now she laughed out loud. "You are so good for my ego!" She reached up and kissed him quickly on the mouth. His blood surged with the power of a roaring ocean storm. "Grab a beer from the fridge," she said, "and go say hello to everyone. You've been hiding out with me long enough...."

"Not nearly long enough." He stepped closer, wrapped her in his arms and kissed her. She was a potpourri of flavors, just like her meals. Sweet, yet tangy. Tender, but strong. Smooth and shivery. And lips…revealing her passionate side, meeting his mouth with equal fervor, definitely hot, hot, hot.

CHAPTER TEN

"Wow." One whispered syllable was all she could manage when Daniel finally ended the kiss to take a breath. She met his gaze. His brown eyes looked black, his lids half-closed, and he stood still as though in shock. "I think you're right," she continued, gulping down a deep breath to keep her voice steady. "I'm not cut out for a summer fling. Emotions could get in the way."

He didn't reply, and Shelley tried to stem a frisson of disappointment. For a moment, for one crazy moment, she'd envisioned possibilities beyond the present.

"It's all right, Dan," she said, squeezing his arm. "You don't have to jump off the fence. Not yet. And, at least, not for me."

He grunted. "The fence is getting awfully uncomfortable."

"Good."

Surprise crossed his face, and then his expression cleared. "A cook who's also a psychologist."

But he didn't look angry, or even annoyed.

Merely thoughtful. "No," she said. "I'm not a shrink. I'm simply a woman who cares."

"Cares? Now there's a word which is never simple—for a man or a woman. In fact, it's damn complicated and…scary."

"Yup," she replied. "But it's what makes life worth living. And you might as well face it, or you'll end up being the loneliest guy on the planet." She handed him a pile of dinner plates. "Would you mind putting this on the dining-room table, please?"

Dan took the plates and left the kitchen, only to be immediately surrounded by what seemed like the entire town of Pilgrim Cove.

"Here's the hero," said Ellen Duffy.

"The man of the hour," added Max Rosen. "Sure knew what to do before I got there this morning."

Dan carefully placed the dishes down and held up his hands. "One more word, folks, and I'm out of here. If you want to applaud someone, give the credit to Jess. She's the one who spotted Emily." He looked around. "Speaking of…where is the hound?"

"In the bedroom with the kids," said Ellen. "Emily's got them all doing an 'arts and crats' project." Her chin started to quiver. "When I think…"

"Then don't," said her husband, patting her hand. "It's all over."

"Just smell that sauce," boomed Bart. "I think my daughters have competition in the kitchen." He wiggled his brows. "Maybe Shelley wants a summer job at the Lobster Pot?"

Ellen Duffy laughed, and the conversation turned general. Dan walked past Bart and clapped him on the shoulder. "Thanks," he whispered, and wondered how many more times that day Bart would need to create a diversion. Dan found himself glancing at the door, ready to escape—and he would have if there was a way not to insult his grateful hostess.

Then Shelley walked into the room, greeting everyone, her face alight with welcome as she urged the small crowd to the table. Dan found himself watching her. A little dimple appeared near the corner of her mouth every time she smiled, which was often. She touched people. On the arm, on the shoulder. A brief hug. She made the room brighter just by being in it.

His thoughts were distracted by a loud commotion as the four children and the dog stampeded into the room. Dan blinked in disbelief when he saw Jessie. The golden was wearing a cardboard crown, painted gold, and tied under her neck with yellow ribbon. A round gold medal, festooned with painted Popsicle sticks like rays of the sun, hung from her collar. On the medal was the misspelled word Curage.

"Like in *The Wizard of Oz*," said Emily, with a big grin.

"Like the Cowardly Lion, who was really brave," Josh explained further.

"The—the Wizard gives him courage!" offered Casey Parker.

"Emily made us do it," sighed Brian, with unusual patience. But he grinned at his brother.

Dan glanced at Shelley. Her mouth formed a perfect O, matching her wide-open eyes. He wanted to kiss that beautiful mouth closed and actually stepped toward her before stopping himself.

"Where's my Daniel p'fessor?" asked Emily, looking around the crowd. Her grin broadened when she spotted her quarry, and Dan reached to catch her after she launched herself at him.

He scooped her up, a tiny flower, fragrant with clean aromas of talc and shampoo. He kissed her cheek, marveling at the baby-soft skin. And at the energy she displayed. No one would believe she'd been under water that morning.

"Look what I made for you, my Daniel." She held up a golden medal that matched Jessie's, with a long ribbon attached. "We got two words on yours," she said. "'Cause we made yours bigger."

He looked. Cur-age on one side. Hero on the reverse.

"Do you like it?" she asked, her eyes shining with hope and happiness.

He nuzzled her little neck. "I love it. It's the best present I ever got." He stole a glance at Shelley, then wished he hadn't. Her eyes also shone as she gave him a thumbs-up, and he turned away. But he wore the medal throughout dinner because Emily watched his every move.

An hour later, Bart approached him. "Now that

we've cleared the table, the women are having a gabfest in the kitchen while they straighten up." He patted his stomach. "Let's walk off some of this dinner, Danny-boy. Got to make room for dessert."

Dan whistled for Jess. "Had the same thought myself. And Jessie needs to go outside."

The night air smelled of the sea but held the left-over chill of the damp, drizzly day. Dan led Bart to the beach at a slow, measured pace. The older man reached into his pocket, took out a pipe and put it in his mouth. Empty.

"Out of tobacco?" asked Daniel.

"Nope. Never touch the stuff. Not anymore. Promised my girls after their mother died." He took the pipe in his hand and looked at it. "But I like the feel of the bowl in my palm, the stem in my mouth. My Rosemary made me smoke it outside. Had to take a walk after dinner, just like this. Imagine! Couldn't smoke in my own house." But he smiled. "Ahh. My Rosemary."

His warm voice revealed all, and Dan nodded. "Yeah, I know the feeling."

"I almost lost her one other time, years before she died. When we were young. In 1959, it was—when the accident happened. A car accident, too, just like your wife. It was touch and go for a while. The broken legs were bad, but those internal injuries…" He shook his head in remembrance. "They were the worst part. And she was out of it for a while. But, sometimes, her mind was clear. Very clear. She understood what had happened. And that's when she made me promise not to live with only a memory if she didn't make it."

Dan glanced at the Irishman, starting to feel annoyed. He didn't have to be a genius to know where this story was going. And he would have told the old man to mind his own business, but, well, he liked him. Bart was one of those people who genuinely cared about others. So, instead, Daniel said, "I'm working on it, Bartholomew." Using the man's full name was the best he could do to create a distance.

"I know you are, son. You had hungry eyes tonight. Couldn't help yourself from watching Shelley all evening. She's in your craw, boyo, whether you want her there or not."

Damn! Everyone probably noticed.

"I'm sure," said Bart, "that if your wife had lived long enough in the hospital, she would have told you the same thing my Rosemary told me. Living with a memory is just not enough."

"You didn't know Nikki, Bartholomew. What makes you so sure?"

"But I know you and that your grieving is from the heart. But just for a moment, change places with Nikki. I want you to think about something." The Realtor looked at him from beneath shaggy brows, and quickly continued. "If you had been the one in the accident, and were looking down from Heaven right now, would you want your Nikki to walk alone for the rest of her natural life?"

Alone? And lonely? His vibrant Nikki? Never! Daniel looked the old man in the eye. "Point well taken, counselor."

"You were on your way. Just wanted to speed things up."

Funny that a fairly bright, educated guy like him needed someone else to point the way. Intellect wasn't enough. Dan had understood all along that his life would have to return to normal in the fullest sense…at some point. But emotionally, he just couldn't face it. Until now. Until he'd come to Pilgrim Cove.

"I'm glad Sea View House was available this summer, Bart Quinn. Very glad."

The Realtor grunted and chewed his pipe stem.

DANIEL SLEPT long and hard that night, and woke up with Shelley on his mind. The sun was higher in the sky than usual when he started his day, and he leaned back to savor the unaccustomed luxury of sleeping late. For about a minute. His stomach growled, and Jess cocked her head and barked. Dan jumped out of bed.

A minute later, he grabbed the leash and jogged downstairs intending to walk Jess along Beach Street and then return home. Parked in front of the house were Bart's Lincoln and the chief's Jeep. Dan glanced at his watch. Still early for visiting, unless there was a reason.

Jess took care of business quickly, and Dan

headed back to the house. He met Josh in the driveway.

"My mom wants to know if you can come to our house now. The chief and Mr. Quinn are here so something's going on, but I don't know what." The boy's expression became resigned. "Something always seems to be happening lately. But mostly not good things. And I don't know why."

Daniel wrapped his arm around Josh's shoulders. "There's a good thing happening later today for you. Baseball practice."

The kid brightened a bit.

"You've got some friends now," said Daniel, "and you'll make more."

"Can I hold Jessie's leash?"

Easy distraction. "Sure," said Dan, handing it over, "but we're going inside. So it's a short walk."

Josh grinned. "That's okay. Next time, you'll let me hold her longer."

Dan chuckled and ruffled the boy's hair. "You've got me figured out, huh?"

They walked around the back and found the adults gathered on the deck. Bart Quinn, Rick O'Brien, Shelley's parents and Shelley.

"Morning, everyone," said Daniel, looking at Shelley and not liking the worried look on her face. "What's going on?"

Shelley shrugged. "Not sure yet. I offered these guys a cup of coffee, but they turned me down. So I guess this isn't a social visit."

Bart coughed. "Actually, Rick needs to tell you something. All of you."

Daniel glanced at the retired officer. "Hang on a sec." He sought out Shelley's son, who stood quietly against the door with Jessie. Big eyes and big ears. "Hey, Josh. How'd you like to practice walking Jess on the leash. Say from Sea View House to our left-side neighbor and back."

Easy-to-read conflict showed on the boy's face. He wanted to take Jess, but he wanted to know what was going on. Dan approached the child and squatted to his eye level. "Everything's cool, Josh. I promise."

He held his breath waiting for Josh's response. The kid had gotten to him, and now Dan cared whether Josh trusted him.

"Okay."

"Way to go, Josh," said Daniel, giving the boy a hug. "And if she's thirsty when you come back, I'll show you how to use the hose on the side of the house. I keep a bowl there all the time."

Josh nodded. "I know." He rubbed the dog's neck. "Come on, Jess. We're going for a walk."

The golden looked at Daniel in query. "It's okay, girl. At heel with Josh." He bent down to pet her. "Easy walk, Jess." He watched the two step off the deck, go through the backyard and onto the beach. Then he turned to the others and stepped closer to Shelley, who offered him a tremulous smile.

"Thank you. I wouldn't have thought to distract him right now."

"Don't think twice about it," said Dan. "You're

caught up in a lot of responsibility, and I've got some distance. That's all." He looked at Rick O'Brien. "So, what's on your mind?"

"When I was on active duty," began the former chief, "I got to know a number of Boston cops. Sometimes because of cases, or regional trainings, or even target practice. One of them, who's retired now, has been hanging around lately. Saw him in town last week and ran into him again yesterday at the harbor. Carries a fancy camera with lots of lenses." Rick paused and scratched his head. "The thing is," he said slowly, "he asked me about Sea View House. And Shelley, in particular."

Daniel heard Shelley's murmured "Oh, no." She shook her head for emphasis, and her rich auburn hair shimmered as it rose and fell back into its sleek cap. Her face turned three shades paler than normal, and he put his arm around her.

"Carl's behind this. I just know it," Shelley said with conviction, as she leaned against him. "He threatened to see me in court, and now he's looking for a reason. He actually hired a spy! And…oh, my God!" She jumped away from Dan, her arms moving as she spoke. "What if the guy was on the beach yesterday when Emily…Emily…and wh-what if—?"

"And what if he wasn't?" Dan reached for her again, his arms tightening around her. "Carl may be behind it. But let's get more information." He spoke quietly. "Hang on, Shel. You're not alone here."

Rick cleared his throat. "The spy has a license.

Had it checked out by one of my buddies about—"
he glanced at his watch "—an hour ago. It's not so
unusual. Lots of retired cops start another career as
private investigators."

"So, what does this mean? Are my grandchildren at risk here?" Phil Duffy looked at his daughter. "Shelley, is he trying to take them?"

"Hold on, everyone," said Dan. "A swimming
accident could have happened if Shelley and Carl
were still married. No one is taking anyone anywhere!"

"And the pictures?" asked the ex-cop.

"Pictures of what? Shelley is divorced. She is
entitled to have friends. Including male friends. So
the P.I. will get pictures of us eating a barbecue dinner. Or walking on the beach. Or walking the dog.
Nothing in our everyday lives warrants censure."

The small crowd broke into chatter, the tone a lot
brighter, and Dan released his own breath. In his
heart, he wanted to break Carl Anderson's jaw. In
fact, his fingers flexed against his side just itching
to connect. He couldn't remember the last time he
felt the need for a visceral release.

He turned Shelley to face him. "I don't want you
to worry about anything. This whole business is
nonsense."

"Oh, Daniel." She averted her eyes, and his heart
almost stopped beating. "I'm so sorry that you're sub-
jected to this whole thing. To this intrusion in your
life."

He reached up, stroked her cheek. "I think I've needed an intrusion in my life."

She chuckled. "But not this kind!"

"I can handle it."

She looked away again, her eyes on the gleaming Atlantic. "Maybe you can, but I can't if Carl gets his way. He's very connected. What if he pays someone off? What if he takes those innocent pictures and doctors them with a computer? What if…?"

"And what if the earth stops spinning? What if people sprouted wings?" He touched his forehead to hers. "Shelley, honey, you're worrying for nothing."

"Daniel's right," said Bart Quinn. "Listen to him. You're in Pilgrim Cove. And we take care of our own."

"You bet we do," seconded Rick. "In fact, I think I'll have a word with my old acquaintance." He rubbed his hands together. "I can still speak to him cop to cop…and let him know how we operate here."

Neither of their suggestions would do much good, thought Shelley, but their hearts were in the right place.

"Hear that, Shel?" asked Dan. "What more could you need?"

"Well, I might need a very smart lawyer." Her eyes began to twinkle and a smile slowly emerged.

"Would the entire faculty of Harvard law suffice?" Daniel replied.

Finally, her face glowed, her laughter rang out

and she became the woman he'd first fallen for. Strong, happy, energetic. From the corner of his eye, he spotted Josh leading Jessie back to the house, talking to her nonstop. Then he heard a soft bark and started to chuckle.

"What are you all laughing at?" asked Josh, coming up the steps. He looked at the assembled adults and started to grin. "How come Jessie and I miss all the fun?"

SHELLEY STOOD at home plate later that afternoon watching her team, Parker Plumbing, run the bases. A group of twelve kids had shown up at the field behind Pilgrim Cove Junior High, including Bart's great-granddaughter, Katie Sullivan, and her new friend, Sara Fielding. Two girls and ten boys. All full of energy and eager for the summer season.

Lila Sullivan had dropped Katie and Casey off at the school, waved to Shelley and disappeared. Adam Fielding, the town's new veterinarian, along with several other parents, decided to hang around for the first practice. Some of the parents were snapping pictures of this small milestone in their kids' lives. It would be difficult for Shelley to make a fuss at the older camera-wielding gentleman sitting in the bleachers, who fit the description of the P.I. Rick O'Brien had given them. He could very well have been someone's grandfather—except he didn't introduce himself as the other parents had.

She shrugged, determined to put the man out of

her mind, and watched the team complete its lap. The children were adorable, and if she had her way, she'd hug and kiss every one of them just for showing up to play. And Josh would kill her. She watched her son as he ran in from third base, eyes shining, face set. Baseball was serious business.

She glanced behind the backstop where Emily had spread her crayons and coloring book out on the lowest bench of the graduated bleachers. Jessie stood next to her, and Shelley was satisfied her daughter would be well protected. As she turned back to the players, Dan jogged toward her from the infield, where he'd been observing the kids run.

"Okay, team," said Shelley. "Today's a skill practice day, so we're going to do some field work. Get your gloves."

As the kids scrambled for their gloves, she murmured, "Maybe I should have said that we're going to shag some flies."

Dan stopped in his tracks. "Shag some flies?"

"It was in the book."

His warm laughter raised her body temperature. And when his eyes shone with desire, she wanted to dissolve in his arms.

Click. Click.

Shelley stiffened. Daniel blinked, but barely. "Let's go, but no shagging. The kids are too small."

"Throw the ball easy, Daniel. They're so little."

"Woman, didn't I just say that?" he teased. "Did you think I'd fire it in at ninety miles an hour? Besides, the kids will be throwing, too. So maybe you should worry about me!"

Ten minutes later, she understood. Some had no control over the ball, and their throws went wild. Some had control but couldn't catch. And some watched the ball sail past them without moving to get it.

"You're doing great, team," she called. "We just need a little practice."

"Coach," said Dan, nodding at the kids. "Do you mind if I give a few directions now?"

"If you can help them not to hurt themselves, go right ahead."

Dan turned to the kids. "Listen up, everybody. And learn. First rule of throwing—step in the direction of where you're throwing and follow through. Step and follow. Get your legs into it. Put your weight behind it. Step and follow. Let's try it without a ball right now."

He demonstrated and they imitated.

"And when you catch, use two hands, not only the gloved one." Daniel again demonstrated the motion. "Get both hands up and don't be afraid. Now, let's try it for real. Everybody get a partner."

He turned to Shelley. "They need adults throwing to them, and I've got an idea. Keep them going."

In two minutes, Daniel returned with the photographer from the bleachers. "George has agreed to help out. Has a grandson who plays Little League in Boston. Loves baseball."

"Uh…th-thanks." Shelley could barely get the words out, didn't know whether to laugh or scream at the man the former chief had told them about. She didn't understand what Daniel was up to. Maybe his tactic was to know the enemy. Maybe he didn't believe she had a real problem and was making light of it for her sake.

Shelley had believed that coaching a team would be a summer challenge. She hadn't realized baseball would be easier than the game Carl was playing with her.

CHAPTER ELEVEN

FOR INFORMATION, Daniel could think of no better place to go than to the diner on any morning of the week. He could always count on the ROMEOs to know what was happening in Pilgrim Cove. And as a bonus, he'd also enjoy a delicious breakfast.

George Delaney, the P.I., hadn't been around since the baseball practice two days before, and now Daniel wanted to check in with Rick O'Brien before returning to the university the next morning. Returning reluctantly. Working from home this week had been a pleasure. More to the point, being with Shelley and the kids had been great.

He approached the reserved table in the back of the eatery, surprised to see Pearl Goodman there with her husband, Lou. Usually, breakfast was a man thing. He also raised his brows at Brian and Casey Parker sitting on either side of their grandpa Sam. As Dan got closer, his surprise changed to concern. Not a smile lit any of the faces around the table. Even Bart's "Good morning" was subdued.

A murmur of quiet greeting followed.

"If I'm intruding…"

"No, no," said the former chief. "You and I need to talk. But first…" He nodded at Sam.

Dan pulled out a chair and sat, noting a glossy flier in the middle of the table in front of Sam Parker. The man's trembling fingers slid back and forth over the print, stroking it as though the paper were something to be either feared or loved.

Bart spoke. "Pearl and Lou flew out west to see their daughter in Kansas, and then went on to California. Just came back yesterday. They saw this announcement at their hotel and brought it home." Bart pointed to the shiny yellow-and-black print.

Appearing in the Starlight Lounge
Our piano man for three nights
J. J. Parks
Hot or cool—the keyboard's his tool
Hearing is believing

A shadowy picture of a man sitting at a stylized grand piano illustrated the announcement.

"We were just showing it to Sam," said Pearl. "We think that this J. J. Parks is really Jason Parker. Sam's younger son. And a solid musician—the best in the musical Parker family."

Dan realized that Matt and Laura were still on their honeymoon. Sam was alone with the boys, but surrounded by friends.

"Of course, we don't know this piano man's iden-

tity for sure," said Lou. "We never saw him. We arrived the day after his last appearance."

"But we spoke to the manager of the hotel,"
added Pearl. She reached for Sam's hand. "You
know we wouldn't just ignore this."

Sam nodded. "Of course," he replied, his voice
gravelly.

"But the manager didn't know where J. J. Parks
was going next," said Pearl. "We bought the local
newspapers hoping he'd be appearing at another
hotel. But we didn't see any advertisements. So we
asked the manager how he'd hired J. J. Parks, thinking we could contact his agent if he had one. No luck
there, either. Seems our hotel manager heard the
piano player in another club and hired him on the
spot. But the man would only commit to three days.
Said he didn't like staying long in one place." Pearl
sat back in her chair and shook her head. She had
nothing more to say.

"Grandpa's crying!" Brian's voice shook, his
face was white and Casey started crying, too.

"It's my Jason," said Sam, looking around the
table, ignoring the tears running down his face. "I
know it is. Can't you see what he's done? Look at
those initials! J.J. That's for 'Jason' and 'Jared.'
He's been carrying his brother around inside since
the day he left home."

Daniel didn't understand everything, but he
recognized love and pain. He turned to Rick
O'Brien. "So instead of watching Sea View House,

why don't we send your old acquaintance out of town to search for Jason Parker?"

"No!" Sam banged his fist on the table. The entire back of the diner fell silent. "No," he repeated quietly, in control once more. "He'll come home when he's ready to stop running."

"Running from what?" asked Daniel.

For a moment, no one seemed able to speak. Perhaps no one wanted to speak. Not Sam, whose lips were now pressed together. Not Bart, whose mouth was quivering. Not Lou, who sighed deeply.

It was Pearl who finally answered, and Dan found himself thinking that women probably were the stronger sex after all.

"Jason is running from guilt," said Pearl. "He blames himself for the death of his twin brother in a car accident on the night of their high-school prom. Every parent's nightmare. But he doesn't understand that no one at this table blames him. Especially not his dad."

Sam held the flier out to Bart. "You want to give this to Lila?"

Bart said nothing for a moment, then nodded his head. "My daughter would kill me if she knew," he said, taking the piece of paper. "Maggie wants Lila to get on with her life. Not hold on to the past."

"And what do you think?" asked Pearl.

"I think," replied the Realtor slowly and deliberately, "that Lila has to come to that decision herself."

Dan watched Bart's hand reach for Sam's. Suddenly, the two old men clasped each other with the strength of younger men.

"Eight years!" whispered Sam.

"Eight years," Bart agreed. "And we've got little Katie to show for it."

"And Jason has no idea at all. Oh, what he's missing!"

So Katie was Sam's granddaughter, too. The relationships clicked into place as Daniel watched the meaning of friendship unroll before his eyes. Maybe that's why the ROMEOs appealed to him so much. They worked hard; they played hard. They knew how to laugh and how to cry. And didn't apologize for any of it.

Dan waited until the group broke up after breakfast before pulling the former chief aside.

"What can you tell me about George Delaney? Incidentally, did you know he's now a member of the Parker Plumbing baseball team?"

"He's getting a hundred bucks an hour for playing baseball with a bunch of eight-year-olds!" exclaimed Rick.

Now Dan's jaw dropped, and he was glad no camera was in sight. "A hundred dollars?" He started to laugh. "Boy, the candidate really knows how to waste money. He'll get nothing worth anything from George no matter how many rolls of film are shot."

"That may be true," admitted Rick, "but I bet Shelley wants him gone. No one likes knowing they're under surveillance."

"That's a fact," said Daniel. "But he hasn't been around since the practice Monday night, and today's Wednesday. I was hoping he'd given up."

But Rick was shaking his head. "No chance. As long as Anderson is paying, George Delaney will be shooting film."

"SON OF A GUN, he's taking pictures of us again!" Shelley jumped from her chair on the back porch that afternoon, her plastic glass of iced tea spattering all over the floor. Her fear had changed to unadulterated anger over the past few days.

Ignoring Dan and her family, she ran to the beach—practically flew—her eyes focusing only on the man and his camera. She was going to give him a piece of her mind. She barely felt the sand beneath her feet as she covered ground.

He was taller than she'd thought. He stared at her, but snapped pictures at the same time. She was almost abreast of him and his camera when she felt a strong arm around her waist. She twisted in Daniel's hold, but he didn't loosen his grip. She glared at him, but his attention was riveted on George.

"You had ample opportunity for pictures at the baseball practice. You should have been content."

"I've got a right to take pictures anywhere."

"I know all about rights. And I know all about the guy that hired you. I did a little research myself. So, you go back and tell him he's wasting his time."

"Everybody says that when they've got something to hide."

"Something to hide?" began Shelley, outraged, her voice an octave higher than usual. Then she felt Dan's arm tighten against her once more.

"The joint-custody agreement hasn't been breached by willful negligence," said Dan.

The other man paused. "What do you think you are? A lawyer?"

Dan chuckled in his usual easy-mannered way. "As a matter of fact, I am."

The guy looked startled, then recovered. "Then you know I'm within my rights—"

"To waste as much film as your employer wants you to. But here's a message to take back."

Suddenly, Shelley found herself free to move around. But ironically, she couldn't budge. In front of her was a Daniel she'd never seen before. All traces of humor had disappeared. His easygoing manner was gone. His eyes darkened as he focused entirely on the other man.

"Tell your boss," said Daniel slowly, "that he's now playing in the big leagues. And he's beginning to piss me off—which is definitely not a good thing."

Silence followed. Shelley glanced at the retired cop. His expression said it all. He'd gotten the message.

Suddenly, coming from behind her, a small tornado in the guise of Joshua Anderson touched ground between Dan and the cop, snatched the camera and ran like the wind back to Sea View House.

Shelley started to follow and heard Dan say, "Seems you ticked off someone else around here, George Delaney. But hang on."

Then he was at her side. "Josh has to return the camera."

"I suppose." Personally, she wanted to smash the thing.

Josh was in the kitchen, the camera on the table. Open. The film exposed. He looked at Shelley and Dan. "Lucky he didn't use a digital."

A smiled tugged at the corners of Shelley's mouth. She wanted to laugh out loud, and glanced at Dan to see his reaction. His eyes were twinkling, but his expression was serious as he sat at the table next to her son.

"It wouldn't matter how many pictures he took, pal. Digital or not."

A look of surprise crossed Josh's face. "How come?" he asked Daniel.

"Because, Josh, we have nothing to hide."

Josh's face crinkled in confusion. "Hide what? I don't understand. First, I thought he was just helping us with baseball. But he's always taking pictures, and Mom doesn't like it. So I thought he was hanging around because Mom's so pretty, and he liked her."

Shelley placed kisses on Josh's forehead. "Sweetie, I don't really know why he's taking so many pictures, but I don't think he'll be hanging around anymore." Not after she called Carl that evening, he wouldn't.

"We've got to return the camera, pal," said Dan. "Otherwise, it's stealing."

Josh shrugged. "Okay."

The P.I. had moved closer to the house. Josh held out the open camera. "Sorry."

"I'll bet," murmured the investigator before turning to Shelley and Daniel. "Looks just like his old man."

Dan replied instantly. "The resemblance ends right there—on the outside."

And that's when Shelley fell totally in love with Daniel Stone.

DANIEL ACTUALLY HATED to leave Pilgrim Cove the next morning to return to the Harvard campus. After his early run on the beach with Jessie, he showered and gently tapped on Shelley's back door.

"Hi." Her cheeks turned rosy. Her soft voice and her smile held more than a mere greeting. Dan gulped. "Have time for a cup of coffee?" she asked.

He shook his head with regret. "Sorry. Not if I want to get back for the kids' practice. Can't disappoint them, or more importantly, the coach."

"There is no possibility of that. Absolutely none."

"Shel…?" He could barely speak. "Remember that fence we talked about? The one I've been sitting on…"

She nodded. "Yes. Yes, I do."

"I'm jumping." He dropped his briefcase on the floor and reached for her. And then she was in his arms, matching his hunger, the hunger he hadn't felt in so long...so long.

He couldn't get enough. She tasted like coffee and mint and sweeter than the sugar she used. He crushed her to him and she pressed against him, on her toes reaching for more. He moved his mouth over hers...again and again...until a voice from afar called, "Mom-my."

He stepped back, his breathing harsh. Panting. Shelley wasn't much better off. In fact, worse. Her lips were full, her eyes...the pupils filled them almost completely. Dark eyes. Now warm and sultry.

"See you later." He grabbed his briefcase, stole another short kiss and closed the door behind him. He took a deep breath and looked around. Was the sun brighter than usual? Was the air crisper? The sky bluer?

He boarded the ferry, then took a taxi to the university and wasted no time in tracking down the dean of the law school. Fifteen minutes later, he had the names of three colleagues whom he'd contact about representing Shelley. He looked at the list and smiled. Hell, yes. He knew them all by reputation, and he'd hire them as a team if they'd prefer.

Dan couldn't function as Shelley's attorney himself, not only because of the conflict of interest, but also because he hadn't sat for the bar in Massachusetts yet.

"One more thing," he said to his boss, "and then I'll get out of your hair."

"You're not bothering me at all," said Howard Dorn. "I'm just delighted at how quickly you've become comfortable in your new life here, not only at the school—I expected that—but also personally. I know you've had a tough time and moving forward hasn't been easy."

Daniel blinked. His private tragedy wasn't a secret—Nikki's life would always be a part of him— but he hadn't expected anyone at work to take more than a cursory interest in his personal life.

"Don't look so surprised, Dan. We want you to be productive and happy—so that you'll stay with us and not return to the West Coast after a year or two."

The day was getting better and better. "I—I came East with the intention of staying, but thank you. Thanks very much for the vote of confidence. Funny, when I haven't taught my first class yet."

The dean laughed. "I've seen your excitement as you've been setting up the new curriculum. I'll be the first one to register for the class!" He sat back in his chair and folded his hands over his stomach, his eyes not wavering from Dan's face. "So, is there another book in the works, Professor Stone? Another book to set the establishment on its keister?"

Daniel laughed with delight. "But Harvard *is* the establishment! Want me to shake 'er up?"

"I think we can handle it." The dean sat forward in his chair. "I'm proud of this school. We've got some of the brightest minds in the country here. The brightest minds in the world! And that includes you."

"Thank you. I don't know the format yet, but I want to integrate a series of roundtable discussions...."

An hour passed. His excitement grew, and for the second time that day, Daniel felt as if he'd gone from living in a black-and-white world to one painted in Technicolor.

He got up to leave, shook the dean's hand and then remembered the question he'd forgotten to ask. "By the way, what can you tell me about a rather prominent alumnus named Carl Anderson?"

The dean shot him a speaking glance. "I can tell you that he's running for Congress and I'm not surprised." Howard Dorn waved his hand at Daniel's chair, and Dan sat down again. This would be time spent well.

AFTER BREAKFAST that morning, Shelley cornered her parents. "Would you mind taking the kids to the library? I need privacy to call Carl. I'm not allowing this intrusion into our lives to continue."

"No problem, Shelley," replied Ellen. "We'll take them to the library and then out for lunch at the diner. And maybe we'll squeeze in a haircut for Dad. Bart recommended the Cove Clippers."

Shelley glanced at her father. Yes, his hair was longer than usual, but it was his worried eyes that held her attention. "You want me to stay with you while you call him? Mom can take the kids."

Shelley shook her head. "No, no. I'm a big girl. I keep reminding myself that Carl really does love his children, and those words keep me sane."

Her dad looked at her and shook his head. "You are quite a woman, Shelley Elizabeth Duffy Anderson. And I'm proud of you, girl. You knew what you were doing all along."

She blinked rapidly, her dad's words of praise unexpected and touching.

"Thanks. Thanks very much." She kissed him on the cheek, then turned to her mother. "I can't ask for a better cheering section than the two of you. I'm glad you're here."

"So are we," replied Ellen. "Now, let's get the children."

Fifteen minutes later, the house was quiet. Shelley stared at the wall phone in the kitchen for a long minute. Then she picked up the receiver and dialed. Carl answered after one ring.

"This is Shelley. Do you have a minute?"

"Absolutely," replied Carl Anderson. "In fact, sweetheart, you beat me to the punch. You were next on my agenda."

She ignored the "sweetheart." "Well, good. What I'm calling about shouldn't take long. I want you to get rid of your private spy, Carl. He's scaring our son."

"Oh?" He elongated the short word, lacing it with a trace of disbelief. "The story I heard had a totally different spin, Shelley. Seems that Josh got scared after seeing his mother run like a madwoman after a poor guy who was minding his own business on the beach."

Now she ignored the "madwoman." "Minding his business, Carl? I think not."

"Now, let's see. He wasn't stalking you. Too far away for that. He wasn't breaking any laws. Furthermore, he's licensed, and he's an ex-cop. I'm pretty sure I've covered all the bases. The man knows what he's doing."

Shelley's grip tightened on the receiver. "If he really knew what he was doing, Carl, I wouldn't have detected him at all. Would I?"

Carl chuckled, an unpleasant sound. "Touché, my dear. But I consider that a small price to pay. He's giving me what I want. Every picture I've got has you and your neighbor together. Living right upstairs, isn't he? How convenient for you. But, more important, how convenient for me."

Any trace of affability disappeared. "I'm going after my kids, Shelley. And I'm going to get them. No judge will find in favor of a woman whose child *almost drowns* while in her care. So what was *that* all about? Too busy with lover boy to watch Emily?"

Blindsided totally by his attack, words stuck in her throat. Shelley could barely breathe let alone speak. Carl was a lawyer, a smart lawyer who knew how to use information to advantage. What if he got full custody, and she had to beg for visitations? Shelley collapsed onto the nearest chair.

"Unless..." continued Carl, his voice tuned with pitchfork precision before pausing.

She'd heard that note hundreds of times over the years as he spoke with clients, associates or opposing counsel and had never given it a second thought. But now he was using that trick on her. Playing her.

She caved. "Unless what?"

"Join me on the campaign trail as a family. A wonderful endorsement. Unique. A former wife who still believes in her first love. It might even work out better than if we were still married."

She doubled over on the chair, tasting the vomit in the back of her throat.

"Think about it," continued Carl smoothly. "And in the meantime, I'm coming for the kids next weekend. Fourth of July. A full itinerary visiting seniors' centers on the third and attending the annual Boston Pops concert on the Fourth. All great photo ops."

She took a deep breath, a spark of hope rising inside her and sat up straight again. "Josh has a game on each of those days. The first actual games of the season. Not just practices. He *lives* for baseball, Carl." Surprisingly, her own voice was steady.

"Then you'll just have to help him reset his priorities. Won't you?"

Without replying, Shelley gently placed the receiver in its cradle. The man was the most selfish, manipulative…and now threatening…individual she'd ever dealt with. She pictured Josh's sweet face and his disappointment, and burst into tears.

CHAPTER TWELVE

ONE LOOK at Shelley's face that afternoon, and Daniel knew her day hadn't gone nearly as well as his. The kids' baseball practice prevented any private conversation, however, and after twenty minutes, Shelley seemed almost like her normal self. Her parents sat in the bleachers today, watching the team, and when the time came, her dad volunteered his help with batting practice. Emily and Jess stayed with Shelley's mom.

"Okay, team. Listen up," called Shelley.

Daniel waited to see what his partner had in mind. They'd had no time to chat before coming to the field today. He'd gotten back to Pilgrim Cove with almost no minutes to spare. "One at a time, each of you will have five turns at bat. Everyone else will start out by playing their field positions. But when your batting turn is over, you're going to replace the person in the field who's coming in next to bat."

Dan frowned. What the heck was she doing? The kids were so new at this, they should be playing their own positions just to get comfortable, not filling in unnecessarily at positions where there were already assigned players.

"Coach Stone is going to pitch to everyone. Keep your eye on the ball. Let's go!"

Daniel gathered several baseballs and put them in his pockets, then walked over to Shelley. "What's with the new routine?"

She turned toward him, her eyes so shadowed, Dan's muscles tightened against an unseen enemy. He cupped her cheek. "What's wrong, Shel?"

Tears welled and she blinked rapidly. "I'll tell you everything later. Bottom line is that Josh won't be here for his games next weekend. I need to get some other kids to try out second base somehow."

Dan glanced at Shelley's son, who was happily jogging to his position right now. "He has no clue, right?"

She nodded.

"Carl?"

She nodded again. "He knows about Emily almost drowning," she whispered. "He said he's going after the kids, and that he's going to win." She blinked hard a few times. "I can lose them, Dan. I can lose my children."

"No! No, you won't." With difficulty, Dan lowered his voice. For the second time in recent memory, anger filled him to the point of explosion. When Nikki was killed he'd raged against the bus driver, the torrential rain, God, himself. But Nikki's death had been an accident. A true accident. Carl's behavior was purposeful and premeditated, aimed not only at unnerving Shelley, but also at manipulating her.

"What happened with Emily wasn't your fault," said Daniel. "It could have happened no matter who was in charge. No judge is going to change custody orders based on that. I promise you."

He leaned into her and kissed her quickly on the mouth. "We'll walk and talk tonight. On the beach. It's going to be okay."

She looked only marginally better, but he had to be content with that for the moment.

He walked to the pitcher's mound, checking to make sure the kids were all in position. "No matter where the ball is hit, throw it home. Step into it and throw. Everybody ready?"

Eleven children in the field nodded. The twelfth gripped the bat.

"Batter up!"

Dan pitched the ball, caught the ball, coached the kids and kept his eye on Shelley while operating on automatic pilot. His mind was listing options for Shelley's defense against Carl.

He managed, however, to note Josh's performance in particular as the kids took their turns. The boy had a natural feel for anticipating where the ball would go. He caught a lot more than he missed, flies or grounders. His swing was solid, and he connected four out of five times when at bat. A very high percentage for an eight-year-old. No wonder the kid really loved the game—he was good at it! What better way to build a child's self-esteem than by allowing him to develop natural skills? Somehow, Josh had to play in the opening game next weekend.

SHELLEY LOVED how Dan's creative mind worked. Not to mention his mouth when he kissed her, his arms when he held her and his hands when he stroked her cheek and tilted her head up for another kiss. She loved his strength that evening as they walked along the beach, arms around each other.

They'd walked a mile from Sea View House and were now lying in the shelter of a small sand dune. The walk had taken a long time. Pauses for kissing. Pauses to gaze and listen to the moonlit ocean waves as they crested in regular rhythm. Pauses to stare at the twinkling stars in the clear night sky.

As they'd approached the dunes, Daniel had pulled out the Parker Plumbing team schedule from his pocket and held it out to her in the moonlight.

"We're the first game of the day on July third," he'd said. "Nine o'clock. Seems to me that a candidate would enjoy a photo op with his own son at America's national sport on America's birthday weekend. He could take the kids after the game, and at least Josh could play the opener."

She'd grabbed the schedule, taken a good look and slapped her own forehead. "Of course! I should have thought of it myself."

"You would have soon enough. It's easier for me. I'm one step removed…or," he'd continued, "maybe only a half step removed."

She'd reached for him, eager to erase the questioning frown from his expression. She'd kissed him with everything she had, and now they lay in each other's arms, content for the moment in the protection of the dune.

"I don't want to think about Carl anymore," whispered Shelley.

Dan chuckled. "Good. Neither do I."

"Look," she said, pointing at the sky. "There's Cassiopeia."

"There's the Big Dipper."

"And the North Star."

"Sure," said Dan in a teasing voice. "Easy for you to say because I found the Big Dipper."

"Phooey. That one's easy. There's the Little Dipper."

"And there's your gorgeous mouth that I want to dip into…like this." And he leaned in.

Shelley turned toward him, as eager as he was. But he took it slow. His tongue traced only the outline of her lips, and she heard herself moan in frustration. "Not…like…that…"

She felt his silent chuckle.

"More?" he whispered. "Like this?"

And now he was inside, exploring her mouth. Then he kissed her. And she returned his touch with equal measure, her pulses pounding everywhere.

"My God," she murmured, her arms tightening around his chest. She lay half over him and wiggled higher, flicking her tongue across his ear, down his neck. She felt him shiver. Heard his breath come and go in rasping pants. His embrace tightened, and she lay on him, breast to chest, every muscle in her body vibrating. Her own breath caught tight in her throat.

"Daniel," she almost whimpered. "It's been so damn long."

And then there was no more talk. Only action. Hot. Hard. Fast. Clothes awry. Some off, some tangled. Nothing registered but the heat. The blazing heat. And the explosion.

Soon, she could breathe again. And hear again. The murmur of Daniel's voice mimicking the whisper of the ocean at their feet.

"I promise, Shel, next time…will take longer."

"I'm not complaining." She lay across him still, content, relaxed, her mind clear. "See, Dan? Kindergarten teachers are as grown-up as anyone else."

She enjoyed the sound of his laughter then. Carefree. Lighthearted. Happy. She cuddled closer and stroked his bare chest. She combed his coarse hairs with her fingers, enjoying the rough texture against her skin. Very masculine. Very wonderful.

"So, are you okay?" she asked.

"Of course. Can't you tell?"

She nodded against his chest. "Just wanted to make sure that the jump you took off the fence was onto a one-way road."

Dan remained quiet for a moment, and Shelley was sorry she'd questioned him.

"Turn over, Shel, and look up at the stars. They're scattered everywhere tonight."

She complied.

"An old Irish leprechaun I know," said Dan, "assured me that if Nikki were a star in the heavens, she'd want to look down and see exactly this scene." He paused. "And I think the old man got it right."

Tears stung Shelley's eyes. "I'm so sorry you lost her."

"Yeah," he whispered. "Thanks. But I'm so glad I found you."

A comfortable silence descended before they stood up and brushed themselves off. Shelley placed her hand on his arm. "Dan?"

"Yes?"

"I'm sorry to arrive in your life with so much baggage. A few months ago, before this congressional race, my world was much calmer. No threats. No photographers. No attempts at blackmail. A very civilized divorce. And now…" Her hands dropped to her sides. "I don't know what to expect from day to day. I can't promise you…normalcy! And I'll understand if…"

"Hold on, Shel! And come here." He opened his arms and she walked into them. "Everybody's got baggage, sweetheart. I've learned that much in thirty-eight years."

"I understand, but this is *extra* baggage, not your

own. And it might get…" She shivered as she spoke, her voice fading as an image of Carl's face flashed into her mind. "It might get uglier than it already is. And you shouldn't have to be part of it. It's not fair. You've already had your share of troubles."

His embrace tightened. "It's too late for regrets. You're part of me already, and so are the kids. It seems to me that you guys are a package deal."

She surprised herself when she chuckled. "Shouldn't *I* be the one saying that to *you*?"

"I guess I'm an easy sell," he replied with another kiss on her mouth.

"It's because," she murmured against him, "you like children. And dogs."

"And you. Especially you."

He kissed her again, this time slowly, sweetly, and she could have stayed right there for hours just being held in his arms and kissed…and kissing back. But finally, Daniel took her hand, and they started the return walk toward Sea View House.

Daniel broke the silence. "Did you know that Nikki was pregnant with our first child? Radiant with it."

"Oh, Daniel. I'm so sorry." Shelley reached on tiptoe and kissed his cheek. "I'm very sorry," she repeated.

"Thanks." His voice was low, gruff, and Shelley strained to hear his next words. "I loved her, Shelley."

Dan pivoted toward her, stopping their progress.

Then he cupped her face in his hands. "But I didn't think about Nikki while I was making love to you," he said. "Not once."

"Well, I know that," she replied in a tone lighter than his. Her heart, however, was filled with wonder and gratitude at his concern for her.

"You do? How?"

She would have laughed at his confusion if the topic hadn't been so important. She reached around his neck and drew him closer. "Because it was *my* name you called out ten minutes ago. Only mine." She peeped at him from under her lashes. "Maybe even shouted."

He understood instantly and grinned. "Well, well, well. Did you say shout?"

She provided a mirror image of his own Cheshire cat imitation and nodded.

"Guess that old Irishman was more on target than he could have dreamed."

"He'll be happy to know that," said Shelley.

"And who's going to tell him?"

"Are you kidding? Just one look at your face—"

He suddenly bent down, scooped her up and twirled her around on the sand. She squealed and held on to him. And couldn't remember the last time she indulged in such carefree play. In the moonlight, Shelley saw the sparkle in Daniel's eyes, the laughter in his expression, and knew that this was a rare event for him, as well. Finally, she slid down his broad body, held him around the waist and leaned on him.

"I could stay like this forever," she sighed.

"Not a very practical arrangement," he replied, squeezing her gently. "Who will coach the team?"

"I get your point." She smiled at him and stepped to his side, clasping his hand as they started walking again.

Sea View House came into sight and with it, for Shelley, the practical realities of her life. "I'll give the esteemed candidate a call tomorrow morning. Hopefully, he'll see the benefits of making an appearance at his son's baseball game on the holiday weekend."

"He'll be here, Shelley. Carl may be selfish, but he's not stupid." He paused and looked at her. "Except with you."

She nodded.

"And I'm grateful for that," he continued. "Carl's loss is my gain. I should thank the man!"

Daniel's words brought a calm to her soul. He was so good for her confidence. They climbed up the back porch steps. A light shone on either side of the doorway. She turned to say good-night, but Daniel looked deep in thought.

"One more thing," he said. "I forgot to mention earlier that I'm putting a legal team together for you...just in case."

Her stomach knotted. "I—I never thought our lives would come to this—Carl's and mine. Everything was settled, and now I need a team!" She took a moment to regroup. "Maybe, just maybe, it will be unnecessary in the end, but thank you."

"I don't know the answer to that one, Shel. I wish I did. So, for now, we'll follow the Boy Scout motto and be prepared."

She forced a smile. "I'll take that advice. Actually, I like it. If we're prepared, there can be no surprises."

SELFISH, but not stupid. That's how Daniel had described her former husband, and he was right. Another photo opportunity was too good to ignore. Shelley held the telephone receiver in her hand the next morning, covered the mouthpiece and called Josh to the phone.

"Daddy's on the line, Josh. He's got some good news for you."

She handed the receiver to her son and watched his joyful reaction to the news that his dad would be at his game. The opening game of the season.

"This is so great, Dad. So great." He twirled around and faced her, his eyes glowing, the picture of happiness.

And once again, Shelley's heart squeezed. Every boy needed a dad. Heck, every child needed a dad. She listened to Josh's end of the conversation and realized that Carl had decided to take her suggestion completely. Josh was nodding in agreement about the rest of the weekend—the seniors' centers, the Boston Pops concert. He didn't even object to missing the team's second game on the Fourth. Obviously, his dad's presence meant the world to him.

"Good job, Carl," said Shelley when Josh handed her the phone. "Just make sure you show up. And on time."

"Oh, I'll be there. In fact, since it's an early game, maybe I'll come over the night before."

"What a good idea! The children will love it. You can stay at the Wayside Inn. It's a pretty place, right in town. Convenient to everything. And if you get here early enough, you can take the kids to Neptune's Park. Lots of rides. A great way to share time with them."

It was quiet on the other end of the line. "That's not quite what I had in mind."

She knew it wasn't. "But that's what you *should* have in mind when you're with the kids. Plan some activities or enjoy quiet routines."

"And what will you be doing while the kids and I are amusing ourselves?"

"No need to be concerned about my activities, Carl. Just let me know when you plan to show up."

She replaced the receiver in its cradle.

ONE BY ONE, the members of the Parker Plumbing team arrived at the middle-school field before the opening game of the season. This time, all the parents stayed and the bleachers filled quickly. For the first time since she'd started coaching the team, Shelley felt nervous.

She glanced at Dan, who'd just deposited the big

duffel bag of equipment in their assigned dugout. "It's too real," she said. "Look at all the people here. Even in Boston, we didn't get such a turnout. I hope the kids don't get as nervous as I am."

Dan chuckled. "But this is Pilgrim Cove, Shel, where everybody participates in everything. The town's in a holiday mood. Baseball and apple pie. That's us!"

But Shelley's butterflies kept dancing. "I don't know, Daniel," she said slowly. "I'm comfortable working with the children, not performing for an audience."

Dan walked over to her, leaned down and whispered, "I loved the performances we indulged in last night."

Heat traveled instantly throughout her body as she recalled the leisurely evening in Dan's apartment. No kids. No grandparents. All of them off to the movies and then to the Diner on the Dunes for ice cream. Last night's activities in the Crow's Nest had been definitely for adults only.

"I know what you mean." She glanced up at him and grinned, suddenly feeling better. She and Daniel were connecting in every way a couple could. Mentally, physically, emotionally. Strength upon strength, they brought out the best in each other.

"Hey, Coach!" She twirled and waved to Laura and Matt Parker, back from their honeymoon. Their older boy, Brian, was dressed in his own uniform, scheduled to play later on. But Casey Parker ran toward her and Dan. "I—I'm here!" He grinned proudly and displayed a new wide empty space where two teeth had once been.

"Well, look at you!"

Then Lila Sullivan waved at them as Katie joined the children. Sara Fielding was right behind her. Shelley noticed Sara's dad sitting next to Lila on the benches.

The Parker Plumbing team had assembled with thirty minutes to spare for warmup. Shelley had to admit that their enthusiasm was still greater than their ability. But what the heck? They were kids, and the game was to be enjoyed. She looked at her son, who always reveled in every moment spent on a ball field.

With his dad's expected arrival on his mind, he'd hopped out of bed before the sun was up that morning, anxious for the day to start. Shelley had had to lie down with him until he relaxed enough to catch another hour's sleep.

She checked the time now, then glanced in the direction of the parking lot. Ten minutes to nine, and no Carl in sight.

She got Dan's attention, pointed at her watch, then to the dugout. Time to assemble.

"Mom! Where is he?"

Josh ran to her side, his worried expression matching his tone of voice. She hugged him tightly.

"He'll be here, honey. He will."

"Maybe he got lost." Josh stepped away from her.

"He's got the directions. It's more likely he got stuck in traffic. You know how Boston can be." She'd suggested the ferry option, but Carl had dismissed it.

"Yeah. Right. I forgot."

She had to get her son's mind back on the game, not only for the team's sake, but also for his own. She put her arm over his shoulder and walked with him toward the dugout.

"Josh, we both have a job to do this morning. The team is depending on us—on every player—to do his best. Dan's been working hard with you to provide backup pitching, as well as to play second base. Do you think you can do the job, no matter what?"

His green eyes shone so earnest and intense. "I want to play, Mom, but I just wish Dad was here, too. He said he was coming!"

"He might show up when you're making a fabulous catch in the field. And you won't even notice."

A tiny smile. "Yeah, I hope so. He's probably just late."

"I'm sure that's what it is, Josh." She kept a smile on her face while she thought about tearing Carl's heart out and cutting it into smithereens. Vicious image, but it made her feel better for the moment.

Dan had gathered the team in the dugout and was chatting up the players. The manager of the Little League Organization walked to center field and held up his arms for quiet. After welcoming everyone to the start of the season, he said the magic words, "Play ball!"

And Coach Shelley Anderson felt her heart rate escalate as her team took to the field in their first game. The kids looked adorable, and she hoped every parent had a camera. She glanced at her son. Josh seemed able to concentrate as he stood on second base. His eyes, however, wandered toward the parking area whenever the ball was thrown home.

Neither team scored for two innings. Then in the bottom of the third, Josh stood at the plate, his face an inscrutable mask, his green eyes focused. Nothing of the disappointed little boy Shelley had seen thirty minutes earlier showed beneath his countenance.

Josh didn't wait. The first pitch was a strike, but Josh was ready to take out his anger on the ball. His bat connected—thwack!—slamming a line drive between second and third. He dropped the bat and ran. None of the children on the opposing team could field his hit until the ball rolled to a stop. He stepped on first, passed second and slid into third, creating a plume of dust around himself.

The crowd went wild. Shelley went wild. In honor of her son, who was motivated by all the wrong reasons. And then, in the midst of the excitement, Shelley saw a man sprinting toward third base from outside the playing field. As though he'd planned an entrance, Carl Anderson, shirtsleeves rolled to the elbow, trim, energetic, arms overhead in a victory salute, strode along the low fence near the baseline toward his son. When Josh picked himself up off the ground, the first person he saw was his dad.

"Like right out of a movie," said Shelley to Dan, pointing at the two male Andersons. She shook her head in disbelief. "How the hell does he do that?"

Dan laughed. "They say timing is everything, and I guess sometimes it really is. Anyway, look at Josh. He's happy."

Shelley looked. "He's happy, but he would have been ecstatic about fifteen minutes ago."

"Salvage what you can, Shelley. Just like your son did." Dan walked to the fence behind home plate. "Now let's see if Casey can bring Josh home."

Shelley heard Dan's soft encouragement to the little boy at bat as she gazed once more toward her own son. Carl still stood at the fence near third, his lips moving as though he were coaching Josh about running home. In the dugout with her team, Shelley sighed in exasperation. No other parent was near the field at all.

Casey swung at the first pitch. The bat whistled by the ball for a strike.

"Easy does it, Casey. Take your time."

Shelley loved the sound of Dan's voice, calm and reassuring to the kids. To her, as well!

Casey let two pitches go by. Two balls.

"Good eye, Case. Good eye."

Then he connected for a ground ball picked up

by the shortstop and thrown home just as Josh's feet touched the plate.

Parker Plumbing had scored their first run. Casey did a jig at first base, but Josh just stood up and brushed himself off. His eyes sought out Shelley as she left the dugout with his teammates for a quick congratulatory high five.

"I did what you said, Mom." His serious expression after his grand feat startled Shelley.

"Did I say to hit a triple?" she asked with a laugh.

He shook his head. "No. But I did my job. No matter what."

Darn her tears! She grabbed her son around his waist and hugged him till he squirmed. "Yes. Yes, you did. I'm proud of you." And now the game he loved had lost its glow. Relegated to a job.

Josh pushed away from her and looked at his father. "Hi, Dad."

"Great slide into third, Josh. Great judgment."

The boy shrugged, started walking to the dugout and then turned back, a tiny gleam of hope in his eye. "Did you…uh…see my hit?"

And that was Josh's challenge to his father. Carl's answer would mean the difference between joy and job. Carl's glance implored Shelley. She could help him…throw him enough information to catch on and remain a hero. She turned to her son, examined his expression. He was eager, yet braced for the truth. His little-boy expectations had started to evaporate. She studied the tableau of three—she, Josh and Carl—poised at a turning point. It was time to move forward.

Shelley met Carl's gaze and lifted her shoulders in a tiny shrug. He was on his own.

Down, but not out, Carl's save was almost good enough. "I heard the bat crack the ball but was just approaching the field. Too far away to see the hit. From the noise, I knew something exciting had happened, and I wasn't surprised to discover it was you. You're a hell of a player, Joshua."

Josh nodded and continued into the dugout.

CHAPTER THIRTEEN

"YOU COULD HAVE GIVEN me some help with Josh." Carl's eyes narrowed as he looked at Shelley.

"The only people needing my help right now are the twelve kids on my team," replied Shelley. "Go sit on the bleachers, Carl, with the other parents. Your daughter is there with my folks. She'll give you what you want."

As Shelley joined Daniel and her team, she saw Emily run to Carl, saw Carl scoop her up and swing her around. The child looked content, and Shelley sighed with relief, happy to be able to focus only on the game. Happy to be partnering with Daniel. They worked well together with the children.

The game ended after seven innings for these youngest players, and Parker Plumbing took the honors with a one-run lead. The two teams walked onto the field, each player giving a high five to the members of the opposite team. Soon parents were swarming the dugout area picking up their children and congratulating the coaches on their win.

"We all had a great time," replied Shelley over and over again.

"I guess a woman can be a coach!" said one father with a grin on his face.

Shelley laughed and nodded at Katie Sullivan and Sara Fielding. "And they can also play the game."

"Thanks, Professor," said another parent.

"No problem," said Dan. "Thanks for coming."

Matt and Laura Parker approached them. "You guys are terrific," said Laura, her arm around Casey. "The coaches and the kids." Casey nodded in agreement, his head bobbing fast.

"And now I can feel less guilty about defecting this summer," said Matt.

"But it was for a good cause," said Shelley, smiling at Laura. "Marriage and a family, not to mention the new house. A lot of changes."

"A lot of new beginnings," said Laura. "New friends, too." She squeezed Shelley's hand before leaving with her husband, and Shelley was warmed by the gesture of friendship.

With the Parkers' departure, the dugout was suddenly empty. Too empty.

"Where's Josh?" Shelley stepped into the sunshine and looked toward the stands. "Well, well. I was wondering when they'd show up."

"Who, honey?"

"Look over there," she replied, pointing to the bleachers. "Photographer and reporter. Carl took our bait for a photo op and now he's getting what he wants. Pictures of him and the kids for the Boston papers." She felt Daniel's presence beside her as he scanned the area.

"They might be from the *Pilgrim Cove Gazette*, and see him as a story—celebrity visiting town," said Daniel, packing away the equipment into the big duffel bags.

"Not a snowball's chance. Besides, the *Gazette* staff has already been here and I know them now. Uh-uh. These guys came with Carl. They're focusing only on him."

Dan shrugged. "So he'll get a headline like Candidate Watches Kids At Little League Baseball Game. He wants to win the election, Shelley. It's reasonable."

"Reasonable would have been getting here on time for Josh," she grumbled.

"Well, he knows that now."

"I hope so. My son will forgive and forget and think his dad is wonderful if Carl comes through next time. And frankly, I hope he does. Even if Carl's an idiot to me, Josh wants to believe his dad is great."

Dan lowered the bag to the ground and turned to her. His left hand rested on her shoulder. He stroked her cheek gently with his right. "If his dad doesn't come through, Josh will look around at other men in his life. I'll be there, Shel. And I'll try not to let him down."

The world around her faded. Shelley remained quiet for a moment, and stared at the man who'd captured her heart. Daniel, who was offering his love and life not only to her, but also to those whom she loved. "You couldn't let him down," she whispered. "You're a good man through and through. An honorable man."

"I'm no saint!" Dan was quick to reply, his complexion turning ruddy.

Shelley grinned at his discomfort and left the dugout just as Carl came striding toward her, the children right behind him.

"I'm on a schedule, Shelley," he said. "Are the kids good to go?"

"After Josh takes a shower, they'll be ready."

Carl glanced at his watch, then at his son. "Make it fast, Josh, but get yourself clean. More pictures later." He motioned to the two men with press badges. "These are stringers for the *Globe*. Since my candidacy is so recent, I need as much coverage as I can get." His gaze veered toward Dan, his expression challenging.

"Makes sense," said Dan, shifting the duffel bag on his shoulder and glancing around the dugout. "New team's claiming this place. Let's get going."

Shelley's gaze lingered on the man who was trying to keep the peace. Knowing his efforts were for her sake filled her with warmth.

"You can all have a glass of iced tea at the house while Josh cleans up," she offered the group of men.

"Thanks," replied the photographer with a grin, "but we're taking a boat ride back to town. Not often we can catch a breeze on the water while at work." He looked at his buddy, who was scribbling in a note-book.

"He's got a point," said the writer.

Carl grunted. "You're not on vacation! I'll see you at four o'clock at the veterans' home. Then we'll hit Grand Acres Seniors' Center. Channel 2 will be covering that visit, too."

Shelley swallowed hard, and glanced at the kids. "That's quite a pace."

"You get used to it," replied Carl. He looked at the newsmen. "Come on. I'll take you to the dock."

"Just a sec," said the reporter, looking at Shelley. "Are you part of this campaign, Mrs. Anderson?"

Startled, Shelley couldn't reply quickly.

"That's still under discussion," said Carl.

"No," said Shelley, now realizing the intent of the conversation. "No, it's not." She turned to the re-porter, forcing a smile and hoping she'd sound artic-ulate. "Give me a break, guys. If you've done your homework, you know the candidate and I have been divorced for over a year. The children will be with him from time to time, and Carl will certainly get my vote in the booth, but as to active campaign-ing…no."

She turned toward Carl. "We'll meet you back at Sea View House."

A curt nod was his only response and Shelley

sighed. How could such a bright man be so stupid? Or was *stubborn* the better word?

Five minutes later, Shelley sat next to Dan in his SUV, eyes closed, head resting against the seat. Josh and Emily were in the back. Daniel turned the key in the ignition, but he didn't shift into gear. Instead he reached for her hand and gently squeezed it. "You're stronger than you think, Shel, and you're not alone."

"I know," she whispered. "I love you standing near me. I love us being together." There was more she wanted to tell him, more she wanted to ask him. But not with the children in the car.

As soon as Dan parked in the driveway, Shelley hopped out, ready to hustle the kids and prepare some sandwiches and soft drinks before they left. The less time she and Carl spent together, the better for everyone.

DAN WATCHED Shelley race into the house. The woman was as nervous as a mouse being stalked by a cat. She'd wanted him to join them for a light lunch, but maybe she'd be better off without him in Carl's face right now. Maybe the kids would be better off, too. Regardless, he needed a shower himself and could take a few minutes to decide.

Ten minutes later, he slid his kitchen door open, and he and Jess walked onto his deck. If Shelley was outside, he'd double-check the need for his presence with her family group. Voices traveled up to him immediately, however, and his decision was made as soon as he heard Carl's voice. "Where's lover man, Shelley? Or should I say boy? Lover boy."

"Have some iced tea, Carl," she replied, her words steady. "Have a sandwich. Then take the kids and go on your campaign." Dan cheered silently at her reply. She hadn't risen to the bait.

But leaving her alone for a long time would accomplish nothing. "Come on, Jess," Daniel whispered, leading the dog back into the apartment. "You're staying up here today. Can't have you in the midst of anything."

He jogged down the outside staircase, making sure his tread was heavy enough to cue Shelley and company that he was on his way. And the first thing he saw when he arrived on the porch was her radiant smile. "Hi, Shelley." It was so natural to walk to her side and give her a small hug. So he did. Then turned to the other man. "Anderson," he greeted.

The candidate ignored him. "Where *is* that boy?" Carl's impatient voice sliced the momentary calm. "He knows I'm in a hurry." He glanced at his watch and started pacing.

Shelley's exasperated glance told its own story. "My dad's helping him, Carl. He'll be right out. And don't take your frustration out on Josh."

"Josh?" he repeated, turning to Shelley. "It's you. I wouldn't be having this problem if we were all back under one roof! I wouldn't have to run back and forth to see him play."

Next to him, Dan felt Shelley stiffen and take a step forward. "Easy, easy," he whispered.

She nodded, but her eyes glowed hot. Her voice, however, was cool. "Commuting is your problem, Carl. You should have thought about your children, if not me, a long time ago. Before you started running around."

"Me?" Carl's voice rose, incredulity coloring his tone. "You're talking about me? At least I'm not shacking up in front of the kids like you are! How convenient he lives upstairs."

Shacking up. The insult exploded in Dan's brain. His mind emptied of everything but those two words, and he found himself walking toward the other man as if in a trance. As if he were someone else. But it was *his* blood pumping with adrenaline, *his* heart pounding like thunder, *his* hands balled into fists. He uncurled his fingers to tap Carl's shoulder. *His* face in Anderson's face.

"You're going to apologize to Shelley, and you're going to do it now," he said in a low voice. They were of a height, and the hate in Carl's eyes was easy to see. The cunning, too.

Carl pivoted to throw a punch, using the momentum of his turn to add power.

Dan blocked with his forearm and pushed.

"It's none of your business what goes on between Shelley and me," Carl said between clenched teeth, taking a step backward.

Like a bee buzzing in the background, Shelley's

voice came through to him, high pitched and indistinct. She'd soon understand that she didn't have to worry. Daniel wasn't going to hurt the candidate, just scare him.

He pushed again, not very hard. But Carl lost his step and had to recover. Dan studied Carl's face. Yes, indeed. His expression was changing. The candidate had gotten the message.

"As I was saying," began Dan in a calm voice, "you're going to apologize to the lady. And you're going to be polite from now on. And if your schedule's tight, you're going to take responsibility for it." He glared at the other man. "Be happy I'm not still eighteen, solving this in the dirt where it belongs. Although," he added, as he felt a grin of pure pleasure cross his face, "the idea is very tempting. Very, very tempting."

Carl's complexion paled.

"That's right, Mr. Candidate. A picture of you in a brawl on the front page sure won't help your campaign, will it? I, fortunately, don't have a campaign to worry about."

The man's Adam's apple bobbed as he swallowed.

"And now," Dan continued, "before your children join us, I'm going to step aside while you apologize to Shelley and speak to her with respect. You're also going to cool off. And if you can't do that, you're going to leave—without the children."

Carl's eyes narrowed.

"Fear of endangerment in a moving vehicle," said Dan. "A lot of us witnessed your temper today. Potential road rage makes Shelley nervous."

Dan stepped back, arms at his sides, giving the candidate room to move around, and signaling the end of the one-on-one episode.

Carl looked at his former wife. "You're not safe with him, Shelley. I think he might be crazy."

"Crazy like a fox, maybe," replied Shelley, laughing between her words. "Meet Professor Daniel Stone, Ph.D., J.D., esteemed member of the Harvard Law School faculty. Your alma mater, Carl. Author of books you have in your own law library. And…a very honorable man." She glanced at Dan and shook her head. "A man just full of surprises."

Daniel watched Carl absorb the information. The man's eyes narrowed and he nodded, as though recalling the facts on Dan's résumé. At their first meeting, when Carl had surprised Shelley with a visit, he'd obviously assumed Daniel was frittering away the summer, and Dan hadn't corrected that assumption. Wasn't the guy's business.

Since then, however, the private investigator would have mentioned Dan's profession to Carl. At the moment, Carl needed to be reminded that the playing field had been leveled. For Shelley's sake. For the children's sakes. Personally, Dan didn't care if Anderson thought Dan dug ditches for a living.

"Why Harvard?" asked Anderson. "Don't they have good schools in California?"

"They do. But Harvard gave me an offer I couldn't refuse. Just as I made you an offer you'd be foolish to refuse." He stared at the man. "Shelley's still waiting."

IF NOTHING ELSE, thought Dan, from his position at the porch railing, his actions today had distracted Carl from his preoccupation with his schedule. If the man's apology to Shelley had been perfunctory, which was probably the case, at least he'd calmed down enough for her to feel comfortable with letting the children drive with him.

Josh and Emily, overnight bags packed, were finishing their sandwiches at the porch table and chatting to their dad, who sat between them. Their grandparents were also having lunch.

"This is good, Mommy," said Emily about her tuna fish sandwich.

"I think you were very hungry," replied Shelley. "Watching a baseball game can knock you out!"

Emily grinned, reached for her drink and knocked it over. Grape juice dribbled everywhere, including on Emily's lap.

"Uh-oh," said Emily, as Shelley blotted the liquid away. "I'm all wet."

"You'll dry off in the car," said her father.

Dan watched the scene play out, and found himself hoping Carl would do the right thing

"But I'm all purple! And it's wet and yucky." Emily's voice started to quiver, and Carl rolled his eyes.

"Okay, okay. Put extra clothes in her bag, would you, Shelley?"

"Sure. And both of you use the bathroom, right now, so Daddy doesn't have to stop."

"Thank you," said Carl.

Shelley and the kids disappeared inside, followed by the Duffys. And Dan released a sigh of relief.

His sigh must have been more audible than he'd thought because Carl glared at him.

"I don't hit my children, so you can stop staring at me."

Daniel chuckled. "I know that. Despite Shelley's efforts, your kids wouldn't have turned out so well if you'd been a real bastard. But I'd be careful if I were you. You're on a slippery slope with Josh." He paused for effect. "And that's an objective assessment from someone with a reputation for objectivity."

"And from someone without a son of his own?"

Daniel silently counted to three. "From someone who cares that Josh grows up secure and happy. He needs his dad. And you'd be a fool to ignore him."

"I have no intention of ignoring him. In fact, I'll probably be with him more often than ever very soon."

The skin on the back of Dan's neck prickled. "You mean, on the campaign trail?"

"Hmm? Sure. I want the kids with me for that. And…more." Carl stared at Dan now, his eyes gleaming.

Daniel hoisted himself onto the railing and casually leaned against the post. "If your grand plan is to the kids' benefit, that's great, and I applaud you." He hoped his voice sounded sincere, even jovial.

"On the other hand," he continued, "if you're planning to use the children to spite Shelley, then that's not so great."

"Then it seems you'll just have to wait and see what I do, Professor, won't you?" Carl's eyes glowed. He was obviously enjoying the debate.

"I'm known to be a patient man," replied Daniel. "But in this case, I won't have to wait long. Your weakness is showing, Counselor. More clearly all the time. The weakness that's going to bring you down—if you're not careful."

The man didn't look quite as smug as before. "An interesting theory. Want to share it?"

Dan waited. Pretended to consider the request. "I never show all my cards," he finally said. "But here's a hint." He nodded toward the kitchen door. "Your weakness—it's *not* Shelley."

Carl's eyes gleamed with suspicion. "What are you getting at?"

Dan pushed himself off the railing. "No, Shelley's not your weak spot," he repeated. "Your Achilles' heel comes from inside, Anderson. Why don't you take some time to figure it out?"

The back door swung open at that moment, Josh in the lead.

Emily followed, with Shelley bringing up the

rear. The kids had never looked as scrubbed as they did then.

"We're ready, Dad," said Josh.

The candidate examined his children, and nodded. "I'll say. You're one handsome devil, son. Chip off the old block."

Josh grinned. Dan winced.

"What about me, Daddy?"

Everyone chuckled now, including Daniel, who was glad to see Emily asserting herself.

"As beautiful as Mommy," said Carl Anderson.

Emily grinned at Shelley, and Dan had to agree with that assessment. The female Andersons were a pair of beauties.

"Listen up, troops," said Shelley. "Last-minute instructions about tomorrow at the big concert in Boston."

"It's the Fourth of July," said Emily to her mother.

"That's right, sweetheart, and there are going to be a lot of people there. Crowds of people who want to hear the music."

She looked at Dan. "The Boston Pops does a fabulous concert every year along the Charles River."

Dan nodded. "I've seen it on television."

"Right. It's broadcast nationally because it's so great." She knelt on the floor, eye level with her children. "You guys have to hold on to Daddy's hands. Tight. Both of you."

"For goodness' sake, Shelley. I won't lose them!" said Carl. "I'm their father."

"I know. I know. But you might be distracted with speech making or whatever you're doing. The crowds are friendly, but they're big."

When she looked up at her ex-husband, Daniel could see a worry line crease her forehead. He wanted to kiss it away.

Carl extended his hand; Shelley took it and stood up.

"If you're that concerned, Shel, come with us. It's a family concert."

That remark got everyone's attention and silence prevailed for a moment. An uncomfortable silence. Daniel watched Emily and Josh step toward each other seeking comfort, an automatic response to the conflict they sensed in the adult world.

Shelley's glance at Carl was eloquent in its disgust, but she smiled. "I have other commitments. You and the children, however, will make a beautiful family portrait."

She turned to the kids. "You know what? I'm going to watch television and try to find you! How's that? If you see a big camera, wave at me."

"If I look real hard, can I see you?" asked Emily.

"No, sweetheart, it doesn't work like that, but I'll see you…when, Carl? I can pick them up at the ferry at Rowes Wharf if you'd like either tomorrow night or on the fifth."

"I'll let you know. My folks will be at the concert, too, so don't worry so much. And watch tonight's news. We may be featured." Carl glanced at his watch. "Come on. We really have to be going."

"Just one more thing," Shelley interrupted him. "Leave me the name and phone number of your campaign manager. You may not be reachable at times for personal calls."

Carl handed her a business card. "Here's the information, and now we're leaving." He motioned the children to him and they walked down the porch steps toward the driveway.

Suddenly, Emily dropped her overnight bag on the ground and ran back straight into Dan's arms. He lifted her automatically, and kissed her cheek.

"Bye, my Daniel p'fessor," she said, her voice as sweet as milk chocolate. "I love you, too."

Dan's eyes stung as he held her close. "And I love you," he whispered. "I'll be waiting for you right here. And Josh, too."

"Good." She jumped down, ran back toward her father and picked up her bag. "I'm ready now, Daddy."

But Carl wasn't paying attention to his daughter then. His glare was only for Daniel.

And then in purposeful slow motion, Carl's eyes roved from Daniel to Shelley and back again, his calculating expression easy to read.

Daniel glanced at Shelley. Her face was whiter than clean beach sand in the moonlight. She'd recognized Carl's message. The candidate was going after custody of his kids.

CHAPTER FOURTEEN

SHELLEY WATCHED in silence as Carl and the children disappeared around the corner and up Outlook Drive. No one on the porch said a word.

"What has happened to that boy?" Ellen Duffy's thin voice finally reflected her confusion. "I don't understand him anymore."

Shelley walked to her mom and embraced her. "Everything will be okay. Don't worry." She nodded at Dan. "The guy over there has a winning team to help me."

"Well, thank God for that!" replied Ellen, and Shelley was delighted to note her mother's renewed spirit. "The lawyer that represented you two years ago isn't up to handling this situation." Ellen's expression hardened, her lips pressed together. "Carl's not thinking about the children at all. And he's jealous of you, Daniel. You know that, don't you?"

"Sure, I do. You realize, of course, that he would resent anyone in Shelley's life right now because he has other plans for her." Dan's calm tone helped to quell Shelley's nerves and seemed to reassure her parents. "And I'm certainly not taking his attitude personally, nor am I intimidated by him."

Now, Phil started to laugh. "I guess not. Geez, there was some excitement here today."

"I'm afraid, Mr. Duffy, that there's going to be more before it's all over," said Dan.

Shelley grimaced at his words, but she knew he was speaking the truth. "I'd hoped he'd simply accept my decision, but I think there's more behind his determination than simply the election. It's become a matter of pride. Now he wants me because I said no—a word he's rarely heard from me. And he doesn't know how to handle it, so he's digging in."

Thoughts and images whirled in her mind. Carl's sneering face, his threatening tone, his overall intimidation tactics. She wanted to curl into a ball and howl. "Now he's getting back at me," she said, her voice quavering, "no matter what's best for the children."

Tears filled her eyes, and despite her effort to remain calm, she couldn't breathe. Fear gagged her, and a wave of nausea hit full force. She ran into the house, to the bathroom and almost missed the bowl. Doubling over, she retched, felt hot then cold.

A strong arm encircled her stomach, supporting her, riding with the waves. A dry towel blotted her forehead.

"Easy, Shel, easy. You'll be fine. Just let it go." Daniel's voice. Confident. Steady. And seeing her at her absolute worst. She heaved again. Nothing she could do about it. Once more and she was done. He helped her up, and his arm stayed around her as she brushed her teeth.

"Thanks," she mumbled when she put the brush away, and then tried to smile. "Very romantic interlude, wasn't it?" she asked.

"I'd definitely give it a ten." Dan's quick grin had her feeling better, especially when he continued to hold her. He kissed her on the neck, the cheek, the ear.

"Hmm," she murmured, nestling closer to him. "Seems like the female Andersons keep upchucking on you."

"As a new courtship ritual, it could use some improvements," he said lightly, "but, so what?"

"I'm sorry to be such a wimp. Guess I'm scared." She sighed. "It seems I have to start fighting all over again when I thought everything was settled for good."

"But this time you're not alone. And in my professional opinion, you're scaring yourself for nothing."

She followed him into the hallway, then into the living room, where he insisted she lie on the couch for a while and sip a cola.

Exhausted, she had no desire to protest. Soon her eyes were closing.

"Stress is a killer," she said with a yawn.

"Yup. And we're going to get rid of it by taking action," said Daniel. "I'll set you up with your legal team next week. We'd be foolish not to lay the groundwork since we've been forewarned, so to speak."

Shelley felt a genuine smile cross her face. "Suddenly, I feel much better." And she did. "Give me an hour and we'll go for a swim."

More kisses feathered her cheek. "Take as long as you need," whispered Dan. "I've got plenty to keep me busy."

She loved this man who seemed to love her. He turned to leave, and she grabbed his arm. "Daniel."

He paused, his brow crinkled. "What, honey?"

"Are you sure you want to stick around? Why should you subject yourself to all this…this…turmoil? You wanted a quiet summer! A quiet life. And I…" She shook her head, unable to speak anymore.

"And you brought me back to life!" He knelt on the floor next to her and took her hands. "Don't ever forget it, Shel. I can't quite explain the change—Bart probably can—but somehow you've got me laughing again. You and your kids. They're terrific, and you're doing a great job with them." He raised her hands to his mouth and kissed every finger. "We're going to change that turmoil into garden-variety chaos," he continued, "the kind that's found in every active family."

"Garden variety?" she asked. "Ordinary? Everyday chaos?"

Now his eyes twinkled when he nodded.

"I'd like that," she whispered. "My favorite brand of excitement."

BY THE TIME Shelley sat with Dan, her parents and Jessie in front of the television that evening waiting for the news to begin, Daniel had arranged a meeting with his colleagues for next week. She knew it hadn't been easy tracking them down on a holiday weekend and organizing a mutually convenient day and time for five people to meet, but he'd done it. Shelley had begun to relax and now felt like her normal self again.

The news started. National events first. Shelley barely blinked as she watched the screen, but she was totally aware of her fingers intertwined with Dan's. She liked the implication, and she liked his touch—cool, smooth, strong. When the focus on screen changed to local news, she gripped hard.

One minute later, Carl, Josh and Emily were shown at the seniors' center. The candidate spoke to the camera after the reporter's lead-in, but Shelley hardly heard the words. She was glued to the kids.

"Just look at my granddaughter," said Phil Duffy. "What a sweet little petunia she is."

Emily stood next to a white-haired lady in a wheelchair, talking to her nonstop, and patting the woman on the arm. The elderly woman seemed to be listening, then suddenly started to laugh and stroke Emily's cheek. Emily leaned over and kissed her.

"That's my girl," whispered Shelley. "So sweet. I wonder what she jabbered about."

"Probably about what a terrific mom she has," replied Dan. "But look at Josh showing off his batting stance to the old men. No need to guess about his topic of conversation."

The camera panned on the children, then back to the candidate, whose beaming expression left no doubt about what a proud father he was.

"That's it!" said Shelley after the piece was over. "He's won the election thanks to the kids."

"So what?" said Daniel, getting up from the couch and starting to pace. "He's no worse than the other party's candidate. So let him win and move to Washington."

Shelley watched him walk back and forth, pure energy in motion. His expression changed constantly, distracted.

"I've got it! A totally different angle," he finally said as he stood in front of her, eyes sparkling and a very satisfied grin on his face. "Shelley, how'd you like to plan a little campaign, too?"

She stared up at him from the sofa. "What are you talking about?"

"How'd you like to help the candidate run as the most eligible bachelor in Boston?"

Shelley jumped out of her seat. "You're a genius!" If dozens of women threw themselves at Carl, he'd quickly forget about her.

"The first call will be to Carl's campaign manager when the time is right," continued Dan. "And you are going to make that call and whisper in his ear."

"With pleasure." The situation was getting better and better.

"How about suggesting the same thing to Carl's parents?" asked Phil Duffy, walking toward Daniel and shaking his head. "Never thought the day would come when I'd be contemplating something like this. But it's the right thing to do. My daughter needs freedom to live her life. And I'd be happy to call them."

"Amen," said Ellen, putting her arms around Shelley. "We have a strategic planning committee, too!"

Shelley spoke next. "Thank you so much." She looked at her parents. "I know it's been very difficult. Not what you envisioned years ago or even more recently. We've been—shall we say—surprised too many times. And I want you to know that the kids and I couldn't have survived as well without you." She kissed them both. "You're my head cheerleaders and I love you."

Next, she walked in front of Daniel. "As for you, Professor, just keep that brain working." She lowered her eyelids suggestively and then peeped up at him from under her lashes. "I like your ideas," she said in a soft, sultry voice. His eyes darkened immediately before he kissed her.

"Uh...uh...why don't we take Jessie for her nightly walk on the beach?" asked Philip, looking at his wife.

"I've got a better idea," said Shelley's mother. "Shelley, why don't you and Dan take her out. It's a beautiful evening, so get out of here."

"And take your time," added Ellen with a grin, "and a blanket!" She poked her husband with her elbow. "Maybe we old geezers could use a little privacy, too!"

"WELL, I GUESS they told us!"

Daniel looked into Shelley's laughing face and felt himself melt inside. She was beautiful, not to mention funny, brave, warm, loving and a whole litany of wonderful adjectives he was rediscovering a use for. He took her hand and led her outside into the moonlight, Jessie at his heels.

"I guess they did," he said. But he wasn't sure her parents' advice was on target. The other two adjectives that described her now were guilty and grateful. And he didn't like the implications of either one of them.

He knew she felt guilty about involving him with her problems. In addition, she was grateful to him for helping her in a concrete way, with more than just emotional support. He understood both feelings, but he didn't want anything to do with them. Gratitude and guilt could only muddy the waters in a relationship.

"Are you up to a short walk?" he asked as they stepped into the backyard. "We can always sit out here after Jess does her business."

Her arms akimbo, Shelley stopped and stared at him. "Daniel, I may have been a little sick earlier, but I'm not dead! I can keep up with you for miles." A grin slowly crossed her face as she stepped closer. "The real question is," she whispered, "do you have a clean blanket in the car?"

It was the grin that got to him, that set him on fire. Followed by her dark eyes, glowing with promise in the moonlight. He wanted to scoop her up and make love to her until she couldn't think about anything else. And he'd want to do it every night of his life.

But he'd saved her daughter, he'd coached the team and he'd help her face up to her ex. And he'd do it all again in a heartbeat. And now she was offering him…what?

He scanned the night sky looking for inspiration. Unlike an earlier time, however, the stars that evening twinkled with an impersonal light, leaving him on his own. He refocused on Shelley, who stood with an air of expectation. Her smile hadn't wavered. Her hand was extended.

He reached for it. "Yes," he said. "I have a blanket, clean and soft and waiting just for us."

If he had regrets later on, if Shelley discovered she had confused gratitude with love, if she discovered that Dan was simply a friend, or merely her first adventure since her divorce, he'd learn to live with it. Right now, he simply wanted to live.

TWO DAYS LATER, on Sunday morning, Shelley and Dan stood at the railing of the ferry heading into Boston to pick up the kids. A light ocean breeze felt delicious against her face, but Shelley's hands were wrapped tightly around the steel bar as she stared ahead through her dark glasses.

"It was really weird coaching the game yesterday without Josh," she said, "and both kids would have loved watching the Pilgrim Cove July Fourth parade."

"It may have been weird, but you know the whole team asked about him. Wanted to make sure he'd be at the next game. Josh has made friends here, Shelley. And you were concerned about that in the beginning."

She nodded. "It's hard to make friends when you're surly," she whispered.

"I think the parents were grateful we showed up to coach!" Dan's teasing grin showed he was kidding, and Shelley punched him lightly on the arm.

"I take my responsibilities seriously!" she said.

"I hadn't noticed," he replied dryly.

She stood on tiptoe and kissed him on the mouth. "I take my kissing seriously, too." Suddenly, Dan's grip tightened, his lips reclaiming hers, demanding a response. She complied happily.

He finally lifted his head. "Now, kissing, I definitely noticed."

She leaned against him, enjoying how his arms automatically encircled her, enjoying the scent of salt and ocean in the air. "Hmm. This is nice."

"Sure is," he whispered. "Make the most of it. Won't be so peaceful on the way home."

She glanced up at him, her stomach tightening. "Are the kids becoming annoying, Dan? Are you tired of them being around?"

A look of surprise preceded a flash of pain before he blinked it away. "Tell you what, Shel," he said quietly, "we're both going to pretend you never asked that question."

She had her answer, but she'd hurt him. He was a sensitive man. More sensitive than that big strong body and finely honed brain would lead a person to believe.

"My watch says nine forty-five and we're meeting them under the arch at the Boston Harbor Hotel at ten-thirty. We've got plenty of time," she said, deliberately changing the subject.

"Good," replied Dan. "I started the day without a cup of coffee. Need to fix that."

By ten-thirty, Shelley's eyes felt strained from constant searching. It was her own fault. Carl and the children weren't even due until now, but she'd begun to look for them as soon as Dan and she had arrived.

"Uh, what's the time on your watch, Dan?"

"Ten thirty-five."

Same as hers. She smiled briefly. "Just checking."

"Just wearing yourself out. For nothing."

She looked at him then, curious.

"Putting everything else aside," began Dan, "he's had a big weekend himself. He could have easily overslept this morning."

"But the kids wouldn't have." She started to smile. "They're early birds who make a lot of noise in the morning. Especially before they've eaten breakfast."

"Well, they could have gotten caught in traffic...."

"Early on a Sunday morning?" She shook her head. "I don't think so. No, this is just Carl trying to make me nuts." She pulled out her cell phone. "However, I'm not totally at his mercy."

"Shelley," said Dan.

Something in the tone of his voice made her respond quickly. "What?"

He nodded toward the hotel's entrance. "Look over there."

She did. Took a moment to focus on the three figures walking toward them. A too familiar blond woman, with Josh and Emily trailing behind her.

"I don't like this at all," Shelley muttered, waving her arm at the trio. She started to walk briskly in their direction, but then stopped and braced herself. The children had spotted her and were running straight at her, their overnight bags dropping to the ground.

"I'm right here," said Dan, over her shoulder. "I'll catch you as you catch them."

And then Emily was in her arms, and she was surrounded by cries of "Mommy, Mommy." Josh hugged her around the waist.

"My Daniel p'fessor!" shouted Emily, reaching over Shelley's shoulder.

Shelley felt Dan take Emily, and she leaned forward to kiss Josh a dozen times. When she looked up, Carl's associate stood waiting, the kids' bags hanging from the ends of her long fingers.

"Carl's in the middle of a strategy session, and I have to get right back," said the woman. Her eyes studied Shelley, the children and Daniel. "But it's probably better this way," she added. "For everyone."

Shelley met the woman's gaze. "I couldn't agree with you more." She took the bags from the blonde, gave them to the children and returned her attention to the woman. No time like the present to start their campaign. "I'll walk you back to the hotel," she said.

The attorney nodded, a quizzical expression on her face.

Shelley turned to Dan, who seemed to be having a sudden coughing problem. He caught her eye and nodded. "I'll be right back," she said to the children, happy to note Josh standing comfortably at Dan's side.

She glanced at the woman. "Alicia, is it?" she asked, as they started walking.

"That's right."

"I'm going to hand you the opportunity of a life-time," began Shelley, glad to note she had the woman's full attention.

"How would you like to capture Boston's most eligible bachelor and candidate for United States Congress?"

The blonde stopped in her tracks. "We've been exclusive for some time now," she replied. "With you out of the picture, we'll be setting a date."

The woman had fallen in love with the image. Or maybe she and Carl were two of a kind. "Then I should have taped the conversations Carl and I had recently," said Shelley, pausing in her stride. "He still has me in his mind, Alicia, and you and he are not a done deal yet."

Shelley waited until the information registered, then continued in a conversational tone. "I see it as a cooperative effort, and we'll have to get— what's his name?—the campaign manager in-volved and every other person of influence who surrounds Carl."

"Go on," said the other woman.

"Urge Carl to run his campaign as a fabulous single dad who has a great relationship with his ex-wife. And I mean ex!"

Alicia smiled. "I guess you really do."

"Count on it," said Shelley. "But there is one more thing."

The smile disappeared, and the woman looked wary.

"The joint-custody agreement I have with him remains in place. No changes. Just remind him how well it's been working for the past two years."

"I'll do what I can," said Alicia. "That much I can promise." Her forehead wrinkled. "On the other hand, those kids were fabulous at the seniors' center and photogenic, as well. Carl seems to have a bug up his…uh…backside about them. And he really wants to win."

Shelley's heart sank; her mind raced. Was all this effort for nothing after all? "And you, Alicia?" She examined the woman slowly from head to toe. "You're a professional woman. An attorney like Carl. But somehow, I see you winding up being responsible for the children's day-to-day care. Not what you bargained for, is it?"

"Me? I'm allergic to kids! I don't even think I have a biological clock." A look of comic horror crossed her face as she stared at Shelley. "In fact, I don't think they've had breakfast today."

"Well, then, you should do your best to persuade Carl to leave the custody agreement as it is."

Shelley walked back to Dan, shaking her head in disbelief. She'd done what she could with her new ally, and she'd tell Dan everything later and get his feedback. But in the meantime, she had two hungry kids to feed.

TEN DAYS LATER, Shelley knew that Alicia couldn't control Carl, either. A subpoena arrived midmorning, delivered in person by a court officer to Shelley Anderson at Sea View House, Beach Street, Pilgrim Cove, Massachusetts. Shelley was alone with the children, Ellen and Phil having returned to Boston after the holiday weekend. Daniel was at the university. As she signed for the delivery, her hand was steady and her signature bold.

Better to face the monster, than worry about it. She smiled at the officer. "Thanks," she said, wanting to laugh at his startled expression. "Guess you don't hear that very often."

"Never can tell what's going to happen when I make my rounds," he replied. "You know what they say about millions of stories in the naked city…"

"And mine is just one of them."

He nodded and waved, but Shelley stood in the doorway for a moment, mulling the words. Just one of many? Yes. But she had the power to influence the outcome of this particular story. To affect her children's future. To affect her own future. In the story of her life, she was the major player, and she wasn't going to waste the opportunity.

She slit the envelope open and read. Two weeks. The last day of July. That's when the Commonwealth of Massachusetts had ordered her to appear in family court. She'd already met with Dan's colleagues from Harvard, had provided them with copies of everything she had, as well as answered a myriad of questions, and was available as needed. She'd agreed that Daniel was not to be part of her defense team, since he might well be named in the complaint. She'd done all she could do, and she was ready.

She reached for the phone and called Dan's cell number. But as soon as she heard the voice she loved, she could barely speak. "The subpoena came." That was all she could manage.

"Good," said Daniel. "Let's get it over with."

She took a deep breath. "Right. Exactly my thoughts. And I was so strong a minute ago. But when I heard your voice…"

"I know, sweetheart." A comfortable silence filled the air for a moment. "I'll be home in a couple of hours," said Daniel. "Or I'll come right now."

"No, no. I'm fine." Pulling Dan away from his own work wouldn't change a thing. "In fact, the kids have a game at four today, so you'll be back a little earlier anyway."

"Where are they now?" Dan asked.

Shelley grinned. "Josh is still working out the team's statistics. That was a great idea you had giving each kid a math assignment. Let's hope they all come up with the same numbers!"

Dan chuckled. "I bet they do. And what's my petunia doing?"

"Emily is making you a picture of Jessie's paw prints."

His chuckle grew into sheer laughter. "I never know what to expect when I hear from you."

"That's where the fun comes in," said Shelley.

"It certainly does."

She disconnected after saying goodbye and realized the next two weeks would pass both quickly and slowly according to her level of anxiety. In the meantime, she had another call to make. She'd ask Laura Parker to look after Emily and Josh on court day.

The Parker answering machine picked up the message and it wasn't until the baseball game that afternoon that Shelley was able to speak with Laura herself.

"I was in Boston today recording Cinderella," said Laura. "It's the third story I've done on the project for Sunrise Books and so far it seems to be going very well." She raised both hands with her second and third fingers crossed.

"Congratulations. I hear you're a talented storyteller."

"You do?"

"Sure. Emily said so. Said you act out all the parts when you tell stories at the library."

"Well, Emily's a sweetie."

"I'm glad you think so, Laura, because I need a favor—if you're free that day."

As Shelley spoke, she watched Laura's warm blue eyes become pinpoints of light. Her calm, happy expression became indignant.

"Of course I'll watch the children. Casey will be thrilled. And if I could be in two places at once, I'd march into that courtroom and tell that judge a thing or two about what a great mother you are!"

Tears stung Shelley's eyes. "Thanks. Thanks so much. It's good to hear nice things from people other than my parents!"

"Hey, girl. Look around you." Laura stretched her arm to include the Pilgrim Cove spectators at the game. "You've got a lot of friends right here who think you're terrific. The professor, too."

Shelley followed Laura's instructions and nodded. She'd gotten to know most of the parents during the previous weeks, and they had become very supportive.

But Laura hadn't finished yet. "And when this travesty is all over," she said, "and everything's back to normal, we'll celebrate at the Lobster Pot. And that's a promise!"

It was a promise Shelley couldn't wait to keep.

SHELLEY FILLED the next few days with activities she'd pictured in her mind when she made the decision to spend the summer with her children in Pilgrim Cove. Morning errands, of course, but afternoon swims and baseball practices, all interspersed with visits to Neptune's Park or breakfast at the diner with the ROMEOs. Sometimes she and the children strolled along the boardwalk eating fresh saltwater taffy or homemade fudge.

Life would have been perfect but for the looming court date. All things considered, however, Shelley thought she was handling her situation well.

What she didn't handle well was not making love with Daniel anymore. Her parents were back in Boston at their jobs, and without them as built-in, trustworthy baby-sitters, nightly walks on the beach with Jessie were taken family-style. No blanket!

"So why don't you invite your folks for the weekends?" suggested Dan impatiently as he kissed her on the back porch five days before the hearing.

"I did. They're coming tomorrow," mumbled Shelley between kisses.

"Thank God!"

She giggled, and the tension was broken. She snuggled against his broad chest, her arms around his waist, and closed her eyes, just listening to the strong, steady beat of his heart. Life was getting better and better, and after next Wednesday, it should be right on track again. Hopefully.

"Want to join us for an early breakfast at the diner tomorrow?" asked Shelley. "I've got to buy some extra groceries afterward."

"And my car needs an oil change. After we eat, I'll drop you at the supermarket while I go to Cavelli's garage."

Shelley nodded. "Perfect." Normal, ordinary conversation and routines. The kind that families everywhere had.

AS USUAL, the diner had a large breakfast crowd on Saturday morning, but as Shelley and Dan were being shown to their own booth, Bart Quinn waved them over and insisted on adding chairs to the ROMEOs' corner table. Shelley counted five Retired Old Men Eating Out that morning. In addition to Bart, there were Lou Goodman, Rick O'Brien, Sam Parker and Mike Lyons.

"Well, if it isn't the world-famous Parker Plumbing second baseman!" said Bart, shaking Josh's hand. "That team is the best."

"Sure is," agreed Sam. "Considering our grandkids are on it!"

"Mom?" asked Josh, a genuine question in his voice. "Am I world-famous?"

Shelley grinned while the men roared with laughter. "How about we start with Pilgrim Cove Little League famous?" she asked her son.

Josh nodded and Shelley ruffled his hair just as Dee O'Brien rushed over to them.

Dee was not smiling. She passed Shelley and Dan without a word, went directly to Lou Goodman and took his hand. "Your wife just called, Lou. Multiple tornadoes have touched down in the part of Kansas where your daughter lives, and Pearl can't get Rachel on the phone. The lines must be down."

All color drained from the librarian's face. "I hope that's the reason," he said. "I've got to go."

"Wait a minute. I have a cell phone," said Shelley, reaching into her purse. "Use this to call Mrs. Goodman before you go."

But the man's hands were trembling too much to

coordinate the effort, so Shelley dialed instead, then handed the phone to Lou.

"The last two hours," he repeated, "just as people were waking up...but sirens did ring a warning...Pearl, doesn't Rachel have a cell phone like the one I'm using? Call that number. Maybe it'll work. I'm coming right home."

He returned the phone to Shelley, distress still on his face. "My daughter—she was coming here next week on vacation. Every summer, she comes back to Pilgrim Cove for a little while. And we just saw her last month on our way to California. She looked wonderful."

"And she still does," insisted Bart. "She'll be here this summer, too." But his mouth trembled when he finished speaking. "Come on, I'll drive you home."

"I'll go, too," said Rick O'Brien. "You drive his car, Bart, and I'll follow in mine. We'll see what's happening, then return here."

The three men left. Sam Parker and Mike Lyons looked at each other. "It's going to be a long morning," said Sam.

"Yes," replied Mike. "But I'm not leaving till we know what's going on."

Sam nodded. "Ever notice how life runs smooth for a time and then, pow! It bites you. Sometimes twice in a row or more."

Shelley agreed with that statement and listened as the men expanded on their observations. She heard Dan place the breakfast order, as well as his conversation with the children, which included Dorothy and Kansas and tornadoes. Actually, Josh and Emily did most of the talking. Dan's contribution was something like "What happened next?"

Just as they were finishing breakfast, Bart and Rick returned—smiling. "Rachel's fine," said Bart. "Smart lass. She used her cell phone to call Lou and Pearl's neighbors since Pearl tied up the line in their house."

"And get this," added Rick with a flourish of his hands. "She's a hero. Seems she couldn't sleep and was up when the sirens went off. She ran from door to door waking the neighbors. Everyone made it to the cellar. Rachel knew what to do. She kept her head."

"That's because we raise great kids in Pilgrim Cove," said Bart.

Shelley smiled at the men and at her own children. "And we have great summer kids, too."

"That's an absolute fact." Dan punched Josh lightly on the shoulder and stroked Emily's soft cheek with his forefinger. "The summer kids are super."

The four ROMEOs glanced at each other. Finally, Bart said, "We'll be wishing you the good luck of the Irish on Wednesday. You hear? And we'll be saying a prayer, as well."

Startled for a moment, Shelley realized that Laura must have told Sam about the hearing. News traveled from many directions to the ROMEOs.

"We'll take all the luck we can get," said Shelley. "Thanks."

CHAPTER FIFTEEN

THE HEARING HAD been set for eleven o'clock in the morning. Shelley received a call the night before, however, asking if she could appear an hour earlier.

"A request from Mr. Anderson's counsel," said her attorney. "If you can't do it, that's okay, too, as long as we're there by eleven."

"I can do it," said Shelley with no hesitation. "The sooner the better."

She hung up the kitchen phone and looked at Daniel, feeling very optimistic. "Think it's a good sign? Maybe they want to drop the whole thing before going in front of the judge."

"Maybe," said Dan, taking her in his arms. "But I wouldn't count on it. As much as I hate to take that smile from your face, I have to be realistic. They probably want to work out some terms before going into the courtroom. Most judges appreciate receiving a possible compromise created by the parties involved before listening to them in their courtrooms."

Shelley sighed and leaned against him. "Hold

me tighter," she whispered. "Hmm," she said. "This is nice." Her eyes closed.

"No sleeping yet," said Dan, bending down and nuzzling her neck. "You need to tell Laura about the time change."

She jumped out of his embrace and grabbed the phone. "Mission accomplished," she said a minute later. "And I'm not tired. In fact," she added, her fingers playing with his ear, stroking his cheek, "I have a great idea."

He caught her hand and kissed the palm. "If it requires a blanket, and I sincerely hope it does, you'll have to wait till your folks show up again."

"Do I really?" she whispered. "When there's a perfectly good couch going to waste in the living room, and the kids are sleeping."

Dan slapped his hand to his head, his face a mask of comic woe. "The woman just wants to use me!"

I want to love you for the rest of my life. "You're my boytoy now," she teased, pulling him by the hand, "so take it like a man!"

"You bet I will."

And he did. His kisses were uncompromising. Full of passion, full of hunger, hard and searching. She responded with an eagerness that made her blood surge. And heat! Heat from the inside out. And she wanted more.

But suddenly, she was free, slightly off balance. Dan stood in front of her, breathing like an exhausted runner, his hands on her shoulders to steady her. "I'm not sure the couch is a good idea, and I'm not continuing what I can't finish," he said in a hoarse voice. "Think you can sleep now?"

He had to be kidding.

"Then take a cold shower." He chuckled without humor. "Just like I intend to." He kissed her hard once more and left.

Shelley locked the kitchen door behind him, taking little comfort that his misery equaled hers. She went to her bedroom, dropped on the mattress and closed her eyes, consciously slowing her breathing until she was calm. Inhale, exhale. She allowed herself to relax and drift off.

The morning sun woke her. She glanced at her watch and bounced out of bed. Three hours to go. She was ready.

"THAT'S THE BUILDING," said Dan, pointing ahead of them to a columned edifice shining in the morning sun.

"Figures," said Shelley. "Cold white concrete. Huge flight of stairs. They want to intimidate us before we go in." But then she flew up the outside staircase as though gravity didn't exist.

Dan was right at her side. "Ha! I can see how much they've scared you. You're like a gorgeous thoroughbred, impatient at the starting gate."

She turned toward him when they reached the top. "Would you hold that thought until later when I can appreciate it?"

He nodded. "Absolutely."

She saw the admiration in his eyes, but now she needed an objective appraisal. "Do I look professional enough?" She wore a simple green summer dress, the only fancy item she'd brought with her to Pilgrim Cove, and small gold jewelry. Lipstick and mascara. Nothing ostentatious, but not frumpy, either.

"You look perfect."

So much for an unbiased assessment. But a boost to her confidence. And for some reason, she did feel confident today. Or maybe she just felt great relief that the wait was over.

"We're earlier than early," said Dan as they approached the entrance. "It's only nine-thirty. Your legal team is probably not here yet."

"That's okay. Early works for me. I'll be cool, calm and collected when Carl shows up. Totally unruffled and unrufflable."

Dan's arm came around her as he guided her inside. "You're one hell of a woman," he whispered. "Very cool."

She was running on nervous energy, but Dan imbued her with more self-assurance every time he spoke. Even if he were merely teasing, his words carried both affection and support.

They walked through the front door, passed through security and approached a bank of elevators.

"There are usually a few benches on either end of the hallway," said Dan as they rode to the third floor. "We can sit there, or if you want a cup of coffee, we can get some. It's not too late."

But Shelley shook her head. "No, thanks. I'm feeling fine right now. Don't want jitters."

The elevator doors opened. "Damn it," whispered Shelley, taken aback when she saw Carl and several men already gathered in the hall.

"Not to worry," said Dan. He nodded at the group, but led Shelley toward the other end of the corridor. "Without counsel present, you're not required to speak with any of them."

Shelley took a deep breath. "I'm okay," she said. "It was just the surprise."

Within five minutes, one of the men approached. "I'm Kevin O'Connor, Carl's campaign manager." He looked at Shelley. "I believe we spoke on the phone."

"Yes, we did." Shelley tilted her head to meet his gaze, wishing she were taller, or had purchased some very high heeled shoes. "And frankly, I'm disappointed. I thought you'd act on my idea regarding the campaign, which would have eliminated the need for this meeting." To her delight, her voice was rock steady.

The man nodded. "Seems you've planted your seeds everywhere," he said. "And made a good point. Now Carl understands how beneficial being a conscientious single dad could be to the campaign. Not to mention being eligible for a new relationship." His words were slow and deliberate, and Shelley understood him perfectly. The blonde had come through after all.

Dan's gentle squeeze on her arm caught her attention. His gaze, however, remained on Kevin O'Connor. "What he's not saying, Shelley, is that Carl's stubbornness in going after the children has not worn well with his supporters in the party. A custody battle between two decent parents will make unwanted headlines and won't make sense to the voters. The party wants to back a winner."

The man coughed. "Let's just say some people were unhappy, and we...that is, Carl, is willing to drop the petition."

Those blessed words! *Drop the petition.* Euphoria beckoned. She couldn't speak. Her whole body quivered as she hovered on the verge of happiness. Dan squeezed her arm again. "Wait. He's not finished."

"You're right," said O'Connor. "We're willing to drop the case if Carl can have access to the children during the campaign even if our schedule doesn't coincide with the prearranged weekend visits."

Shelley stared at the man in disbelief. Felt her temper start to rise. "Which weekends are you talking about, Mr. O'Connor? The ones he remembers or the ones he forgets?"

Next to her, Dan burst out laughing. "Be nice, Shelley, and maybe you'll get what you want."

The other man gave Daniel a look of gratitude. "We're conducting a clean campaign here, and we believe in Carl Anderson's vision for his district and for the state." He shrugged. "Divorces happen. It's not a crime. But we need a successful divorce. A cordial relationship between the parents with the children as first priority."

"I don't believe this," said Shelley, looking at Daniel. "He's lecturing me about putting the children first!"

She turned quickly back toward the campaign manager. "Get the candidate over here," she demanded. "I'm not doing this twice." Then she spoke to Dan again. "As far as I'm concerned, my conversation with Carl is private with no need for attorneys at all."

"It depends what you say. I'll be right here and will stop you if necessary."

Standing straight, with shoulders back and chin up, she felt like a general going into battle. For her children, she'd emerge from this skirmish wearing five stars.

Carl approached, stopping two steps in front of her. Shelley moved into his space, her body taut, ready to take him on.

"You and your people want me to cooperate after you had the nerve to hound us with a private investigator? A man who couldn't even stay hidden? Who harassed us for no reason? You want my cooperation after you tried to intimidate me with threats? And worst of all, after you took the kids all over Boston with insufficient supervision and no breakfasts?"

She poked him in the chest with her index finger. "Now you listen to me, Carl Anderson, because I'm calling the shots. If you want the kids while you're campaigning, you will provide a nanny. In fact, a licensed nurse would be even better. And I will meet this person first and approve her. Furthermore," she said distinctly, "this item is not negotiable."

Stunned silence was the immediate reaction. Then Carl reacted. "A licensed nurse! That's not necessary. The kids aren't sick."

"Then we'll just have to wait and see what the judge says," replied Shelley, holding his gaze. "When it comes to the health and safety of our children, I'm not budging. You've proved that your judgment can't be trusted." Her voice was strong with conviction.

The campaign manager looked hard at Carl, seeming to send him a silent message. Carl nodded briefly, then looked at Shelley. "You win."

"We all win," replied Shelley, "but you're too blind to see that. Here's a free tip for Boston's most eligible bachelor—if you want your next relationship to succeed—try sitting on your ego. It would make a nice change."

She scanned the small crowd. "So, where's an attorney when you need one? I want this agreement in writing and witnessed, legal and tight. And until I get it, the kids aren't available."

"For God's sake!" said Carl. "Listen to the lioness roar."

Laughter bubbled up inside her. "That's the nicest thing you could have said to me," replied Shelley. "But the sad part is, Carl, I shouldn't have to."

She stepped closer to Daniel. "Is there anything else we need to do here?"

He shook his head, his eyes twinkling. "You've handled it all, Counselor. I'm taking lessons."

"Oh, Daniel," she whispered, squeezing his hand. The guy made her feel ten feet tall just by being himself.

The elevator door opened, and Dan's colleagues emerged. "Perfect timing," said Shelley. "If you guys could just wrap this up, we'll all be on our way."

She would have loved to leave the building right then and let the attorneys do what they had to do. But the judge was expecting her to appear, and until she heard and saw the words she wanted, she wasn't going anywhere.

With nerves on edge, Shelley maintained her composure and vigilance through the judge's final words reinstating the current custody arrangement plus amendments for child visitation during Carl's campaign, including the presence of a nurse. She listened, she spoke, she focused. She sometimes remembered to breathe.

But when she and Dan were alone again, outside the building in the sun, she started shaking so hard, she had to sit down on a concrete bench.

"I can't believe we did it," she said. "I can't believe the good guys won."

"Not 'we,' honey. You did it. You."

She shook her head in disbelief. "But you don't understand. I'm just a kindergarten teacher. I don't like conflict. I teach children how to play together, how to share. I live a calm life."

Dan's laughter silenced her words. "You, my dear, are not 'just' an anybody. You're ferocious!"

She didn't *feel* ferocious! "I never want to go through anything like that again." She shivered at the thought.

"Daniel," she said, placing her hand on his arm. "No matter what happens between us in the future, I want you to know that it wasn't only about the children. Carl was going to tear your reputation to shreds if he could...living upstairs and all."

He kissed her lightly on the mouth. "Thank you. But I wasn't worried about it. Not a bit." He started chuckling again. "With you in my corner, how could I lose?"

She liked the sound of his laughter and silently vowed to help him laugh more often.

They debarked the ferry in Pilgrim Cove almost two hours later. "I'll rephrase my recent argument," said Dan, pointing at the crowd on the pier. "With those guys in your corner, how could you lose?"

Laura had spread the word again. Bart Quinn and the ROMEOs, with every thumb up, had come to welcome them home.

WITH CARL TOTALLY OUT of the picture, there was nothing to stop Daniel from making his move. Except…Shelley seemed so happy with the way things were between them. All the joy was back; no shadows darkened her expression anymore. Within mere days, the children were infected with their mom's lightheartedness and started to blossom before his eyes.

Josh acted like a typical eight-year-old with normal exuberance and normal downtimes. Many chips had fallen off his shoulders. No more suspicion or defensiveness. According to Shelley, he fell asleep within seconds at the end of the day. And Emily had turned into a chatterbox, making her wishes clearly known about everything.

It was as though a spigot of happiness had been turned on in Shelley's house, and Dan had no wish to change anything, especially since he was part of it all. He and Jessie.

And that was the kicker. Shelley loved him. He knew she did, with every kiss, with every thoughtful act and loving gesture. But that didn't mean she wanted to get married again. In fact, if he were in her shoes, he might very well avoid the married state for a long time. So, he said nothing for a week and simply enjoyed their relationship.

On a Saturday morning in early August, Dan joined Shelley and the kids for breakfast. Halfway through the delicious French toast, Josh pointed to the Parker Plumbing baseball team schedule that hung on the refrigerator. "Look, Mom. Tomorrow's our last game. Darn! It's over too fast." His wistful tone reinforced his words.

"But we still have a couple of more weeks at Sea View House," replied Shelley. "Summer's not gone yet."

"But…but…" The youngster shifted in his chair and looked at Dan. "Are we going to see you again…after…?" Now his voice trembled, and the question lingered in the air.

Dan seized the opportunity. "How about we discuss that while we take a walk? Or would you rather fish off the jetty?"

"Fish!" replied Josh, jumping from his chair. "Let's go!" He glanced at Shelley. "Okay, Mom?"

"Y-yes." Shelley's color was high. The woman was blushing.

"I'll get my rod, and I saved some bait in the door of the fridge. Be right back," said Josh.

Confidence surged in Dan, and he stepped toward Shelley, his arms open. She walked into them. He leaned down until his forehead gently touched hers. "I'm going to tell him what I think he wants to hear. So, if a summer romance is all you want, stop me right now."

"Wouldn't dream of it," she replied. "I'm not stopping you." She tilted her head back, stood on her toes and kissed him. "I love you, Daniel. Emily already loves her Daniel p'fessor. So, go fishing with Josh. Throw in your line, and hook my son."

He couldn't speak for several moments. Her permission was the greatest gift she could have given him. "I love you, Shelley Anderson."

"I know," she whispered, burying her face in the crook of his neck, then nipping his earlobe. "And I love you." He shivered. A delicious shiver that reverberated down to his toes. He held her tighter, not wanting to ever let go. Not believing he could be this lucky twice in a lifetime.

"Are you ready, Daniel?" asked Josh, holding his fishing rod aloft.

"You bet, tiger. Let's go."

"Jess, too?"

"Absolutely."

They walked two blocks along the shoreline until they came to the jetty, a concrete structure about ten feet wide and reaching a football field's length into the ocean. They walked along the top, then dangled their legs over the edge as they baited their hooks with clams.

"Remember the question you asked me back at the house?" began Daniel.

Josh eyed him warily. "Yeah. I just wanted to know…you know…about later…."

"Yeah," said Dan. "I've been thinking about that, too. And the truth is that I've had a great summer with you and your mom and Emily. I want to see all of you again—a lot."

"Good." Josh grinned, and threw his line out.

"In fact, I'm planning to see you guys every single day."

That got the boy's full attention. "Every day? Just like here in Pilgrim Cove? Are you buying the house next door to us?"

"Even closer than that."

Dan watched the boy's expressions change as he processed the information. Saw the exact moment when the connection was made. And saw a big question mark on Josh's face as the youngster turned to face him. "You're going to live with us?"

"I love your mom, Josh. Very, very much. And I love you and Emily, too. I would be honored to spend the rest of my life with all of you, living together every day."

The boy's hazel eyes brightened at first, but then turned dark green. His lips tightened. And he stared at Dan so intently, that Dan began to feel nervous.

"You mean get married?"

Dan nodded.

"No!"

The kid's eyes were shiny, his fishing rod clutched so tightly in his hand that his knuckles were as white as his face. Dan stared at the child. A boy in pain stared back. Personal history had already left its mark. Dan knew what Josh was thinking.

"No more divorces, Josh. This time the family is forever."

The kid's whole body flinched. "How do you

know that? Everybody gets divorced and then life sucks."

"Not everybody. Not me!" Dan put his fishing rod down and leaned back on his hands. How could he reach an eight-year-old in a way he'd understand? His gaze fell on Jessie. Dan waved the dog over and rubbed her head. "Think I'd ever divorce Jess? Get rid of her?"

"No!" The horror on Josh's face spoke for itself.

"Why not?" asked Dan.

"Because you love her. And she's the best dog in the world." Josh dropped his rod and crept over to the hound. He laid his head on her ruff while his arm went around her neck.

"I love your mom even more than I love Jessie." Dan spoke quietly, hoping his solemn tone would reinforce his words.

Josh's eyes widened in astonishment. If the boy and the subject weren't so serious, Dan would have laughed.

"Did you tell her?"

Dan nodded. "And she's very happy about it. But you can ask her yourself."

"Okay."

"One more thing, Josh. I love you and Emily, too. More than Jessie. And I promise not to get rid of any of you. No matter what."

Finally, Josh was ready to explore the idea. "I have a lot of friends, and we make a lot of noise."

Dan sighed in relief. Success. He'd hooked him

and negotiations had started. "I'm glad. Friends are very important. Just like baseball teams."

"And what's my dad going to say?"

"Your dad has already figured it out. Not a problem."

"Oh." His thoughtful look was soon replaced with one of delight. Josh rolled on his belly and got nose to nose with Jess. "Did you hear that, Jessie? You're going to live with us. Forever! And Dan, too."

Daniel didn't mind coming in second. Not when the rewards would be incalculable. "Josh? How would you like to help me plan a surprise for your mom? A terrific surprise?"

The boy looked at him eagerly. "Sure."

"But you have to keep it a secret, even from Emily."

The boy wrinkled his nose. "You mean, *especially* from Emily. She can't keep any secrets."

Dan chuckled and held out his hand. "Shake? Man to man?"

Josh nodded and put his hand in Dan's. "Shake."

"Thank you," said Dan before hauling the boy close and hugging him. "You are some kid, Joshua. The best. And don't forget it."

Shelley met them at the back door, questions in her eyes. Daniel nodded and winked. "Hook, line and sinker."

WHAT HAD POSSESSED him to propose to her on a baseball field in front of the whole town, or rather, part of the town? The part that would attend the last game of the season. Nuts. How could he have considered it, much less put the plan into action? But he had.

In the beginning, he thought his reasons sound. He'd spent as much time with Shelley coaching kids as he had on the beach or in Sea View House or at the diner. The Parker Plumbing team had been along for the ride from the beginning. But more than that, he wanted Shelley's kids to experience his commitment to them and to their mom in a way they'd remember.

But still...Daniel could hardly believe that he was consciously putting himself out there. He scanned the crowd from the dugout at the top of the fifth on Sunday afternoon, surprised at the large attendance. Maybe because the season was ending. Baseball was everybody's game after all.

Bart Quinn, Lila and Lila's mom were there. And Matt and Laura Parker with Brian, of course. And Rick and Dee O'Brien, who didn't have any kids in the league. For that matter, neither did Lou and Pearl Goodman or Mike and Kate Lyons. Heck! All the ROMEOs and wives were in the bleachers.

Josh was at bat and slammed the ball out to right field for a home run. In the dugout, Emily cheered for her brother, but cheers from both teams' supporters filled the air.

"Wow," said Shelley. "Everyone's in a good mood today. Even the competition."

"Yeah. Who's up next?"

"Dan! You've got the order memorized. What's wrong with you?"

"Sorry. Is Casey ready?"

He had to pay attention or she'd think he'd lost his mind. Which might be true. Time moved slowly through the sixth inning with no runs being made on either side. Parker Plumbing was up at the top of the seventh. When the third out was struck, Dan splashed some water on his face, then approached Shelley while wiping his brow. "Would you mind getting some more water from the car? Whatever we had here is gone."

"You're really perspiring, Dan. Are you not feeling well?"

"Just need some water."

"Be right back," she said, and ran off.

Dan turned to his three basemen, shortstop and pitcher and gave each a rolled-up paper bound with a rubber band. "You all know what to do?"

They nodded.

"Remember, wait for my signal."

They nodded again and ran to take their positions.

"Here's the water, honey." A worry line marred Shelley's brow and Dan kissed it. "I'm fine. Thanks." But he took the bottle and drank, just to reassure her. Then stayed next to her in their dugout while the other team was at bat.

Finally, the inning ended. "Step outside, Shel. Want to show you something."

Dan led Shelley by the hand to home plate, and motioned for Emily, Jess and their grandparents to follow. The children on the Parker Plumbing team stood quietly at their places. Slowly, a hush fell over the field. Something Dan hadn't expected. And then he realized for the first time, that the entire crowd knew what was coming next. There were no secrets in Pilgrim Cove.

"What's going on here, Dan?" Shelley whispered. "I don't like this. It's weird."

"I hope not." His stomach was churning. Why had he ever thought this idiocy was a good idea? And it was too late to change his mind now.

He raised his team cap in the air, held it up, then lowered it quickly to his side. Across the field, five children held up signs painted in block letters by Dan in the wee hours of the night.

SHELLEY, WILL YOU MARRY ME?

He watched her face until he knew she'd absorbed the message. "I love you, Shelley. With all my heart. Will you…?"

"Yes, yes, yes." She threw her arms around his neck. And he twirled her around and around to the cheers of Pilgrim Cove.

When he finally put Shelley down, he picked up Emily and kissed her. Still holding the child, he waved to the crowd. "In case you couldn't hear the answer," he bellowed. "She said yes."

Another cheer greeted his words. Emily pointed at the big signs, then leaned into him and said, "You did arts and crats, too!"

"SEA VIEW HOUSE did it again!" Bart Quinn's voice left no doubt as to whom the credit belonged. He patted himself on the stomach. "The gut still works."

Shelley grinned at the Realtor, who sat across the table from her at the Lobster Pot. Dan had insisted on celebrating with the children that evening, as well as with her parents. Somehow they all wound up sharing a large table with the Parkers, Quinns, Sullivans and anyone else who wanted to be with them.

Laura Parker spoke up. "You'll be writing your Sea View House story in its official journal before you leave town. Bart's got the book in his office. What a collection. I read for hours before I wrote our story." The loving glance she gave her new husband revealed the happy ending. But Shelley knew that Laura and Matt's romance was defined by painful twists and turns along the way.

"I'm sure I'll be just as fascinated," said Shelley.

"Are y-you going to l-live here now, Josh?" asked Casey. "That would be cool. W-way cool."

Josh's eyes lit up when he looked at Shelley, but it was Dan who answered.

"Would you settle for summers, kiddo? I think we know someone sitting right at this table who could help us find a house to lease."

"He's got that right," said Bart Quinn.

Shelley turned toward Dan, her heart overflowing with love. "That's such a wonderful idea. Just perfect." She reached for his hand.

"My pleasure." His eyes devoured her, and she felt herself blush. No question, she and Dan would be celebrating later on that night.

"Are you going to tell them about the phone call we got today, Granddad?" asked Lila. The young woman scanned the table. "It's unusual that Sea View House is in demand during the off-season. But it's happened twice now. Laura had it in the spring, and now we'll be leasing it in the fall after you leave."

"He's a marine biologist who's going to double as a science teacher in the high school. Last-minute hire. Don't know the details yet," said Bart.

Shelley's attention was caught by Maggie Sullivan and her sister, Thea Cavelli. The women were approaching with a large poster in their hands. They paused between her and Daniel.

"Boy, oh, boy," said Maggie. "Events happen so fast around here, we can barely keep up. But today, we were there at the baseball field. We saw it all."

"So we've got another piece of community art for the restaurant," added Thea. "Hope you like it."

The ladies stepped back as they held up the picture so everyone at the table could see their latest effort.

A beach scene, the sand covered with pretty sea shells. A caricature of Daniel wore a graduation cap and tassel and dragged a wide-toothed rake behind him. He peered down at one of the shells, which was a caricature of Shelley.

The caption read: Professor Dan Combed The Beach Till He Found The Perfect Shell-ey.

The entire table broke into applause.

"Look!" said Emily, pointing at the picture. "There's Mommy and my Daniel!" Her eyes shone with excitement. "Where's Jessie?"

Katie's grandma, Maggie, put her hand on her cheek and rocked her head in dismay. "My goodness! We almost forgot."

She whipped out a piece of thin charcoal from her pocket and sketched in the golden retriever trailing after Daniel.

"How's that, sweetheart?"

"Oh, yes!" said Emily. "It's perfect. Just perfect. I'm so glad we came here."

"So am I," said Josh.

"Don't leave me out," added Daniel.

"Or me," said Shelley, looking at each member of her family and basking in their happiness. Reveling in her own. She glanced at Bart Quinn for a moment. Amazing how one phone call to an ad in the newspaper changed her whole life. One phone call. Which led her to one special town and to one special house…where she'd met one special man. Her gaze rested on Daniel. The right man.

* * * * *

*Please turn the page for an excerpt
from the third book in
Linda Barrett's engaging series,*

PILGRIM COVE.

Reluctant Housemates *will be available in
February 2005.*

TOTAL DEVASTATION. No roof. Barely a wall. No classrooms remained intact. Rachel Goodman stared at what remained of Round Rock High School, trying to equate the scattered mounds of rubble with the neat brick building that had stood on the spot only yesterday before the twister touched ground.

"Tornadoes in Kansas," she murmured to her friend and colleague. "A genuine cliché that's proved itself again. Thank goodness it's summertime, and the building was empty."

"We were lucky, but…darn it! This one shouldn't have happened." Beverly Arnold put her hands on her hips. "Not only is it a month after the season, but…the early-morning hours? Give me a break!"

Rachel blinked at the ruins and nodded. "You're right. Tornadoes usually form in the afternoon. This one was unusual. But whatever the hour, they're scary as hell."

"That's true," replied Beverly. "At least during the season you're sort of prepared. The worry sits on your shoulder, and you're always figuring out the best places to hide if necessary. Like the nearest ditch or whatever cellar you can find."

"Cellar is right," Rachel said in a tight voice. "That's where I was with old Mrs. Potter and the rest of my neighbors when it hit. But…oh God, Bev! I had to carry her, frail as she is—I knocked on all the doors, and she took forever to open hers. And she's stubborn! We didn't have time for stubborn. I just picked her up and carried her to the cellar with me."

Beverly chuckled. "I'm sorry. It's not funny, and you had no choice. But I'm picturing the scene. She probably wanted to bash you."

Rachel sighed. "Don't worry. She had her revenge." She looked Beverly in the eye. "She made me call home."

Beverly squeezed Rachel's hand. "She did the right thing."

Rachel sighed. "I suppose. But I feel like a five-year-old again. I'm the assistant principal of Round Rock High, and everyone keeps reminding me to call home. Is my name E.T.?"

"No," said Beverly, a smile lingering.

"Then as soon as the all-clear sounded—" Rachel continued "—all my neighbors joined Mrs. Potter in insisting I contact my folks to reassure them of my safety." It was her own fault, she thought. She shouldn't have invited everyone to meet her parents at a cookout the month before, when they'd visited her on their way to California. Now all the residents of her building felt connected to Rachel's family.

"I would have called anyway. I know that tornadoes make national news," said Rachel. She read and ignored the hastily erected warning signs on the school site and took the lead as the two women picked their way around the perimeter of the foundation.

"Had they heard about it?"

"Oh, yes. And they were frantic." She gestured toward the town. "Our phone lines were down here, but they kept trying to reach me. They didn't know my new mobile number and kept calling the old one. With all their button pushing, they tied up their own phone. By the time I thought of dialing their neighbor on my cell, my mom was…barely coherent. What a mess!"

"She's a mother," said Beverly. "You're her daughter. Her only daughter. What do you expect?"

Rachel shrugged. An automatic gesture. She wasn't the favorite child. That honor went to her older brother, Alex. A straight A student and well liked by everyone. Liked? The teachers *loved* him, but they'd shaken their heads at her. "Amazing how two children in the same family could be so different."

Her dad had been disappointed, too. But she'd never felt smart enough or attractive enough to compete with her brother. She was, however, better than Alex in one area: Getting into trouble. Was there ever a time she *hadn't been* in trouble?

She grinned at her friend as she scanned the remains of the building trying to locate where her office had been. "Point taken, Bev... But do we have to suffer a tornado for my own parents to show they love me?" Suddenly, her mouth trembled, all vestiges of her smile gone. Damn! She was an adult now. When would she outgrow that pain? She pressed her lips together.

"Some people have a hard time showing love," said Beverly. "And older people rarely change their ways."

Rachel managed her usual grin again. Beverly was a peacemaker. Always searching for a reasonable explanation, and there was no need to upset her, especially when she was right.

"I should remember that," replied Rachel. *And stop being disappointed.*

Leaving home when she started college was the best decision she'd ever made. Thirteen years later, she felt the same way, still thankful for the swimming scholarship that had provided the opportunity.

As a tall and awkward teenager with shiny braces on her teeth, she tripped in the hallways every day, but swam like a shark in the water. Through her membership in the USA Swim Club, she was able to compete and show her stuff. And was recruited by a university in the Midwest. In the end, growing up in Pilgrim Cove with the Atlantic as her personal swimming hole, had paid off.

Rachel squared her shoulders and focused on the

present. On the destroyed high school. She had more important matters to consider than remembrances of her home town.

"John Thompson's called a meeting for the senior staff tomorrow morning," she said, shading her eyes to view the destroyed building one more time. "He's a strong principal, but even he will need help deciding how to open school this year."

"Not much time to figure it out," replied Beverly. "It's the end of July. School's scheduled to start in three weeks."

"We'll come up with something. In the meantime," said Rachel, her words coming slowly, "I'll cancel my flight to Boston."

Beverly shook her head. "I'd forgotten about your vacation."

"Not exactly a vacation. More of a pilgrimage to Pilgrim Cove," Rachel said with a wink.

"It's too bad you have to cancel. It's important to visit with your family."

"Our situation here is more important," replied Rachel with a clear conscience, knowing she was speaking the truth. She tried to ignore the sense of relief she felt about remaining in Kansas. She always had such mixed feelings about going back home.

She was a poor fit in Pilgrim Cove. A poor fit with her family. Always had been. No reason to think this year would be any different. Of course, she'd miss seeing her niece and nephew—the bright spots in her visits—and she was sorry about that.

But in the end, Pilgrim Cove, Massachusetts, was her past. Round Rock, Kansas, was her future. She had no intention of leaving the Midwest.

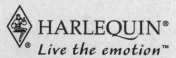

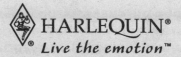

eHARLEQUIN.com
The Ultimate Destination for Women's Fiction

Visit eHarlequin.com's Bookstore today
for today's most popular books at great prices.

- An extensive selection of romance books by top authors!
- Choose our convenient "bill me" option. No credit card required.
- New releases, Themed Collections and hard-to-find backlist.
- A sneak peek at upcoming books.
- Check out book excerpts, book summaries and Reader Recommendations from other members and post your own too.
- Find out what everybody's reading in Bestsellers.
- Save BIG with everyday discounts and exclusive online offers!
- Our Category Legend will help you select reading that's exactly right for you!
- Visit our Bargain Outlet often for huge savings and special offers!
- Sweepstakes offers. Enter for your chance to win special prizes, autographed books and more.

Your purchases are 100% guaranteed—so shop online at www.eHarlequin.com today!

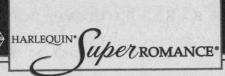

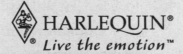

Receive a FREE hardcover book from

HARLEQUIN ROMANCE®

in September!

Harlequin Romance celebrates the launch of the line's new cover design by offering you this exclusive offer valid only in September, only in Harlequin Romance.

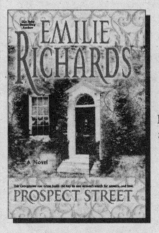

To receive your FREE HARDCOVER BOOK written by bestselling author Emilie Richards, send us four proofs of purchase from any September 2004 Harlequin Romance books. Further details and proofs of purchase can be found in all September 2004 Harlequin Romance books.

Must be postmarked no later than October 31.

Don't forget to be one of the first to pick up a copy of the new-look Harlequin Romance novels in September!

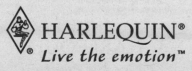

HARLEQUIN®
Live the emotion™

Visit us at www.eHarlequin.com

HRPOP0904